# LONG NIGHTS & LONG KNIVES

1st Edition

Published in 2014 by
Woodfield Publishing Ltd
Bognor Regis PO21 5EL England
www.woodfieldpublishing.co.uk

ISBN 1-84683-156-3


Printed and bound in England
by Woodfield Publishing Ltd

Book/cover design: Klaus & Pastorius

# Long Nights & Long Knives

*A novel set in Kenya at the time of the
1952 Mau Mau insurgency*

ALASTAIR TOMPKINS

Woodfield

## Woodfield Publishing Ltd

Bognor Regis ~ West Sussex ~ England ~ PO21 5EL
tel 01243 821234 ~ e/m info@woodfieldpublishing.co.uk

*Interesting and informative books on a variety of subjects*

For full details of all our published titles, visit our website at
**www.woodfieldpublishing.co.uk**

*To Pauline*

# About The Author

Alastair Tompkins was one of the 600 extra officers recruited by the British Colonial Service in 1952 to reinforce the Kenya Police following attacks on European-owned farms by native insurgents and the declaration of a State of Emergency. After undergoing an accelerated induction programme he and his colleagues were engaged in a variety of anti-terrorist activities and it is these experiences upon which he has drawn in writing this fictional account.

Alastair was to remain in the Kenya Police for ten years, until the former Crown Colony gained its independence in 1963.

# Preface

This book is fiction, however the places mentioned exist, although the characters in the story are entirely fictitious and do not refer to any person either living or dead. The incidents at Lari and Naivasha are undisputed facts but the other incidents that appear in this book are fictitious. Having served as a Police Officer in Kenya at the time, I have attempted to recapture the atmosphere that existed within the European farming community during the early 1950s and to reveal how evil men within the Kikuyu tribe persuaded their fellow tribesmen to support and engage in acts of brutality and murder.

The first Europeans arrived on the East African coast during the 1890s. They discovered a land teeming with game and a climate that ranged from high humidity on the coast to sub-tropical in the hinterland. They also discovered that Arab slave traders were constantly raiding deep into the interior, capturing innocent people who were never seen again. Within a very short period, the Arab slave-traders had been crushed and a rule of law imposed.

Within less than sixty years, Kenya was transformed and a Crown Colony created. Nairobi, once swampland, was now Kenya's capital. A rail network linked Kenya to Uganda and Tanganyika; Nairobi had a first class airport; the Civil Service and the Police were efficient. Coffee, tea and canned beef were major exports. Dairy products were placed on a proper commercial footing. It was a safe, prosperous land and everyone had a full stomach. What could possibly destroy this tranquillity?

Kenya's native population is made up of numerous tribes, each with their own beliefs, values and customs. As long as anyone could remember, these tribes had waged constant warfare on their neighbours. In order to prevent this constant bloodshed on what was seen as 'non-native land', a string of European farms were created from virgin bush into prosperous, fertile land to act as 'buffers zones'. This policy proved highly successful.

The Kikuyu had a system whereby when a father died, if he had two sons, each would receive half of the father's land. Upon their deaths, if they had two sons, their grandfather's original holding was now sub-divided into four. With a rising birth-rate and this constant sub-division, there was a hunger within the Kikuyu Reserve to acquire more land. On their borders were the well-managed and prosperous European farms, many employing Kikuyu in various capacities from farm labourers to cooks, house servants and supervisors.

A secret society was formed with the intention to take these farms from their European owners by force. At night Mau-Mau witchdoctors visited each farm, telling the Kikuyu workforce that the land could be theirs. The Kikuyu believed deeply in witchcraft. Taking oaths, sipping chicken's blood, piercing a goat's eye with a thorn and crawling through an arc of thorns were common tribal rituals. Ritual oaths were used to recruit participants to the Mau-Mau cause. An example of one of the milder oaths was, *"If I am asked to bring my mother's little finger, I will do so."* The oaths were considered completely binding and to refuse to take them could result in death. It was not unknown for a daughter to assist in killing her father if he had refused to take the oath.

No other Kenyan tribes were involved in the Mau Mau and when called upon they rallied to support the Crown, as indeed did many Kikuyu, who actively supported the security forces.

My story begins in 1952, when a series of apparently unconnected but disturbing incidents occurred, heralding the start of what would become known as Mau Mau.

**Alastair Tompkins**
Crowthorne, Berkshire,
June 2013

# CHAPTER ONE

The year was 1952. Chief Inspector Dundas of the Kenya Police Provincial C.I.D. Nakuru drove his Morris Oxford saloon into the entrance of his Government bungalow. The day had been uneventful and he was looking forward to a relaxing evening with his wife Joanne and their baby son, Ian.

Of late things had been quiet. However, this was not the case within Nairobi and its surrounding area. A European couple had been murdered; a Chief in the Kiambu area, which was not so far from Nairobi, had been found strangled, and a Police Constable had been attacked and his rifle stolen. These events were both unusual and disturbing.

He stopped the car on the drive as his wife Joanne, with their son in her arms, came down the four steps that led to the bungalow's entrance.

"Darling, you're home early, I didn't expect you until at least five o'clock."

Dundas put his arm around Joanne's waist as they made their way up the steps and onto the cool veranda, framed with the vivid red of large-flowered hibiscus. It was good to be home. He sank down into one of the cane armchairs, then stretched out his six-foot frame and briefly closed his eyes. He mused that life was good. He loved Kenya; its peoples; his job, and most of all, his wife and son Ian. He opened his eyes and looked out at the garden with its well-trimmed lawn; the frangipani bushes that lined the drive, their crocus like pale cream blooms that emitted a delicate perfume that no man-made scent could emulate; the ochre coloured earth of the drive itself. He switched his attention to Joanne.

"Well, what's been happening today?"

Joanne placed Ian onto her lap.

"Apart from our son trying to wear me out, the major thing is that Kamau has left."

Dundas was surprised. Kamau, their gardener, was always cheerful and maintained the garden in excellent condition.

"So he left just like that? Did he give a reason?"

Joanne shook her head.

"No. The first thing I knew was when Steven said that Kamau had just walked off."

Dundas frowned.

"Are you sure that he's left?"

"It would appear so. Steven is positive that he will not return."

Dundas was puzzled; it was very strange. Steven, their cook, and Kamau had been with them for over two years. There had never been any friction.

"Joanne, do you know if he had any family problems?"

Joanne smiled and shook her head.

"Darling, my Kiswahili is very limited and doesn't extend to holding detailed conversations!"

Dundas nodded.

"Hmm... It seems a strange thing to do. I'll have a word with Steven after dinner."

With dinner over and Steven having served the coffee, it was time to listen to the evening news. Dundas went over to the bookcase and switched on their Pye battery radio. The European broadcaster, having announced that it was 9pm, began to read the news:

> "A report has just been received from Police Headquarters Nairobi that within the Ngong area an African gang consisting of six men attacked a European farmer and his wife. One of the attackers was shot dead, the others escaped. The farmer and his wife were slightly injured. John Sullivan has the details."
>
> "At about eight fifteen this evening, a gang of six men armed with pangas (machetes) forced their way into the house. The farmer and his wife managed to lock themselves in the dining room and shot one of the attackers through the door. Police are at the scene and we will give more details as these become available."

The rest of the news followed, but apart from the weather report there was of little interest. Dundas went over to the bookcase and switched off the radio, then returned to his armchair. Joanne looked up from her knitting.

"Robert you have that 'policeman's frown', which tells me that you are deep in thought."

Dundas lay back in the armchair and stretched out his legs.

"It's just that these recent reports of attacks are both very unusual and disturbing. For example, stealing that constable's rifle."

Joanne's knitting needles clicked as she completed three more stitches, and then looked up.

"I have little doubt that the culprits will be caught and then things will return to normal."

Joanne glanced down at her knitting pattern.

"Darling, Kiambu and Ngong are at least a hundred miles away. This is Nakuru. Quiet, friendly and safe."

Dundas grunted.

"I hear what you say Joanne, but from now on we need to be more cautious."

Joanne placed her knitting onto the low, square table beside her chair.

"Robert, you have an early start in the morning, it's time for bed. Don't forget to lock up."

The following morning as Steven was serving his breakfast, Dundas raised yet again Kamau's unexpected departure.

"Steven, Memsahib cannot think of any reason why Kamau has left us. Can you think of anything?"

Steven placed the pot of steaming coffee onto the heat resistant mat and looked at Dundas.

"*Hapana Effendi* (No Sir), all I know is he has removed all his things."

"Did he say why he was leaving?"

"*Hapana Effendi.*"

"But Steven, I must owe him some money. It's four days since pay day, so he is due four days' pay."

"Perhaps Effendi he will return to collect his money, and then you can ask him why he decided to go."

Having given Joanne and little Ian their usual departing kiss, he started the car and set off down the drive to Provincial Headquarters. At the bottom of the hill, he turned right onto the main tarmac road and headed into town. It was the usual warm sunny morning and at this early hour the shops lining the High Street were opening. As he passed the French Bakery to his left, a delicious smell of newly-baked bread wafted through the car's open window. Passing the Nakuru Hotel, he turned left at the traffic lights and headed down the road that led to Provincial Headquarters and the Law Courts and entered the gates of Provincial Police Headquarters. Having parked his car in its designated place, he made his way towards the entrance to the Police Station, which was attached to the Headquarters building.

As per standard practice, he paused by the Charge Office counter to peruse the Daily Occurrence Book as Inspector Farrell, who had been the Night Duty Officer, exited from his office and greeted Dundas.

"Morning Robert, it's been a very quiet night, no assaults, no stabbings and no major thefts. All we have are two drunks, who are currently fast asleep in King George's Hotel."

Dundas grinned. This was the nickname given to the Police Station cells by the local African population, pronounced as *"Hoteli ya King George"*. Inspector Farrell continued.

"So Robert, whilst you were having sweet dreams, some of us had to work. If ever C.I.D. has a vacancy, let me know."

Dundas made his way to his office and sat heavily into his chair. Purely out of habit, he glanced at his watch – it was just three minutes to eight. He looked out of the office window; the early morning sunlight was casting long shadows across the grass. Within the next two hours, the heat of the day would be making its presence felt. His mind drifted back to the incidents around the Nairobi area. Attacks on

Europeans were almost unknown and, as for attacking the police, the last incident had been in the Suk District, which had a border with Uganda, when a group of religious fanatics had attacked a party of police, killing the European officer in charge and some ten native constables. This same group had also attacked a Police Station at Cherangani, killing several police and setting fire to some of the thatched buildings. But the tribe living around the area of Nairobi were not Suk but Kikuyu – the Suk District was several hundred miles away – not only that, it was highly unlikely that the two tribes knew of each other's existence, particularly the Suk, who were still regarded as being 'wild and woolly'.

Anyway, it was time for work. Dundas went over to the safe and re-moved the file marked *INFORMERS' – Restricted Circulation*, then returned to his desk and opened the cover. The first report was regard-ing a Sikh contractor currently employed by the local Council. The allegation was that false invoices were being submitted or that the quantities of materials being used were being exaggerated. This would require a visit to the Council's Surveyor and visiting the sites where the work had been carried out. He turned the page just as the telephone on his desk jangled and invaded his thoughts. He picked up the hand-set.

"Chief Inspector Dundas C.I.D."

"Morning Robert, are you busy?" Dundas recognised the voice as that of his boss, Superintendent Lewis.

"Sir, what I'm doing is not urgent."

"Good, then step round to my office."

There was a click and the line went dead.

Superintendent Lewis, who was now in his early fifties, was seated behind his desk, with his familiar pipe situated in the ashtray. He was tall and well-built, with a tanned face, a deeply-furrowed forehead and sandy-coloured hair with slightly greying sideburns. Dundas never failed to notice the man's vivid blue eyes with their 'crow's feet', matching those on his forehead, denoting his years of service under the East African sun. As usual, he was dressed in an immaculate white short-sleeved shirt, set off with what could be a military tie, and long, light, khaki cotton slacks. On his feet, which protruded from underneath the desk, were the familiar light tan, suede, desert boots. He was looking very affable.

"Come in Robert and take a seat."

He gestured at the chair situated to the right of his desk.

"The reason why I've asked you round is regarding local information. You are aware of these reports from the Kiambu and Ngong areas. I know they are over a hundred miles away, but I want you to 'keep your ear to the ground'. These incidents are few and far between, but I need not tell you that they are both unusual and disturbing."

Superintendent Lewis leaned back in his chair.

"I take it you've heard nothing?"

Dundas shook his head. "No Sir, not a thing."

Superintendent Lewis placed his hands behind his head.

"I'm attending an 'O Group' meeting and Special Branch will be there. If they provide any worthwhile information I'll let you know."

Dundas walked back to his office.

As far as he knew, all was quiet.

# CHAPTER TWO

TWO DAYS HAD PASSED since his meeting with Superintendent Lewis and the information provided by Provincial Special Branch, who were responsible for the whole of the Rift Valley Province, had revealed very little, apart from the fact that only Kikuyu were suspected in the incidents around the Kiambu and the Ngong areas. Investigations were proceeding but no arrests had been made.

❖ ❖ ❖

The gardener employed by the Dundas household had not returned to collect his wages and within a few days another gardener had been employed, so things were back to normal. Dundas pursued the Public Works case and the evidence gathered so far pointed to a 'fiddle', the extent of which was yet to be established.

Four evenings later, Steven had served their after dinner coffee. As per usual, Dundas switched on their 'Pye' battery radio and out of habit glanced at his watch – almost news-time. The European male announcer having given details of forthcoming programmes, said:

*"Here is the nine o'clock news, read to you by Alastair McDowell... Traffic Police in Nairobi have reported a record number of cases involving expired road fund licences and state that their current operation will be extended to cover other areas outside Nairobi. The price of coffee has fallen by seven shillings per hundred pound bag and this follows the current downward trend in the World market. An outbreak of foot-and-mouth has been reported on two farms in the Kitale area. All livestock movements in the area have been stopped..."*

Dundas went over to the bookcase and switched the set off, then returned to his armchair, stretched out his legs and glanced across at Joanne who was, as usual, knitting.

"Not another woolly jacket?"

Joanne looked up.

"Yes it is, but not for now. When we go on home leave it will be cold and Ian will need to be kept warm – and before you ask, yes, I am also knitting him a woollen hat and some mitts."

Dundas gestured.

"But Joanne, our leave is over a year away!"

"It doesn't matter, I believe in being prepared."

Dundas grinned.

Joanne had a very determined nature and he knew from experience arguing was pointless. He decided to read last Sunday's newspaper, and then head for bed.

The ringing of the bedside telephone startled Dundas into semi-comatose wakefulness. He lifted the mosquito net and fumbled for the telephone, then lifted the handset. It was Superintendent Lewis.

"Robert, there's been a dual murder on a farm in the North Kinankop area. The local police are in attendance. Meet me at Headquarters as soon as possible. I propose that we should be armed."

There was a click and the line went dead. Joanne looked up.

"What is it darling?"

"There's been an incident and I have to go. Shield your eyes, as I'm about to switch on the bedside light."

The impact of the sixty-watt light-bulb made Dundas screw up his eyes. He swung his legs out of the bed onto the cool, polished floor and ran his fingers through his short dark hair.

He rubbed the bristles on his chin.

Was there time to shave? He made his way to the bathroom and ran some cold water into the washbasin, then splashed it onto his face to clear his semi-comatose state. He rubbed his chin with his right hand. Yes, he'd quickly shave. Within eight minutes of the telephone call and having given Joanne a kiss, he exited into the starlit night, started his car and headed for Headquarters.

Driving along the now quiet High Street at this 'ungodly hour' was almost a new experience. In shop doorways there were night-watchmen crouching over small charcoal stoves to obtain a modicum of warmth during their long vigil. The combination of his car's head-lights and the streetlights picked out their huddled figures. Just before arriving at the traffic-lights, he passed a lonely Police Constable doing his beat. The traffic-lights were red but Dundas ignored them and gunned the car, turning left down the road to Headquarters.

Superintendent Lewis was at the Charge Office counter talking to the Night Duty Officer. He turned as he heard the main entrance door swing open.

"Robert, I've just been receiving more details about these deaths at North Kinankop. Everything is being left pending our arrival, but it's a bloody mess in every sense of the word. Evidently, they were butch-ered in their dining room whilst having dinner. Even their cat has been killed. It's a bad business. I have alerted Bill Stewart, he will follow with all his paraphernalia, so we can go."

The lights of the Land Rover cut into the darkness ahead, as, having cleared the township boundary, it sped along the tarmac road towards Naivasha. With Ndibo at the wheel, each man was alone with his thoughts and hunched against the cold night air seeping through the gaps in the Land Rover's loose fitting sliding windows and canvas canopy. Ndibo slowed as a herd of zebra, no doubt startled by the headlights, galloped across the road and off into the sparse bush that lined either side of their route, their eyes and stripes clearly visible in the headlights. Ndibo broke the silence and intruded into their thoughts.

"Effendi, it's not so far from here that a young European couple, who were driving back to Nakuru at night, hit a zebra. The girl was thrown through the windscreen."

Superintendent Lewis grunted in reply.

"In that case Ndibo, drive fast but carefully."

"Ndiyo Effendi."

Having accelerated, Ndibo drove with the needle of the speedometer hovering between seventy and eighty on the softly illuminated dial. For some minutes nothing was said. This time Dundas broke the silence.

"Sir, have we any idea as to why this couple were killed?"

Superintendent Lewis shrugged.

"Not an inkling Robert. According to the local Police Inspector, they were well liked by their labour, their house servants had been with them for years – it's all very strange."

"But Sir, as their cat was also killed, it sounds like some form of revenge attack. How was the crime discovered?"

"The intruders fired two shots, which disturbed the cook. By the time he had plucked up courage to investigate, the intruders had fled."

Dundas raised his voice against the road and wind noise.

"Sir, I cannot recall any previous incidents where burglars have been armed."

Superintendent Lewis grunted.

"For all we know, the shots could have been fired from weapons stolen from the house."

Superintendent Lewis turned to Ndibo.

"Ndibo. As soon as we enter Naivasha, go past the Naivasha Hotel, which is on your left, then take the next left, it's the road that goes past Divisional Police Headquarters. Then just keep going."

"Ndiyo Effendi."

As they entered Naivasha it was like a ghost town; not a glimmer of light anywhere and not a soul to be seen. Dundas glanced at the luminous dial on his watch. It was 2.12am. Despite the zebra crossing the road, Ndibo had made good time. Dundas recalled taking this selfsame road when he had taken Joanne to the 'Brown Trout' at Njabini, which was in the South Kinankop area, but this time, at the 'T' junction they would turn left and head in the direction of the North Kinankop.

The Land Rover was now on the usual dirt road, the recent rains having gouged out numerous corrugations in the road's surface making conversation difficult. Dundas grasped the Land Rovers' metal facia and was glad that the heavy dew would be holding down the usual daytime dust. The Land Rover continued to climb and some thirty minutes later, having reached the plateau, turned left, heading towards the North Kinankop. At this height of over seven thousand feet, the cold night air was crisp and Dundas hunched his shoulders against the cold air seeping into the vehicle.

Some ten minutes later the Land Rovers' headlights picked out two Police Constables armed with standard .303 Lee Enfield rifles, who signalled them to stop. They then cautiously approached the Land Rover's near-side window, pointing their rifles at the interior of the cab. The taller of the two spoke in Kiswahili.

"*Nani wewe* (who are you) and where are you going?"

Dundas was conscious that the rifle was pointing directly at him and in the reflected lights of the Land Rover he could see that the man's finger was on the trigger. Superintendent Lewis carefully opened the Land Rovers sliding window.

"We're from C.I.D. Nakuru."

The tall Constable stepped closer and peered in the window as his companion shone his torch onto their faces.

"Sorry Effendi, but we have been ordered to stop all vehicles as two Europeans have been killed at the farm here."

He gestured over his shoulder.

"The Bwana A.S.P. from Naivasha is there and the Inspector from the local Police Station. At the signpost just ahead, turn left and follow the dirt road to the farmhouse."

With the rifle now pointing in a different direction, Dundas breathed a sigh of relief.

"Thank you Constable – and stay vigilant."

The tall Constable saluted.

"*Ndiyo Effendi!*"

Superintendent Lewis turned to Ndibo.

"*Ndibo, endelea.*" (Carry on).

Ndibo engaged the gearbox and moved off in the direction of the farmhouse. Their headlights picked out two Police Land Rovers and six African Police, all armed with rifles. The lights of the farmhouse were on, the soft yellow light, denoting that, as on many farms, oil lanterns were the sole method of illumination. Ndibo stopped the Land Rover beside the other two vehicles and switched off the engine. Superintendent Lewis turned to Dundas.

"Based on the initial report, I have little doubt that we are about to face complete and utter carnage."

Superintendent Lewis opened the Land Rover's door and stepped down onto the ground quickly followed by Dundas.

"Evidently Robert, they were surprised by the intruders when having dinner."

In the light cast by the open veranda door, a uniformed figure came down the three steps and walked over to where they were standing. From the three 'pips' on his epaulettes, Dundas realised it must be the Assistant Superintendent from Naivasha. The figure stopped and saluted Superintendent Lewis.

"Sir, Assistant Superintendent Smith, Naivasha H.Q. Nothing has been disturbed and I'm afraid it's an awful bloody mess. All we have been able to discover so far is that the houseboy is missing. I've sent for a tracker dog. At dawn we can try to track the persons responsible."

Dundas glanced towards the East; already the night sky was tinged with pink and purple. He hunched his shoulders against the cold, thinking about the coming dawn. At this height, now some eight thousand feet, frosts were not unknown and, having been trout fishing in the area, Dundas was aware that the dawn would produce a very heavy dew. Superintendent Lewis turned to Dundas.

"Bill Stewart and his Scenes of Crime team are on their way and should be here about dawn. In the meantime, until they have completed their work we should confine our activities to questioning the labour force."

The Assistant Superintendent interjected.

"Excuse me Sir, the Government Doctor at Naivasha has been alerted and should be here about seven a.m. I thought this was the best course of action pending the arrival of Provincial Scenes of Crime."

Superintendent Lewis grunted in reply.

"Why the huge delay in reporting this incident?"

"The phone lines had been cut Sir, and the nearest farm is about five miles away. Their cook had to cycle there to raise the alarm."

"Hmm..." Superintendent Lewis grunted again. "Where's the cook at the moment?"

The Assistant Superintendent pointed. "He's over there, giving a statement."

Superintendent Lewis turned to Dundas. "Robert, go and find this cook and see what you can find out. I'll speak to some of the labour."

Dundas found the cook seated in one of the Land Rovers giving his statement. Dundas opened the door and spoke to the European Police Officer.

"Robert Dundas Provincial C.I.D. so what's he saying?"

"Basically, what we already know is that the cook here heard some shots and when he went to check at the house, he found the two bodies."

Dundas nodded his head. "Do you mind if I ask him some questions?"

"Not at all, I was just taking a routine statement."

Dundas hunched his shoulders against the cold night air.

"I thought dawns at Nakuru were cold, but here it's bloody freezing!"

He turned to the cook, speaking in Kiswahili.

"What's your name?"

*"Njeroge Effendi."*

"So you're a Kikuyu?"

*"Ndiyo Effendi."*

"And the houseboy?"

*"Kikuyu Effendi."*

"And you hand the food to him and he serves it at the table?"

The cook nodded.

*"Ndiyo Effendi."*

"What time do Bwana and Memsahib have dinner?"

"About eight o'clock Effendi."

"And last night?"

"It was later Effendi."

"Why was this?"

"I was late and I had to put more wood into the stove as the oven was too cold."

Dundas noted the cook was shivering.

"Are you cold?"

"Just a little Effendi."

"So Ngeroge, you served the meal about nine p.m. What time did you go to your hut?"

"Soon after Effendi."

"So who washed up?"

"The houseboy Effendi."

"This noise that you heard, what time was it?"

"I don't know Effendi I was just about to go to sleep, perhaps it was ten o'clock."

"So you heard this noise, went to investigate, found Bwana and Memsahib dead. Where were they?"

The cook shivered again. "In the dining room."

"Seated at the table?"

*"Ndiyo Effendi."*

The cook shivered again. Dundas turned to the European Inspector.

"This doesn't add up. What time did you receive this report?"

"At about one forty-five."

"So the cook here finds the bodies, the phone lines have been cut and he rides off on his bicycle to raise the alarm. Let's assume that it was now ten thirty. On a bicycle at night, how long would it take to reach the nearest farm, remembering that he would be stressed and going like the clappers?"

"At the outside, one and a half hours."

"That takes us to midnight or thereabouts. So what has happened to the other hour and a quarter? Not only that, the murdered couple were eating. Do you know what it was?"

"It was the main course and from what I have seen, they were surprised by the intruders whilst eating it."

Dundas nodded his head.

"Exactly! Have you ever known a cook to go off duty before the sweet and coffee have been served?"

The Inspector nodded. "It would be highly unusual."

Dundas noted that the cook was shivering again as he lapsed into Kiswahili.

"I don't believe your story."

The cook looked down at his linked hands and stayed silent.

"It's all very convenient. You are late preparing the dinner. You leave before sweet and coffee have been served and, having heard this noise and finding that the telephone didn't work, it took you from ten thirty until one thirty to cycle five miles. How old are you?"

"Forty one Effendi."

The cook shivered again, without looking up. Dundas placed his forefinger under the cook's chin.

"Look at me."

The cook raised his head and continued to shiver, his eyes avoiding Dundas's face.

"Now Ngeroge, I'm not a fool. Tell me what really happened?"

There was a long silence and the cook made several involuntary twitches.

"I didn't kill them Effendi. I was told to serve the soup and the main course and then go to my hut."

"Who told you this?"

"The houseboy and two men came to my hut just after dark, saying they wanted to steal Bwana's guns. They said if I told anyone they would kill me, my wife and children... but no mention was made of killing Bwana and Memsahib."

"And the delay in reporting the incident?"

"I was told to leave it as late as possible Effendi, in order for them to get away."

Dundas turned to the European Inspector. "Go and find this man's wife and see if her story is the same as his. I'll look after this one."

He faced the cook again. "Ngeroge, how long have you worked for Bwana and Memsahib?"

"Over twelve years Effendi."

"How did they treat you?"

"Very well Effendi."

The cook twitched again and looked down at his hands.

"What about the houseboy?"

"He had been with them for nearly eight years Effendi."

"Do you know of any reason why he should want to kill them?"

There was a long silence and the cook's body shook with a series of shivers and he continued to look at his hands.

"Well?"

The cook looked up at Dundas. Even in the dim light cast by the Land Rovers' interior light, Dundas could see raw fear as it screwed up the cook's face.

"Well?"

"Effendi, I dare not tell you. If I do, I will die!"

"So who are you afraid of?"

"Effendi, I cannot tell you, please! I didn't want Bwana and Memsahib harmed."

"Right Ngeroge, you are under arrest for being implicated in this murder. Anything that you do say will be taken down in writing and may be used in evidence. Do you understand what I have said?"

The cook nodded his head and continued to twitch.

"Right Ngeroge, you come with me."

Dundas waited as the cook slid off the Land Rover squab seat and put his feet onto the ground.

"Walk ahead of me and go over to the veranda where the light is."

Superintendent Lewis was at the foot of the steps and turned as Dundas and his prisoner approached.

"Robert, is this man under arrest?"

"Yes Sir. He's up to his eyeballs in this murder, but for some reason refuses to say why." Dundas spoke to the cook. "You sit on the step there." He turned to the nearest armed Constable. "I want this man handcuffed and placed under guard."

The Constable saluted and proceeded to handcuff the cook.

Superintendent Lewis felt in his right-hand jacket pocket and produced a large torch.

"Robert, before you give me the details, let me show you this."

Superintendent Lewis, using the torch, led the way to the right of the veranda and stopped by the kitchen door.

"What do you make of this?"

In the light of the torch, Dundas could see a black and white cat hanging by a cord around its neck, which was attached to a stick about five feet long. The eyes were closed and its pink tongue protruded from between its teeth. His boss intruded into his thoughts.

"Evidently it was the couples' pet cat. So why kill their cat?"

Dundas shook his head.

"All I can say, Sir, is that the hate must be very extreme." Dundas stood there, his eyes fixed on the dead cat's face. "I have never ever seen anything like this before."

"Neither have I Robert. From what I've been told by the Assistant Superintendent, the scene in the dining room is horrific."

Superintendent Lewis shone the torch onto his watch.

"In less than an hour Bill Stewart will be here, so once he's finished and the Government Doctor has done his stuff, we can get down to work. Now, tell me about the cook..."

# CHAPTER THREE

DUNDAS GLANCED TOWARDS the East again. The dark purple sky was tinged with pink and in the soft light of the coming dawn he was able to see his surroundings in more detail. The farmhouse was of typical Colonial construction, single-storey and surrounded by a large wooden veranda some ten feet wide, the whole being capped with a corrugated iron roof. The entrance steps led up to a pair of natural wooden French doors, one of which was open. To the left of the French doors was a small, round wooden table and in the growing dawn light he was able to discern two cane easy chairs placed either side of the table. There was utter silence. Dundas could well imagine the once young couple arriving here on this virgin patch of land; perhaps initially living under canvas, full of hope and determined to convert this untamed place into a home and a farm of their own. How many months, perhaps even years, had gone into making their dream a reality?

From his position on the steps he could now see the rose beds, surrounded by a neatly-cut lawn and, some fifty yards away, a row of tall 'blue gum' trees silhouetted against the pink dawn sky. Again, he was conscious of the utter silence that would soon be broken by the lowing of the farm's cattle and, perhaps, the noise of a tractor being started. With the coming dawn, wisps of smoke would curl up into the crisp air as the farm labour prepared for another working day.

The noise of an approaching vehicle disturbed his thoughts. The Land Rover stopped beside the other vehicles. There was a sound of a door being opened and slammed shut and then a moment of silence as the familiar lanky figure of Bill Stewart, the Scenes of Crime Officer, came into view carrying a large valise and a camera tripod. Out of habit, Dundas glanced at his watch.

"Morning Bill, what kept you in Nakuru?"

Bill Stewart grinned. "It should have been sleep. Bloody hell, it's a bit nippy in these parts!"

Dundas grinned. "It'll soon warm up."

"It needs to. So what can you tell me?" Bill Stewart dumped his equipment onto the ground.

"The farm owners have been hacked to death in their dining room. Evidently, the farm's firearms have been stolen. The houseboy is suspected to be involved, as he's missing and their cook is under arrest as a strong suspect. Nothing has been touched and the Government Doctor from Naivasha is on his way."

Bill Stewart gestured at the house. "Have you seen the murder scene?"

"No, but from what I have heard, it's pretty gory. One other thing... their cat has been killed and it's by the kitchen door, so I'd like some shots taken."

Bill Stewart bent down and started to pick up his equipment. "Is Superintendent Lewis around?"

"I believe he's showing the Assistant Superintendent from Naivasha the dead cat."

"Right Robert, I'll get stuck in." With these words, Bill Stewart made his way up the steps and began dusting the French doors for fingerprints.

The sky had lightened and the colour of the sky to the East had lost its purple tinge; orange was now the predominant colour captured by the sparse clouds floating overhead. Dundas stood near the farmhouse entrance and looked across the neatly cut lawn, now soaked with overnight dew. In the distance, a cow could be heard lowing. Apart from this, there was still utter silence. He glanced at his watch, almost 5.50am. The Dog Master would be on his way to commence following the tracks of the persons involved in this senseless killing. A uniformed figure was approaching from the direction of the line of Blue Gum trees; it was the Police Inspector from North Kinankop. As he drew closer, he raised his right hand in a gesture of recognition. In his left hand, supported on a short stick, was what appeared to be a garment. He stopped upon reaching Dundas.

"Sorry I've been so long, Sir, but I decided to have a look around the labour camp. The cook's wife confirms his story but it was obvious she was hiding something. Not once did she look me in the eyes. I searched the hut but there was nothing unusual. The wife also took me to the houseboy's hut. It was unoccupied and the bed had been stripped and the blankets, clothing and cooking utensils were also missing. So it would appear that both the houseboy and his wife have done a runner. However, I did find this..." The Inspector held up the garment on the stick for Dundas to inspect.

"It was under the bed and must have been missed. I thought the Dog Master could use it to track the suspects. I also spotted something very odd; in the light of my torch it looked like a sheep or cow's eye with a thorn stuck through it. I decided not to disturb things too much until daylight. The camp is now stirring, so the labour can be questioned."

Dundas shivered against the cold dawn air and hunched his shoulders inside his jacket. "This animal eye with the thorn, have you come across anything like it before?"

"No Sir. The Kikuyu are steeped in witchcraft and no doubt this was used in some form of ceremony."

"Hmm..." Dundas nodded his head. "The cook knows more about this murder than he cares to admit, so mentioning this eye may unlock the door. When I have conferred with my boss, it is highly likely that he will wish to see the two huts for himself."

A Police Land Rover arrived and stopped on the drive. A uniformed figure alighted from the passenger side of the vehicle, went round to the rear and undid the canvas flap. A large Doberman Pincer jumped to the ground and immediately started sniffing, then cocked its leg against the Assistant Superintendent's Land Rover to send a steaming jet of urine onto the front offside tyre before scuffing the ground with its rear feet and sniffing at the ground again.

Superintendent Lewis and the Assistant Superintendent appeared from around the side of the farmhouse. The Dog Master saluted.

"Good morning Sir, we are ready to go. Are there any signs of tracks or an item of clothing that the dog can scent?"

The Inspector from North Kinankop stepped forward, with the garment still on the stick.

"Sir, I found this in the houseboy's hut. I haven't touched it." He held the garment aloft as all eyes turned on him.

Superintendent Lewis turned to the Dog Master. "It should be ideal."

The Dog Master nodded in agreement. "It is Sir, so if I can be shown the point of entry, the dog can scent this garment and we will be on our way."

The Assistant Superintendent spoke to the Inspector from North Kinankop.

"Inspector Davies, detail two of your armed men to accompany the Dog Master."

The Inspector snapped to attention and saluted. "Sir." He then handed the garment on the stick to Dundas. "Can you look after this?" Then hurried away.

Superintendent Lewis addressed the Dog Master. "We have checked all around the building. There are no signs of a forced entry; the persons involved entered by the steps here." He gestured towards the entrance.

The Dog Master looked up at the open French door. "In that case Sir, if the other C.I.D. officer will place the garment about three feet from the foot of the steps, we'll get started."

Dundas carefully placed the garment on the ground, removed the stick and stood well back. The Dog Master clipped a long, thin rope onto the dog's collar, led it over to the garment and said, "Suk!"

The Doberman sniffed the garment twice and then, with its nose to the ground, set off up the drive as the Dog Master began to uncoil the thin rope, trailed by the two armed constables. As they moved out of sight, Dundas walked over to Superintendent Lewis.

"Sir, the Inspector here has checked on the cook's story and has also briefly searched the houseboys' hut. The man's wife is also missing and from what he has told me the hut has almost been stripped bare. He also found what appears to be a sheep or cow's eye, impaled with a thorn."

Superintendent Lewis pursed his lips and nodded. "Interesting. Obviously some form of witchcraft, but I doubt if it's involved in this murder. This type of 'mumbo-jumbo' is confined to their own kind."

He turned to the Assistant Superintendent.

"Have you any idea of the make-up of the labour force here?"

"No Sir, but based on other farms in the area, mostly Kikuyu."

Superintendent Lewis nodded. "Hmm, they're a clannish lot, but perhaps someone will talk. Robert, we'll take a closer look at these two huts and perhaps, Superintendent, in the meantime can you arrange to have the cook booked into custody?"

The Assistant Superintendent saluted and walked over to the parked vehicles. Superintendent Lewis turned to Dundas.

"How's Bill Stewart progressing?"

"The last time I saw him, Sir, he was dusting the French doors. I'll go and check."

Dundas went up the steps two at a time, paused by the French doors and raised his voice.

"Bill, the boss wants to know if you're making progress."

Bill Stewart's voice emerged from somewhere within the farmhouse.

"Tell the boss that until now I've been working by the light of the farm's paraffin lamps, so progress has been slow. Now it's daylight, it will still take ages and I've yet to photograph the crime scene and the cat. I'll be here until lunchtime at least."

Dundas raised his voice again. "O.K. I'll pass on the message." He retraced his way down the steps and back to Superintendent Lewis.

"He says, Sir, lunchtime at the earliest."

"In that case Robert, let's search those two huts."

# CHAPTER FOUR

BY NOW THE SUN WAS CASTING long shadows and in its warm light a slight mist was rising from the ground. The heavy dew was still evident and, as Dundas and Superintendent Lewis made their way to the labour camp, their footprints could be clearly seen on the dew soaked grass. Ahead, wisps of smoke could be seen curling up into the almost still air as the labourers' wives prepared for another day of toil to support their husbands' needs.

Dundas never failed to marvel at the huge weights these women were able to carry on the hollows of their backs, the carrying strap positioned across the tops of their heads which, due to the pressure over the years, caused a groove in their skulls. It was a common sight to see these women staggering along under these heavy loads of firewood, or large cans of water, whilst their husbands rode ahead on a bicycle.

The camp consisted of some twenty neatly-thatched round native style huts. To the side of each hut was a smaller version, supported off the ground on short stilts. These were the individual maize stores. Chickens, mostly with deep brown feathers, were doing what all chickens do, scratching at the bare ground or settling into shallow hollows for a dust bath. Small children were running around and stopped as Dundas and Superintendent Lewis approached, then either ran off to peep at the two strangers from the safety of their doorways, or stood looking curiously with large brown eyes. One of the women was pounding maize into flour. A large pole, some six feet long and about four inches in diameter, rose and fell in a regular rhythm into a hollowed-out log containing the seed. Dundas went over to where she was working and spoke in Kiswahili.

"*Jambo.* Which is the cook's hut?"

The woman paused and rested the pole on top of the partly pounded maize flour, then pointed.

"*Jambo Bwana*, it's the one over there with the black chicken outside." She picked up the pole and continued with her labours.

The hut door was open and Dundas knocked, making the usual greeting, "*Hodi*." A woman came to the door and emerged into the bright sunlight. Dundas put her age around the mid-twenties; she was about five feet four in height, well-built and had the usual cotton *shuka* (cloth) knotted on her left shoulder, covering a short-sleeved cotton top and skirt. Her head was covered with a simple cotton scarf worn like a bandana and knotted at the nape of her neck. Dundas noted that she looked either stressed or scared and she avoided his eyes.

"*Jambo Bwana.*"

Dundas glanced at Superintendent Lewis, then faced the woman again. "Are you the wife of the cook?"

"*Ndiyo Bwana.*"

"What time did he start work yesterday evening?" Dundas noted that she was trembling very slightly.

"He was late going to the house."

Dundas nodded again. "What caused this?"

The woman, with her eyes still on the ground, started to wring her hands and her trembling became more apparent. There was no response to the question.

"Well?"

"I don't know Bwana."

"Who came to see your husband, either last night or the night before?"

Suddenly the woman darted into the hut and slammed the door.

Superintendent Lewis interjected.

"Leave her for the time being, Robert. I don't know how you feel, but there is an atmosphere here that you can almost touch. The woman who was pounding the maize – no smile and very curt. This woman is so scared that she has fled into her hut. My instincts tell me that something has been going on. Add to this, the houseboy has apparently fled with his wife plus most of his goods and chattels."

Dundas looked around. "You're right Sir, there is a definite atmosphere. I thought it strange when the other woman was so curt. So, shall we check on the houseboy's hut?"

Nearby, a little girl, perhaps no more than six years old and who had been watching intently the contact with the cook's wife, when asked pointed to the houseboy's hut, then giggled and ran off to join her two friends, who were peeping around the side of one of the huts.

The hut door was ajar and the hinges creaked as Superintendent Lewis pushed it open. The interior smelled strongly of woodsmoke and, apart from a bed and a table, the hut was bare. At this early hour, the shaft of sunlight from the open doorway penetrated deeply into the interior, adding to the light coming through the two small windows. Dundas glanced up at the thatched roof, then around the walls and the floor.

"There's not much here Sir, but why take everything? Is it possible that he and his wife have been abducted?"

Superintendent Lewis bent down and examined the earthen floor.

"I can't see any signs of a struggle Robert, and the door's not damaged. You were saying that there's an eye impaled on a thorn."

"Yes Sir. The Inspector from North Kinankop said it was just under the bed." Dundas bent down. "Here it is Sir." He stood up, holding the grisly exhibit by its thorn. "Looking at this, Sir, I would say that it's not more than forty-eight hours old."

Superintendent Lewis looked at the exhibit closely. "Without any doubt Robert, witchcraft is involved here, but the question is, how does this link in with the murders of Mr and Mrs Blake? And why should their houseboy depart with his wife, goods and chattels? Let's have a look at their maize store..."

Just ten yards away, situated beside a patch of land sown with cabbages, was the maize store. Dundas opened the small door. It was empty! Dundas went to an adjoining store. It was nearly full of dried maize cobs. Returning to the houseboy's store, he noted that Superintendent Lewis was crouching over the stumps of cabbages. He glanced up as Dundas approached.

"Robert, take a look at these cabbage stumps. It's my guess that they were cut either late last night or first thing this morning. Now, is it possible that the houseboy also took with him twenty cabbages?"

"With the houseboy gone, Sir, perhaps some of the people in the camp decided to help themselves. On the other hand, it is not possible for two people to carry most of their belongings plus at least ten sacks of maize and now twenty cabbages. I am beginning to think that a gang of men must have been involved in this murder."

Superintendent Lewis stood up and glanced at his watch.

"Almost nine o-five. I suggest that we return to the farmhouse and I'll have a word with the Assistant Superintendent. I'll make the necessary entry in my notebook and then he can conduct a thorough search of every hut and maize store. You can see what progress Bill Stewart has made, then later we'll return here to interview the cook's wife."

Dundas went up the steps of the farmhouse and stopped at the French doors, then raised his voice.

"Bill are you there?"

Bill Stewart's voice responded from somewhere inside.

"Robert, stay within the taped area. I'm in the dining room and I hope that you have a strong stomach."

Dundas carefully made his way inside, noting the white and black fingerprint powder on every object. Despite Bill Stewart's warning, he was not fully prepared for the sight that met his eyes. The man was slumped over the dining table, his face buried in his plate of food, his head almost cleft in two; his blood had spread across the white tablecloth and dripped onto the polished wooden floor. He must have died instantly. His wife was slumped back in her chair and had obviously raised her arms to protect herself; the right arm had been severed below the elbow and had fallen onto the floor. Like her husband, she had a huge gash diagonally across her skull, causing blood to spurt onto the ceiling and down onto her cream blouse, her chair and the floor. Dundas stood there, stunned.

"My God, whatever made anyone do this?" He looked at Bill Stewart. "I never expected to see anything like this."

Bill Stewart looked up from adjusting his camera tripod. "The guns have also been taken. I've told the Assistant Superintendent and he's getting in touch with Central Firearms Bureau to ascertain the types and their serial numbers. The gun case has been smashed open and, from what I can see, all the ammunition has been removed. The good thing is, I should be able to obtain some first-class fingerprints. On that note, can I ask you to assist me with a rather unpleasant task? I need to fingerprint the bodies in order to obtain lawful access prints. I've some spare rubber gloves. Can I count you in?"

Dundas nodded and found it difficult to take his eyes away from the gory scene.

"Right Robert, in the black valise there you'll find some spare white surgical gloves and in the side pocket the ruler-sized copper pad and roller. Then, if you'll ink the pad, we can begin. If it concerns you, I'll ask the Government Doctor to help me with the severed forearm."

Dundas placed the copper-sheathed pad onto a side table, squeezed on some fingerprint ink and then, using the roller, made a thin film of ink on the pad. He then slipped on the white rubber gloves, bent down and picked up the woman's forearm. He was surprised how heavy it was.

The Government Doctor had been and gone and the two bodies had been removed to Naivasha. It was nearly four o'clock before Bill Stewart had completed his many tasks. The search of the labour camp had not produced any evidence and the Inspector from North Kinankop reported that the cook's wife could not be found; her door was shut and the two small windows were closed and shuttered.

At about four-twenty, the Dog Master and the two constables returned empty-handed. However, the report was interesting. The dog had tracked the houseboy's scent, initially along the earthen main road and then across fields and open land but the visual tracks indicated perhaps some ten or eleven persons. All had gone well until the gang had passed close to another farm's diesel and petrol store. This had caused the dog to lose the scent. They had circled the store at a distance of some two hundred yards and regained the trail, only to lose it again when the gang had crossed two small streams. It was the opinion of the Dog Master and the two constables that the gang were heading towards the forest. Despite everyone's efforts, the trail had been lost. Dundas calculated that the tracking team must have covered in excess of twenty miles. He looked towards the North. In the far distance was the outline of the Aberdare Range, which he knew was thickly forested.

"Well Robert, what do you make of the Dog Master's report?"

Dundas turned and faced Superintendent Lewis.

"It seems difficult to believe Sir, but I would suggest that this was a planned attack to obtain weapons and supplies. Hence the cut telephone line, the missing cabbages, the empty maize store and the almost empty hut."

Superintendent Lewis gestured.

"Hmm... or is it that this houseboy has fled into the forest and joined some criminals to avoid arrest and hopes that some weeks later he can reappear elsewhere. The guns could be used to shoot game. Any comments?"

"Yes Sir. It is my belief that we have stumbled across something very sinister here. The persons involved were not ordinary thieves. They are well organised and ruthless. There was no need to kill the Blakes. We have the cook's admission, the curtness of the woman pounding the maize, the cook's wife shutting her door and refusing to speak to us. Add to this the couple's dead cat and the eye impaled on a thorn. Something odd has taken place at this farm and native witchcraft is involved."

Superintendent Lewis stood there nodding his head and looking very thoughtful.

"You could well be right. Back at base I'll have a chat with Special Branch, perhaps they have heard the odd rumour. I've sent to the Brown Trout Hotel at Njabini for some flasks of coffee and some assorted sandwiches, so before my stomach collapses, I suggest that we eat."

At five o'clock Dundas and Superintendent Lewis once again made their way to the labour camp to see if the cook's wife had returned. The door was still shut and the windows still secured. Several calls of "*Hodi*" failed to produce any response. Dundas looked at his boss.

"I suggest, Sir, that we force the door."

"With what in mind?"

"We know the cook is implicated and we may find some evidence."

Superintendent Lewis gestured. "Do it!"

Dundas barged the door with his left shoulder and it flew open. Swinging by the neck from the hut's crossbeam was the cook's wife. Her head was to one side and her lifeless eyes were bulging. The tip of her tongue protruded from between her lips, her arms hung limply at her sides. Dundas noted that, as was usual in cases such as this, her urine had run down her legs and soaked into the earthen floor below. Dundas stepped forward and felt her pulse. There was nothing, but the body was still warm. Near her dangling feet was a small wooden box that perhaps she had used to stand on. He swore.

"If only we had made her open the door and not gone off!"

"Robert, don't blame yourself. Assuming that it was suicide, something that she knew was of such magnitude that she dare not tell us. This whole case has become ever more sinister since we arrived. You stay here and I'll alert the Assistant Superintendent, the Government Doctor has already left, so I'll alert Bill Stewart."

Dundas checked the floor very carefully; there were no signs of any scuff marks that would indicate a struggle. The woman's clothing was unsoiled. He next looked at her wrists. No signs of bruising or rope marks. Dundas went outside. The same little girl was standing some way off. Dundas emerged from the hut, gently pulling the door shut and smiled at the girl.

"Have you been here all day?"

The girl grinned and nodded her head several times.

"Do you know the wife of the cook? Her husband works at the Bwana's house."

The little girl nodded her head again, put her hand to her mouth and raised her shoulders in a typical childlike reaction.

"Did she go anywhere today?"

The little girl shook her head.

"Are you sure?"

At least five head nods and she repeated her previous gesture, giggled and ran off to join her two friends who were, as before, peeping around the side of one of the huts.

Some two hours later, following the visit from the Government Doctor, extensive enquiries by the European Police Officers and the African Constables, plus Bill Stewart photographing the body, the knot used, and an overall picture of the scene, the initial conclusion was suicide, but in view of the general situation at the farm, Superintendent Lewis decided to reserve judgement.

# CHAPTER FIVE

THE FOLLOWING MORNING, after a good night's rest at the Brown Trout and having consumed a substantial breakfast, Superintendent Lewis and Dundas were in the small car park at the hotel awaiting the arrival of Ndibo with the Land Rover. At this early hour, it was just 7:22, the air felt crisp, almost frosty.

"Well Robert, how was the Brown Trout?"

"In a word, Sir, excellent! I have been here before but have never stayed here."

Superintendent Lewis turned around and gestured at the rising slopes of the Aberdare Range. "Take a look behind you Robert. The far peak to your left is called Fey's Peak and is named after one of Kenya's original settlers."

Dundas looked at the skyline, the dense forestation stretched in both directions as far as the eye could see; a faint mist was rising above the trees.

"What's the height of the Aberdare Range Sir?"

Superintendent Lewis pointed, sweeping his right hand from left to right. "At the top, over eleven thousand feet and where we are standing must be close to eight thousand."

Their conversation was disturbed by the distinctive sound of an approaching Land Rover. Ndibo swept into the entrance and, having quickly reversed, stopped beside them, then jumped out and opened the passenger door. He gave them a big welcoming grin.

"*Jambo Effendi!*"

Dundas clambered in first, his feet straddling the central gearbox housing, followed by Superintendent Lewis. Ndibo returned to the driver's seat, turned the ignition key and started the engine.

"So Ndibo, how was Njabini Police Station?"

"Very good Effendi, I stayed with one of the constables, who knows my brother."

Ndibo steered the Land Rover up to the entrance, then turned right onto the murram-surfaced road, passing the Police Station to their left. Some two miles later, they passed the 'T' junction that led to Naivasha and headed towards the North Kinankop Police Station.

Dundas glanced past Ndibo at the vast Aberdare Range and wondered if a small gang were up there somewhere in that mist-shrouded forest. If so, just how long would it be before cold and hunger drove them to return to a normal environment?

Superintendent Lewis disturbed his thoughts.

"I was going over in my mind your comments about the emerging sinister aspects of this case. The cook was obviously scared and is afraid to talk. His wife, to avoid further questions, hanged herself, or so we believe. And, based on the report of the Dog Master, some ten or more people were either directly or indirectly involved in this murder and the theft of the firearms. So, is something brewing?"

Dundas shrugged. "I don't know Sir, but what really concerns me is how do we make contact and arrest the people involved? If they are hiding in the Aberdare forest, it covers hundreds of square miles. My other concern is what if their success 'goes to their heads' and they repeat the same *modus operandi*? As we have often discussed, Sir, the best deterrent is a rapid detection, arrest and conviction."

Superintendent Lewis looked very thoughtful and nodded his head several times. "Hmm... so, considering the huge area involved, how would you go about bringing them to justice?"

There was a thump that almost loosened their fillings as Ndibo, in trying to avoid a small dik-dik running across the road, hit a pothole. Ndibo looked anxiously at Superintendent Lewis.

"*Sorry Effendi.*"

Superintendent Lewis grunted. "Just make sure that we arrive at North Kinankop in one piece!"

"*Ndiyo Effendi.*"

"And slow down!"

"*Ndiyo Effendi.*"

"Are you OK Robert?"

"Yes Sir, but I'm not too sure about the springs!"

The blue Kenya Police flag suspended on its white flagpole soon came into view.

"We'll continue this conversation Robert, after we've questioned the cook."

The Land Rover slowed and stopped beside the neat, stone-clad and corrugated iron roofed Police Station Charge Office. Even before they had alighted, the European Inspector whom they had met during the previous day came out and stopped beside the passenger door, then saluted.

"Good morning Sir!"

Superintendent Lewis, followed by Dundas, clambered out and held out his hand.

"Good morning Inspector, is it always this cold?"

"It's worse when it rains Sir. We've kept a close eye on the cook and he has not been informed about his wife's death. Also Sir, sometime today he must be taken before a Magistrate and officially charged. In the cell register I have recorded murder. Is this the official charge?"

Superintendent Lewis nodded.

"It will do for now. So where's the cook?"

❖ ❖ ❖

The cook was led into the Charge Office under the escort of two constables. Superintendent Lewis indicated the chair on the opposite side of the table and the cook, looking very dejected, sat down, with the two constables standing directly behind him. The cook looked down at the table and fiddled with his fingers. Superintendent Lewis remained silent for another thirty seconds and then asked.

"So which dish did Bwana and Memsahib like best of all?"

The question caught the cook off guard and he looked up at Superintendent Lewis in disbelief.

"Well... what did they like best of all?"

The cook shrugged his shoulders, paused and then said,

"Roast beef with roast potatoes, cabbage and Yorkshire pudding."

"And what about sweet?"

"Apple pie and custard."

"So where did you learn to cook like this?"

"At the Church of England Mission, near Nairobi." The cook looked down at the table again and a shiver went through his body.

"What's your name?"

"At the Mission I was christened John, John Kimathi, but my Kikuyu name is Ngeroge."

"John, you shivered just now. Are you cold?"

The cook remained silent. Superintendent Lewis continued.

"You said yesterday that you didn't expect Bwana and Memsahib to be harmed. Why did you say this?"

The cook shivered again and continued to fiddle with his hands.

"What can you tell me about this?" Superintendent Lewis placed the animal eye speared with a thorn onto the table. The cook looked shocked and started to tremble violently. Superintendent Lewis gestured at the grisly exhibit.

"Well? Is it yours?"

The cook shook his head, looked at the open door and half rose from his seat. One of the constables stepped forward and pushed him down again. Superintendent Lewis picked up the grisly exhibit.

"This was found under the houseboy's bed, so was a witchdoctor involved in this?"

The cook shook his head and remained silent.

"So then you know who it was?"

The cook shook violently again and looked desperate.

"John, you raised the alarm, is that correct?"

The cook nodded his head but didn't look up.

"But your hut is as least a hundred and fifty paces from the farm-house, so what did you hear at such a distance?"

The cook looked very furtive, then stared at the eye impaled on the thorn. Superintendent Lewis continued.

"John, look at me and tell me what went on before Bwana and Memsahib were killed?"

There was a long silence and the cook looked down again and fiddled with his fingers. The pressure created by this silence was intense. Finally the cook spoke.

"I didn't know they were to be harmed Effendi. James..."

"Who is James?"

"The houseboy, Effendi. He said they would threaten them and then steal the Bwana's guns."

"So who are *they?*"

"I was told by James that ten men would be involved and that he planned to join them."

Superintendent Lewis gestured. "Did you see any of these men?"

"Only one, Effendi, and he was called Kamau."

"Can you describe him to me?"

The cook looked down at the table and shivered.

"If I tell you, Effendi, I will die!"

He broke into a series of violent shivers.

Superintendent Lewis spoke again.

"So you took some kind of oath?"

The cook nodded and continued to shake. Superintendent Lewis turned to Dundas and said in English, "Robert, the Kikuyu are very superstitious and an oath can be completely binding. Normally some form of sacrifice is involved and the participants drink the blood. I suspect that as each person took the oath, they speared a sheep's eye with a thorn."

He turned back to the cook and reverted to Kiswahili.

"Was it chicken's blood that you drank when you took this oath?"

John Kimathi visibly paled.

"And was it this man called Kamau who administered this oath to you?"

John Kimathi gave a cry of despair and buried his head in his hands and shook violently. Superintendent Lewis continued speaking in a soft voice.

"John, until a few days ago you were very happy doing your job as a cook. Now you are in custody and will be charged for assisting a gang to murder your employers. But I have even more bad news for you. Because your wife was so scared after taking this oath, rather than answer our questions she hanged herself. I'm sorry to have to tell you this, but it's true."

The cook stared at Superintendent Lewis in utter disbelief and then the tears started to run down his cheeks and onto his chin and shirt front.

Superintendent Lewis glanced at Dundas and jerked his head at the door.

"John, we'll leave you for a while and I'll have a mug of tea sent in. What you have to ask yourself is, have all these deaths been worth the oath that you and your wife took?"

Superintendent Lewis stood and followed by Dundas exited the Charge Office out into the bright sunlight.

"Thank God, it's warmed up!"

Dundas grinned as Superintendent Lewis closed his eyes and let the morning sun bathe his face in warmth.

"Well Robert, any comments?"

Superintendent Lewis felt in his right hand jacket pocket where he normally kept his pipe and tobacco pouch. Having extracted both, he proceeded to fill the pipe's bowl.

"As you remarked Sir, these oaths are obviously very binding; it was not due to us that he was shaking."

Superintendent Lewis applied a match to the pipe's bowl, drew deeply, then removed the pipe from his mouth and blew a plume of blue/grey smoke into the morning air.

"The Kikuyu have many beliefs tied to witchcraft. For example, old women can, at night, transform themselves into hyenas and roam at will, looking for victims. During oathing ceremonies, chicken blood is often used and participants have to crawl through an archway of thorns. Sheep's' eyes are normally used and a thorn is thrust through the eye as the oath is taken."

Dundas interjected. "Excuse me for asking Sir, but where did you obtain all this information?"

"It was a long time ago. I was newly qualified and I was assisting an Inspector with several years' service to investigate a series of native murders. Basically, it involved a Kikuyu witchdoctor who by mumbo-jumbo scared the hell out of two men, then used them to commit his crimes." Superintendent Lewis glanced at his watch. "It's time to return to John Kimathi."

The cook was still sat at the table guarded by the two constables. In front of him was an enamel mug of partly consumed tea. He looked up as Superintendent Lewis and Dundas took their seats.

"So, John Kimathi, you are in deep trouble."

Having said this, Superintendent Lewis remained silent and let the pressure of silence do its work. A minute passed. Even Dundas could feel the pressure of this simple but effective technique. The cook gave an involuntary shiver and looked up.

"Effendi, if I break the oath, I will die."

Superintendent Lewis leaned forward and gestured.

"This oath that you took... has it protected you from being arrested by the police? Has this oath kept your wife safe? Did this oath protect the lives of Bwana and Memsahib Blake?"

John Kimathi sat at the table, his eyes cast down, looking very distressed. Again there was a long silence.

Superintendent Lewis spoke again. "All this oath has brought you is misery. Is this what you expected when you drank the chickens' blood and crawled through the archway of thorns?"

Without looking up, the cook shook his head.

"So what more can you tell us?"

Again there was a long silence then the cook looked up at Superintendent Lewis.

"Effendi, you are not a *mganga* (witchdoctor) and cannot free me from my oath. I will tell you all I know and then the oath will take my life."

Having been cautioned, John Kimathi's statement was even more sinister than either Superintendent Lewis or Dundas had realised. The Kikuyu stranger Kamau had arrived on the farm at night, saying that the European farmers must be driven off their land. As far as this farm was concerned, the land would be divided equally between each family. Everyone who worked on the farm was a Kikuyu and the head of each household gave five shillings to the man Kamau, who then proceeded to oath every adult, binding them to secrecy. Part of the oath consisted of agreeing to help drive the European farmers off the land.

The houseboy had stayed behind after the ceremony and later stated that he had taken a very powerful and special oath, but refused to say what it was. Kamau had told everyone that he was recruiting men to assist in driving out the Europeans and guns were being stolen from European farmhouses. In view of the fact that the houseboy had departed with most of his goods and chattels, plus his maize, it was assumed that he had gone to join the gang alluded to by Kamau. The description of Kamau was rather vague, except for one thing; his hair was long and multi-plaited.

Once John Kimathi had been officially charged, Dundas excused himself, went outside into the warm sunlight and looked towards the Aberdare Range. It looked vast and foreboding. Assuming that this gang was still hiding within this vast forest, how would one set about finding them and bringing them to justice? His thoughts were disturbed by the European Inspector.

"Excuse me Sir, I've organised some coffee in my quarters; it will be ready in less than five minutes. So, has the cook given a statement?"

Dundas nodded. "He has. In view of what he has said, has there been any increase of thefts in the area? For example, farm produce, animals, chickens?"

"Yes there has, mainly from the farms bordering the forest."

Dundas continued. "Has anyone been arrested?"

"Yes. Two months ago a sheep was stolen. Two men were arrested, pleaded guilty and were convicted."

"Two questions. One, what tribe were they?"

"Kikuyu Sir."

"And two, was the sheep recovered?"

"No, it was never traced. It was bloodstains on the clothing of the thieves that led to their arrest."

"Did they say what happened to the sheep?"

"No, the assumption was they sold the meat."

Dundas nodded. "Hmm... I'll need their names. Keep in touch and let me know if any more of these thefts occur. It would help if map references could be included for these and any future thefts."

Having consumed their coffee and thanked their host, Superintendent Lewis and Dundas, with Ndibo at the wheel, set off for the scene of the murders.

Ndibo stopped the Land Rover by the steps leading up to the French doors of the farmhouse. Superintendent Lewis clambered out and spoke to Ndibo.

"Ndibo, drive back to the South Kinankop Police Station at Njabini. See this friend of your brother and ask if there has been an increase in thefts from local farms in the last three months. Then about twelve thirty call in at the 'Brown Trout Hotel' and ask the two ladies in charge if they can provide coffee and sandwiches."

"Ndiyo Effendi."

"And what about you?"

"My friend's wife will feed me Effendi."

"Ndibo, one final thing, make sure the Inspector in charge knows you are around."

Ndibo gave a great big grin, started the Land Rover, quickly reversed and sped up the earthen drive, leaving a faint dust trail in his wake. Superintendent Lewis turned to Dundas.

"Robert, I am not trying to undercut the Inspector's authority. It will give Ndibo something to do – and it is far better than having him hanging around."

Superintendent Lewis and Dundas made their way down the pathway towards the labour lines. The position of the sun indicated that it was close to 11am. In the distance, a tractor could be heard working, cattle were lowing and the sound of a rooster in the labour camp could be clearly heard. In the line of blue gum trees, a pigeon was making its familiar cooing noise that always ended so abruptly. Dundas found it difficult to believe that some 36 hours ago two innocent people had been butchered and a third had taken her life due to an oath administered by some witchdoctor called Kamau.

His boss invaded his train of thought.

"Robert, I find it difficult to believe after what has happened but it would appear that work on the farm continues unabated!"

"Sir, I was just thinking exactly the same thing."

Despite their enquiries, no one had seen anything, heard anything and knew nothing whatsoever about a man called Kamau. Yet again, there was an atmosphere that it was difficult to 'put one's finger on'. Superintendent Lewis sat down on the grass close to the houseboy's hut, reached into his jacket pocket and produced his pipe.

"Robert, they've clammed up! With some, there is a sullenness that I have rarely encountered in the past, but with some of the younger wives there's an element of fear. All we have to go on is the cook's account of events."

"Do you think he was telling the truth, Sir?"

"On balance, yes. I'm sure that he was instructed to serve dinner outside normal hours and, having dished up the main course, was told to leave the kitchen. While the houseboy served the main course, the gang must have waited outside until they felt it was the ideal time to attack. Let's hope that Bill Stewart found some useful fingerprints. Incidentally, I forgot to tell you. The Assistant Superintendent from Naivasha has checked up on the missing firearms. According to the Central Firearms Bureau, the couple owned a twelve-bore over-and-under shotgun and an old Mauser rifle. It's difficult to estimate the number of rounds of ammunition stolen, but for certain we are now facing an armed gang."

Dundas sat down beside Superintendent Lewis.

"Let's hope Sir, that they can't shoot straight!"

Superintendent Lewis drew on his pipe, blew the smoke into the air and looked very thoughtful. "Let's hope you're right."

Some two hours later, a Constable came running down the path that led to the labour camp, stopped before Superintendent Lewis and saluted.

"Effendi, a message has just been received over your radio from the Inspector at North Kinankop. The cook was found hanged in his cell."

Superintendent Lewis erupted. "How the bloody hell did he manage to do that?"

"I don't know Effendi, but the Inspector is on the radio wishing to speak to you."

Superintendent Lewis turned to Dundas.

"I don't swear very often, but he was our only bloody witness!"

Superintendent Lewis lifted the VHF microphone from its clip on the Land Rover facia and pressed the transmit button.

"North Kinankop this is Mike Baker Five, do you read me, over?"

There was a faint crackle from the loudspeaker. The transmission did nothing to disguise the apprehension in the Inspector's voice.

"Mike Baker Five this is North Kinankop reading you at strength five, over."

Superintendent Lewis pressed down the microphone button with more force than was usual and ignoring radio procedure.

"Inspector, this man was our only witness. How the hell did he manage to commit suicide?"

"Sir, all normal precautions were taken. His belt and shoelaces had been removed. He used his trousers twisted into a rope. He had attached one end to the bars on the door of his cell and the other around his neck. Then, in a squatting position, he must have twisted round and round until he was asphyxiated."

Superintendent Lewis pressed the microphone button again and, as before, ignored radio procedure.

"And how often was he checked?"

"Every hour Sir, as per normal standing instructions."

Superintendent Lewis shook his head and made a "tch" sound, then pressed the microphone button again.

"Inspector, as this was a death in custody, it will be subject to an enquiry and an inquest."

He swore again and replaced the microphone into its clip.

Despite the tension, Dundas decided to speak.

"Very annoying Sir."

"Annoyed? I'm bloody furious!"

❖ ❖ ❖

# CHAPTER SIX

THREE DAYS OF ENQUIRIES at the farm drew a blank. No one was willing to talk. However, Bill Stewart had obtained masses of fingerprints and with the death of the cook, had the unpleasant task of obtaining prints from the body for elimination purposes. As Superintendent Lewis remarked, the only highlight so far, had been the quality of the food from the Brown Trout.

As a result of Ndibo's information, it was decided to call at the Njabini Police Station and speak to the Inspector in charge. He too had reported an increase in thefts of produce from some of the local farms. The trail of one group of thieves, estimated to be at least four men, had passed by the sawmill situated on the edge of the forest and had then broken up into individual tracks, which had finally petered out.

Dundas was seated in Superintendent Lewis's office, thankful that his boss's pipe was inert in the ashtray.

"Robert, the reason I have called you here is, as promised, I have had a word with my opposite number in Special Branch. There are rumours of a secret society being formed within the Kikuyu tribe."

"What about all the other tribes Sir?"

Superintendent Lewis shook his head.

"Nothing. The Kipsigis, the Nandi, Masai, Luo and all the rest, not even a whisper of any problems. Evidently, we have been the first to produce any form of evidence that some Kikuyu witchdoctors are going around oathing people. We have had reports and evidence of small gangs of Kikuyu entering the Aberdare Forest range. For my money, something is afoot."

Superintendent Lewis picked up his pipe, then arose from his chair and went over to the map on the wall. He tapped the stem of his pipe at the map.

"The murder took place just about here, and you will recall that the police dog tracked the houseboy and his murderous bunch to about here..." He tapped the stem of his pipe at another location.

"The approximate position of the Njabini sawmill is here. If we draw an imaginary line from the Blake's farm to where the houseboy and his gang entered the forest, and do the same from where the theft took place at Njabini to where the trail was lost, and if we extend both of these lines, they cross here, about ten miles inside the forest. Any comments Robert?"

"Yes Sir. So it's highly likely that it's the same gang or that the stolen food is being delivered to a common place."

"That's my thinking Robert. The next question. Assuming that my theory is correct, our houseboy is holed up somewhere in that vicinity, so if we can find him, with this bunch of murderous bastards and in possession of the stolen firearms, backed up by Bill Stewart's finger-print evidence, hopefully the whole lot will be for the chop."

"Sir, I was going to speak to you about allowing me to try to find and arrest the houseboy and his gang."

Superintendent Lewis returned to his chair. "Even if I agreed, it would take at least months, if not longer to find them. And, we are not equipped for this type of activity."

"No Sir, but what if we contact the Kenya Regiment in Nairobi? They must have everything that we need: rucksacks, clothing, special rations... the lot."

Superintendent Lewis nodded several times. "You have missed something off the list. Firearms! We know they have a shotgun and a Mauser rifle, so a truncheon, a pair of handcuffs and a revolver will not exactly scare them to death." Superintendent Lewis gestured. "And, let us not forget, you will have to operate within the law. You are well aware of the strict controls on the use of firearms."

Dundas nodded. "Yes Sir, under the rules we can only shoot back if we are shot at, or to protect life and property. Providing we outnumber them, or they see that we are heavily armed, I'm sure they'll surrender."

Superintendent Lewis shook his head. "Don't count on it Robert, they will know that if proven guilty a hangman's rope awaits them. Desperate men do desperate things. However, reverting to your suggestion, in my opinion this type of operation that you have described is normal police work. Our job is to investigate and apprehend. At present we have no witnesses, a suspect who may be in hiding somewhere in the depths of the Aberdare Range and four dead bodies."

# CHAPTER SEVEN

JAMES NGITHI SAT ON THE EDGE of his bed, watching his wife stir the fire and add two more 'green' logs. Within minutes, the logs started to hiss and their smoke rose into the grass thatch above their heads. His wife now knelt close to the fire and blew on the embers, causing tiny sparks to fly. He noted as he had done so many times before, how this caused the fire's glow to enhance the deep brown of his wife's face. He recalled haggling with her father over the bride price. Ten cows, one thousand shillings, plus many gallons of home-made beer had been difficult to fund. As per their custom, all his new wife had brought with her were the five large stones from the river that now circled and contained their hut's fire. His wife placed the alloy cooking pot onto the fire, then stirred the contents. There was a tap on the door. It was unexpected and they looked at each other and shrugged their shoulders. James Ngithi stood up.

"Who is it?"

The door was tapped again. This time he raised his voice.

"Who is it?"

This time there was a reply but he did not recognise the voice.

"There's a special meeting tonight at midnight, it's inside the farm's barn. Everyone will be there."

James Ngithi glanced at the large alarm clock that stood beside the oil lamp on a low table beside their bed. It was almost 8.35 and outside it had been dark for over an hour.

"What's it all about?"

His question wasn't answered. The voice continued.

"Make sure you are there and bring five shillings."

"What's the money for?"

There was no reply, whoever it was had gone away.

Close to midnight, and carrying an oil lantern, James Ngithi made his way towards the barn. There was faint moonlight and, due to the crisp night air, his breath was clearly visible. The light from the lantern picked out the tall grasses and reflected off his khaki shorts and bare legs. Ahead, other lanterns could be seen heading in the same direction. A meeting at this late hour called by a person unknown was strange, mysterious and intriguing.

By the time James Ngithi arrived, most of the farm's male labour were already there, squatting on the floor. Standing at the front of this gathering were two men; one was dressed like a witchdoctor, the other had long plaited hair, was carrying a shotgun and wore an army great-coat. He noted that, attached to the left lapel of the greatcoat was a small bunch of black and white feathers. The glow from the scores of oil lamps sent flickering shadows onto the walls and gave the two standing figures a sinister appearance. The man with the shotgun raised his right arm and the babble of voices ceased immediately. He scanned the assembled gathering and then spoke.

"Is it true to say that this land, this soil that you nurture for a white farmer is good farming land?"

There were grunts and nods of agreement. The man continued.

"And the cattle here... are they not fat and give many churns of milk?"

Again there was a positive response. He continued.

"Raise your hand anyone here who can afford to buy a tractor like the white farmer's."

Everyone looked around. Not a hand was raised. The man scanned the gathering again.

"Now raise your hand if you would like to own a tractor."

Every hand went up!

"And cows and land?"

Again, every hand was raised. He swept his hand across his chest in a grand gesture.

"My Kikuyu brothers. Each and every one of you can have a share of this farm, its land, its cattle, its farm machinery and even the white farmer's house!"

A voice spoke up from the centre of the crowd.

"But how is this possible? These things cost money."

The man scanned the gathering again and the hubbub died down.

"My Kikuyu brothers, we will drive the white farmers off their land, our land, and then distribute their wealth to all of you! I am a major in the Kikuyu Freedom Army. What we need is your support. Both money and food. We need to know where this farmer keeps his guns and ammunition and we are prepared to kill to obtain them. Some members of our army have already killed white farmers and their wives. A wave of fear is spreading and many will leave. What I have told you is a secret that must not be revealed to anyone. If you do so, the oath that you are about to take will kill you."

James Ngithi felt a shiver run down his spine. Oaths were powerful things, his father had told him that old Kikuyu women could, at night, turn themselves into hyenas and go searching for their victims. As he watched, the witchdoctor reached into a sack at his feet, dragged out a white chicken, quickly slit its throat, then held the flapping bird upside down and let the blood run into a small wooden bowl. Three more chickens were despatched in a similar manner. He then held the four dead birds aloft.

"On this night we will all share in this sacrifice and become as one, dedicated to driving the white farmers from their land!"

He threw the dead birds at his feet, bent down, picked up what appeared to be an arch made from thorn bushes, and held it above his head.

"Every man here will crawl through this arch and then, having sipped chickens' blood, will take the following oath.

*If I am asked to bring the left little finger of my mother, father, wife, son or daughter, I will do so.*

*If I am asked to kill a white farmer and his wife, I will do so.*

*If I am asked to steal guns and ammunition, I will do so.*

*I will give the Kenya Freedom Army every support that I can, including money, food and shelter. To break any of these sacred oaths, then the oath will kill you!"*

A man who James Ngithi recognised as one of the tractor drivers spoke up. "But I don't want to take this oath. I am happy here; the white farmer is good to us. His wife nurses the sick and has opened a school for our children."

The man with the shotgun scowled. "Then you are not one of us. Refuse to join your brothers and tonight you will be strangled and your body will be dumped down a pit latrine, so that everyone can defecate onto your worthless body."

There were mutterings in the crowd and James Ngithi felt a shiver of fear pass through his body. The man with the shotgun spoke again.

"Now each man will crawl through the archway of thorns, sip the blood and take these sacred oaths. Having done this, place your five shillings on the ground to the right of the archway."

He paused and scanned the squatting men, then pointed to the barn door.

"Then leave immediately and return to your homes. Tell no one of what you have seen or heard this night, or the oath will kill you!"

James Ngithi was one of the last to crawl through the arch of thorns and sip the chickens' blood. The enormity of what he had done shocked him and he was unable to stop trembling.

The following morning there was an atmosphere of fear on the farm, people avoided each other's eyes. James Ngithi's wife had asked what had happened at the meeting. No doubt like many other men, he avoided her eyes and mumbled some excuse.

Three weeks had passed and, although the workers on the farm were more relaxed, the underlying element of fear continued. If James Ngithi could have known what the future held, he would have fled.

A month had passed and the night of the oathing ceremony and the terrible things that he had agreed to was starting to fade as the work on Mr Myers' farm followed its normal routine. As the head clerk, James Ngithi was in a trusted position and looked up to by the other Kikuyu labour. He liked his job and was happy with his lot.

"So James, how is our milk yield this month?"

Mr Myers had entered the small, brick, single-storey office attached to the dairy. He was in his mid-fifties, medium height, slim, his dark, straight hair now showing traces of grey. His small clipped moustache and bearing gave away his military background. Like most European male farmers, he favoured a lightweight cotton short-sleeved shirt, long cotton trousers and a pair of sturdy brown boots. He was deeply tanned and looked fit. James Ngithi reached across the bare wooden desk for the daily milk record, then opened it and briefly studied a page.

"Thanks to the recent rains, we are twenty-six gallons up on last month, and that is a direct comparison to the same number of days."

Mr Myers nodded his head.

"Excellent! So James, if this improved yield continues, can we expect a big cheque from the K.F.A. (Kenya Farmers Association)?"

*"Ndiyo Bwana."*

Mr Myers went to turn away, and then paused.

"James, have you heard any rumours about the recent attack at North Kinankop? If you hear anything, let me know."

*"Ndiyo Bwana."*

James Ngithi dared not turn around, he stared at the brick wall of the office with unseeing eyes as the memories of that night came flooding back. It all seemed to be so very normal. Bwana Myers asking about milk yields, maintaining the records to pay the farm labour. He and two others had discussed the meeting in the barn and had decided that perhaps the real reason was to obtain money from everyone. Peter the tractor driver, said that the farm next door had also been visited by the man in the army greatcoat and the witchdoctor. As James turned these thoughts over in his mind, the power of his oath dominated his mind. An involuntary shiver passed through his body.

That same evening, following dinner, Mr Myers switched on their battery radio. He glanced at his watch, nearly news time. His wife Betty was in her usual armchair beside the Tilley pressure lamp reading a novel. The lamp threw deep shadows into the corners of the room; its soft, soothing hiss accompanied the crackle of the logs burning in the fireplace.

Phillip Myers reached for his pipe which was on the plain blue gum mantelpiece, then returned to his chair. He looked across at his wife.

"Betty, the nine o'clock news is about to begin."

Betty put her book down.

"Why is it that they always report the price of coffee but never milk?"

Her husband's retort was stopped short as the news began:

*"Good evening, this is the nine o'clock news, read by Robert Marsh. In the last 24 hours, two attacks have been made against farms within the White Highlands. There is growing concern over the number of incidents and a delegation of Kenya farmers will be holding a meeting with the Governor. Andy Macpherson has the details..."*

*"...Just before midnight, two European farms situated within ten miles of each other, were attacked by gangs of men estimated to be at least twenty strong. In the first attack, a storage barn was set on fire, some livestock were hamstrung and had to be destroyed. When fired upon by the farmer, the gang fled. In the second incident, horses in the paddock were slashed and farm machinery set on fire. The gang then attacked the house, but fled when fired upon. The farmer involved in this incident was slightly injured by flying glass. The Assistant Superintendent in charge of the area said 'investigations were continuing and early arrests were expected'. As a result of the rising number of incidents, a twenty strong delegation..."*

Phillip Myers eased himself out of his chair, went over to the radio and turned it off. "Betty, more attacks, and not so many weeks ago the Blakes were murdered." He returned to his chair, 'fluffed up' the two chintz cushions and sat down, looking very thoughtful. "Betty, we need to take precautions."

His wife placed her book onto the small side table. "I agree these reports are concerning, but Phillip, we already lock the doors and secure the windows."

Phillip Myers nodded his head several times. "However, we have to face reality. We are at least twenty miles from the nearest police station, and if the phone lines were cut, how could we obtain help?"

His wife leaned back in her armchair. "Phillip, you are not in the army in Palestine now and I'm sure that all these problems will soon go away."

Phillip Myers grunted. "Hmm... Betty it may never happen, but I want to make some changes. I suggest that we have dinner before 7PM."

"But Phillip, we've always had dinner at 8.15!"

Phillip Myers continued. "I also suggest that soon after dusk I carry my Webley revolver and that we keep the shotgun and the old ex-army .303 rifle with us at all times. I'll teach you how to handle all three weapons."

His wife picked up her book again. "I agree that for you to carry your revolver is sensible, but I couldn't hit a barn door at ten paces. I think you are being over dramatic. And anyway, we've had most of our workers for years. If we were attacked I'm sure that they would come to our aid."

As she opened the page of her book and began reading, her husband went over to the sideboard, opened the left hand drawer and withdrew a .455 Webley revolver. His wife looked up from her book.

"The last time you used that was to shoot a cow that had broken its leg – that must be at least six years ago."

Having said this, she returned to the imaginary world between the covers of her book.

❖ ❖ ❖

That same night, James Ngithi sat beside an old storm lantern and, in its yellow light, studied the milk yield; with a semi-sharp pencil he calculated the amount of money it would bring. He had to admit to himself that to share in this with the other farm labour and to have a share in the farm's lands would be far better than his current monthly pay and the half-acre plot allocated to him by Bwana Myers. Also, due to his position he should be given an extra piece of land. Perhaps he would even be responsible for dividing up the farm. In his mind's eye he pictured himself as the new Bwana Myers, issuing orders, driving a dusty old car.

A tapping at the door brought him back to reality. He looked at his wife, and then called. "Who is it?"

There was a pause for several seconds. "A friend."

James Ngithi glanced at the old alarm clock on the small table beside the lamp. It was after 9PM.

"Who are you?"

"I once had four dead chickens." The unknown voice continued.

James Ngithi's heart started to thump in his chest. The voice outside was now urgent. "Open the door and come outside."

James Ngithi arose from his wooden chair and carefully opened the door. In the soft moonlight, he could see three figures. Each one had long plaited hair and was dressed in an army greatcoat. One was carrying what appeared to be a rifle. He stepped outside and shivered, partly from the cold night air but more from the fear that he felt in the pit of his stomach.

The man with the rifle said, "Come with us."

James Ngithi's blood ran cold. "But what have I done?"

The man spoke again. "Nothing as yet, there's a special meeting in the barn."

In the soft light of just two oil lamps, he recognised the figures of the cook and houseboy. The man with the gun addressed them.

"The time has come to act. Let me remind you of your sacred oath." He scanned the small group. "In three nights' time we will attack this farm, kill the farmer and his wife, seize their guns and to obtain fresh meat, slaughter as many cattle as possible. We now need some information..."

James Ngithi broke out in a series of trembles. Thinking about a share in the farm was one thing, but killing Bwana and Memsahib? The mention of his name brought him back to stark reality.

"As the farmer and his wife eat early, to attack at dusk would not be to our advantage. Your job, James, will be to concoct some story that will make the farmer open the door. We will then rush in and complete our task."

James Ngithi's mouth was so dry he could hardly speak. "Will I be involved in the killing?"

The man with the gun had a sneering expression on his face that the soft yellow lamplight could not conceal. "Not this time, perhaps another night. So what would make the farmer here open his door?"

James Ngithi searched for suitable words, but due to a lack of saliva and a very dry mouth, found it difficult to string them together.

"Perhaps... perhaps I could say one of the cows had been attacked by hyena."

The discussions continued. Finally, the man with the gun held up his hand. "This is the plan. The farmer and his wife will be given extra portions of food to make them feel lazy. You (pointing to the houseboy) will check that the two guns are in their usual place. At 9.30PM we will arrive here with fifteen men and commence slaughtering the cattle. At the same time you James will knock on the farmer's door and say that a cow is sick. We three and some others will be hiding out of sight. When the door opens, we will rush in, kill him with a single blow to the head with a *simi* (machete), then find his wife, kill her and seize their guns. The telephone line will be cut and as the police are miles away, we will be back in the forest well before daybreak. One final thing, remember the power of your oath."

James Ngithi returned to his hut, undressed, lifted the blanket and lay beside his sleeping wife. A series of trembles wracked his body. Sleep did not come easily. In his mind's eye he conjured up gory images of Bwana and Memsahib Myers being hacked to death.

❖ ❖ ❖

Phillip Myers stretched out his legs towards the crackling log fire. He had to admit life was good. The farm was not in debt, they couldn't afford a new car, but the farm provided most of their needs and, from time to time, he and Betty would drive down to Naivasha to pick up essential supplies from the local *duka* (shop) in the High Street. The routine was always the same, leave the shopping list with Mr Desai, the shop's owner, have lunch at the Naivasha Hotel, which was almost next door to the shop, then, feeling replete, pick up their order and head for home.

He looked across at his wife who, as usual, was deeply engrossed in a book, no doubt a love story! Betty had been the ideal army wife. When they had purchased what was then a piece of virgin bush, she had 'roughed it' under canvas without a word of complaint. He looked around the room, remembering how he had helped the Asian carpenter set the adzed blue gum beams in the ceiling and lay the mahogany floor. With the house completed, Betty had been in her element, making curtains and cushions as he turned the handle of their second-hand Singer sewing machine. He glanced at his watch; nearly 9.20. The news was finished and, thank goodness, no more attacks. The meeting with the Governor had been completed with promises of increased security. Phillip Myers leaned across, picked up the heavy .455 Webley and felt the weight in his hand. All six chambers were loaded and when he had examined the box of cartridges, just as Betty had said, only one had been used. He replaced the Webley on the side table.

"Betty, I'll give Peter Solomons a call to see if he's planning to attend the cricket match in Nairobi."

His wife looked up, grunted a reply and continued with her book.

Phillip Myers lifted the telephone handset, turned the handle vigorously to alert the operator at the exchange in Naivasha, then put the handset to his ear. There was utter silence.

"Damn!" He turned the handle again, with increased vigour, but still nothing.

Betty looked up from the book. "Anything wrong dear?"

"Yes, the damn phone's as dead as a dodo!" He sat heavily into his chair. "It means going over to Peter's place to report the fault, or driving all the way to Naivasha. It's a damned nuisance!"

There was a knocking at the French door. The knock was repeated. Phillip Myers looked at his wife.

"At this hour it can only mean trouble." He picked up the Webley, went out into the wide hallway and up to the French door.

He spoke in Kiswahili. "Who is it?"

"James Bwana. One of the cow's is very sick."

"Do you know which one?"

"It's the one you call 'Bluebell' Bwana."

"Right, I'll get a jacket and a torch."

Phillip Myers entered the dining room, went over to the sideboard and picked up the large chrome Eveready torch, then turned and made for the hall and his jacket. Betty looked up from her book.

"What is it dear?"

"James has reported that 'Bluebell' is sick, so I'll go and take a look."

At the curtained French door he paused, transferred the torch to the left jacket pocket, then placed the Webley into his left hand, released the top bolt, then bent down to release the second.

There was a tremendous crash, as some heavy object hit the door. With a second crash the door almost gave way. He shouted at his wife.

"My God, it's an attack!"

From his crouching position and despite being right handed, he fired through the French door, which then gave way. A figure burst through the door and he instinctively fired a second shot. The impact of the bullet stopped the man in his tracks, he staggered, paused, then crashed face down onto the wooden floor. A second figure sprang into view but before he could cross the threshold, Phillip Myers fired again. The man staggered and collapsed at his feet. All was confusion with Betty screaming and the almost blinding flashes from the Webley.

He changed the revolver to his right hand and shouted, "Betty, I'm O.K. Keep low and bring the rifle and shotgun... and if you can, douse the oil lamps!"

He waited by the open French door, tense, listening for the slightest sound. There was utter silence.

"So where was that two-faced bastard James?"

Betty appeared, clutching a shotgun and a rifle, and then stared in horror at the three bodies sprawled in the entrance to their hall.

"Oh my God Phillip, are they dead?"

"Yes, I shot the first one through the door. Now give me a hand to drag them clear and we'll try to bolt the door."

"Phillip, I'm trembling too much. Thank God you are unharmed!"

He handed her the Webley. "In that case take this revolver. If anyone appears at the door just pull the trigger!"

The bodies were heavy, but thanks to the blood on the polished wooden floor, it was possible to slide them to one side and re-bolt the door. Phillip Myers whispered to his wife. "Stay here. If anyone tries to force the door, even if you can't see them, shoot through the door."

Crouching low, Phillip made for the lounge, opened the drawer where he kept the spare bullets for the revolver and slipped the packet into his pocket. Still crouching low, he made his way to the kitchen. Being as quiet as possible he paused, then listened for any movement on the other side of the door. All was still; there was no sound. He inserted the key into the door and quietly turned it. There was a soft click. Keeping low, he gently pushed the door open, then, staying close to the outer wall, carefully peered outside. Nothing. Having relocked the kitchen door, he returned to the lounge. Through the window he could see flames.

"It must be the barn!" He returned to where Betty was crouching on the floor and put his arm around her shoulders. "Betty, don't worry, we'll survive. The bastards have set fire to the barn, but at least some neighbour might see the flames and when they find the phone's dead, they will alert the police."

He gave her another hug. As he did so, there was a sound of smashing glass from the direction of their bedroom. Phillip Myers grabbed the shotgun and burst into the bedroom to see a figure clambering through the aperture where once there had been glass and a wooden frame. He fired from the hip, the flash from the muzzle and the volume of noise within the confined space of the darkness was deafening. The buckshot ripped into the man's face. There was a huge gasp and the terrorist slumped across the windowsill, his head hanging down into the room. The man twitched twice and then went still. Keeping low, Phillip carefully made his way to the window, then, hugging the wall, stood up and peered outside. There was no one to be seen. Again crouching low, he made his way back to his wife.

"One of them was trying to break into our bedroom. Are you OK?"

He placed an arm around her shoulders and hugged her very close.

"Help must be on its way due to the fire. We'll survive. Having killed four of them, perhaps they've had enough."

He gave her trembling body another hug and kissed her on the forehead.

James Ngithi realised that he was now a fugitive from justice and the only thing that awaited him was a hangman's rope. 'If only the gang had waited for the key to be turned in the lock. He could have lied to the police and still be employed on the farm. That Bwana Myers would be armed had not been considered. It had all happened so quickly. The man charging the door, the shots! For a space of maybe seconds, he had been bewildered by the noise and confusion. Now there was only one place to run to – his hut.

In the turmoil of his confused mind, he ran and stumbled towards his hut. Within its confines was the only place where he could feel safe. With the flames from the barn illuminating his flight and with his mind recalling the scene at the farmhouse, one thought predominated – Bwana Myers had recognised his voice! He may be dead, but the risk was too great. It was time to flee! But to where? There was only one place – with the raiding gang in the forest.'

❖ ❖ ❖

Phillip Myers and his wife were still crouched on the floor, hyper-sensitive to every sound. There was a faint noise. Betty stiffened.

"What was that?"

The whisper could not disguise the fear in her voice. Phillip Myers placed his mouth close to her ear.

"I think it's just the house structure creaking. I'll go and check. Stay here and guard the door. Remember, do not hesitate to shoot."

Phillip Myers crawled towards the dining room until he was just inside. There was a very slight sound from the door connecting to the kitchen. What was it? The noise was unmistakable; a key was being carefully tried in the lock. He aimed the shotgun at waist height and just left of centre. As the flash erupted from the barrels, the sound of the shot in the confines of the dining room was almost deafening. Phillip Myers waited, tense. He snapped the shotgun open, quickly inserted two more twelve-bore cartridges and snapped the gun shut, placing his finger on the trigger, ready to fire again. He could hear groaning on the other side of the kitchen door. He eased himself back into the doorway of the dining room, then, using the wall as cover, called to his wife.

"Betty I'm still OK. Someone was trying to get into the dining room from the kitchen, but I shot the bastard! Are you OK?"

Her trembling voice conveyed urgency. "Phillip, I can hear a vehicle!"

"Stay low Betty, I'm coming to join you."

Crouching low, Phillip Myers returned to his wife's side.

"Let's hope it's the police from Njabini, but unless we hear a European voice, the door stays closed."

A vehicle stopped outside on the driveway. There was shouting of order and the unmistakable accent of a European. Phillip Myers, again using the wall as cover, peered around the side of the curtained French

~ 60 ~

door. "Betty it's the police!" He bent down and hugged his wife very tightly. "We're safe now."

He kissed his wife on her forehead, then stood up and began to open the French door.

# CHAPTER EIGHT

JAMES NGITHI'S MIND was in turmoil. Bwana Myers had recognised his voice, then, as he crouched beside the farmhouse door, three rapid loud reports, the three men in greatcoats falling and writhing on the ground. In seconds, his whole life was changed. Panting, partly from running to his hut but more from fear, he hammered on the hut door shouting, "Let me in, let me in let me in!"

His wife's scared face appeared at the door. He pushed past her and sat on the bed, trying to control his trembling. His wife knelt before him and gently lifted his head. "James, James what is the matter?"

He remained silent and once again stared at the floor.

She crouched before him and looked up into his face. "James, what have you done? Have you killed someone?"

He shook his head and continued to tremble. His wife attempted to lift his head again. "Have you stolen something?"

He shook his head again, and then looked up. "I helped three men try to kill Bwana Myers but he killed all three and he knew it was me!"

She reached up and clutched his left arm. "James! Why did you do this? We have nothing against Bwana Myers."

In the soft yellow light of their single oil lamp, he looked his wife in the face, shaking his head as he did so. "I had no choice, I had taken the oath."

She shook his arm, as if urging him to speak. "What kind of oath? Tell me!"

He placed his right hand onto the top of his wife's head. "This I cannot tell you." He trembled again and stood up, looking very furtive and avoiding her eyes. "I must flee, as the police will be here very soon and if they catch me I'll be hanged!"

His wife looked shocked. "Flee? Are you sure that Bwana Myers isn't dead? I heard five bangs from the direction of the farmhouse."

James Ngithi didn't answer but went over to the hook that held his old ex-army greatcoat, quickly slipped it on, then went over and removed a blanket from the bed, quickly folded it and placed it on his shoulder.

His wife clutched him from behind. "James don't leave me! Where will you go?"

Still gripped by fear, he roughly disentangled her arms and went out into the night. To his right the barn was on fire, sending showers of sparks into the night sky; there was a lot of shouting and men and women rushing around, which added to his confusion. Silhouetted against the flames, he saw a figure carrying what appeared to be a large object on his shoulder. As the man passed by, he could see the object was the hind leg of a cow. What was happening? Which direction should he take? Who could help him? Without any warning, someone thrust him hard in the back.

"Don't just stand there, come with me and help carry the meat."

The voice had authority and, before James Ngithi could turn around, another violent push sent him stumbling forward.

"Head for the paddock, there's still lots of meat to carry!"

James was confused. Carry meat? But where to?

The stranger shoved him in the back again. "Come on you idle bastard – move! Follow me!"

In the light cast from the blazing barn, James could see that the stranger had what appeared to be a gun over his shoulder and, like the three men he had assisted, long plaited hair. The stranger strode ahead at speed as James stumbled along in his wake. Arriving at the paddock, five men were using *pangas* (machetes) to hack up the remains of two cows. The stranger immediately took charge.

"We leave in under five minutes, as the police from Njabini must be on the way. Give this man one of those legs."

A very heavy warm lump of meat was placed onto James's shoulder. The other men shouldered the other lumps of the roughly butchered cow.

The stranger spoke again. "Right, follow me and stay together!"

By now they were at least a mile from the farm and, having crossed the main dirt road some ten minutes before, they were now on another farm track. The leader's pace never slackened and James was now very aware that a whole cow's leg was extremely heavy. Suddenly, the leader stopped.

"We rest for just three minutes."

James gratefully placed his burden onto the grass beside the track, then sat heavily onto the ground. Was this really happening to him? In the faint moonlight he was able to see some of his new companions. All but one had this same long, plaited hair. He could see a figure approaching, it was the stranger. The man stopped before him.

"Stand up in the presence of an officer!"

James Ngithi struggled to his feet.

The man looked closely into his face. "So who are you?"

"James Ngithi Sir, I'm the head clerk at Bwana Myers farm."

"Bwana Myers." There was mockery in the stranger's voice.

"Bwana Myers. The bastard's dead – and his wife."

James Ngithi hesitated for a moment.

"I don't think so, Sir, he shot and killed the men I was with."

"Liar!"

The slap across his face was completely unexpected, making James reel back under the force of the blow. Before he could recover his composure, the 'officer' strode away to the head of the group. The order was simple and succinct. "Move! We rest again in one hour."

James Ngithi bent down and shouldered his heavy load.

During the next brief rest period James spoke to one of the other men.

"Surely the police dogs will follow our scent and we'll be caught?"

The man flicked back his long hair. "Do you think that we are stupid? As we pass by the next farm it has been arranged that they will release a bitch on heat. No police dog can refuse an offer like that! By dawn we will be miles away, deep in the forest."

James felt a shudder pass through his body. "Is that where you live?"

"Well it's a lot better than being in prison," the man sneered. "You'll soon get used to it. And don't ask any more stupid questions."

As dawn was breaking, their party of seven entered the forest. In the dawn's early light, James was able to see his companions in more detail. Their leader had a small bunch of three white feathers attached to the lapel of his greatcoat. He was of medium height and had a small scar on his right cheek. Over his shoulder he carried a shotgun, the sling being made from some form of antelope skin. He wore long khaki trousers that matched his greatcoat and James noted that he constantly scowled. James turned to another of his new companions.

"What's the officer's name?"

"It's Colonel Tom. A word of warning, always obey his orders. He's ruthless and doesn't hesitate to kill."

Not for the first time in the last twelve hours, James felt a shudder of fear pass through his body.

The camp in the forest was situated beside a small, fast flowing stream of clear water. On either side of the stream, the ground rose steeply and the forest canopy allowed shafts of sunlight to seep through. There were numerous birdcalls, the overhead and distant shrieks of the hyraxes adding to the cacophony of forest sounds. The camp itself consisted of fifteen lean-to shelters made mainly of bamboo, with a simple sloping roof of lapped banana leaves, some now starting to wither with age. The front of each lean-to was about four feet high, with the rear wall being about three feet in height, the front being open to the elements. James estimated that each one could 'house' at least three men. Close to the stream, two small fires were burning, sending spirals of smoke into the forest canopy.

Since dumping his load, he had been ignored, so he sat beside a lean-to, watching the other thirty or so men busy themselves around the camp. Three men were cutting up the hunks of raw meat, splitting them into thin strips and placing them onto bamboo poles suspended over the fires. He noted that most of the men had long multi-plaited hair and nearly every man had a *simi* (a razor-sharp, double-sided

Kikuyu machete) slung under the left shoulder. He also noted that a few of the men carried either shotguns or rifles. He looked around for Colonel Tom and then noted one of the men approaching. Not knowing what to do, but remembering Colonel Tom's words about 'officers', he stood up.

The man stopped before him and scanned him from head to toe.

"So you've just joined us?"

James was not sure if this was a question or a statement, and decided to assume the former. "Yes Sir."

The man poked him in the chest. It's Sergeant, understand?"

"Yes Sir, Sergeant."

The man scanned him very closely. "What have you brought with you?"

"What I am wearing and this blanket."

"No food?"

"No Sergeant. I was told to carry a cow's leg by Colonel Tom."

The man looked closely into his face. "Have you ever killed anyone?"

"No Sergeant."

"In that case, you'll be in the next squad sent on a raid. How about firing a gun?"

Yet again James Ngithi felt fear take hold of his stomach. The man looked closely into his face again, so close he could smell the stench of his breath. "Then we'll show you. Now for a few rules. Obey every order without question. Do not take another man's food. Don't pee in the stream and don't make eyes at the girl in camp, she's reserved for Colonel Tom. Any questions?"

"Yes Sergeant. Where do I sleep?"

"You're in number six with another new recruit. He also worked on a farm serving food to two Europeans."

"Excuse me for asking Sergeant, how did he come to join you?"

"He helped our men kill the Europeans."

With these words the Sergeant turned on his heel and strode away. Not knowing what to do James sat down again. He would be sharing a shelter with a murderer! He looked at the ground and contemplated how quickly he had become implicated in this new environment. His mind turned to his wife and what could have been their future.

About thirty minutes later, another man approached. Unlike most of the others, his hair was short and he wasn't wearing the usual ex-army greatcoat. James Ngithi stood up. To his surprise, the man held out his hand.

"I'm Thomas, and you are?"

"James Ngithi Sir."

The man smiled. "I'm the same rank as you. Only say 'Sir' to anyone wearing a small bunch of feathers on the lapel of their coat. Have they told you that we are to share shelter number six?"

"Yes they have."

"Then I'll take you there. It's easy to find, it's the sixth shelter from downstream."

James followed his new companion, who then stopped beside one of the shelters. "This is it!"

James bent down and looked inside the structure. The walls consisted of bamboo split lengthways and woven into bamboo uprights spaced about every twelve inches. The banana leaves on the roof looked reasonably new and the floor was covered in dry leaves to a depth of about two inches. The floor area was some nine feet by seven feet, and as per the other shelters, the front was open to the elements.

"Well James Ngithi, what do you think?"

James pointed to the open front. "Isn't it cold at night with an open front?"

His new companion nodded. "Yes, but this is to allow us to quickly resist any attack."

"And have you been attacked?"

"Not to my knowledge, but it's a good precautionary measure."

James stood up. "What do we do about food?"

"We steal it from farms bordering onto the forest. We also snare small game and we have lots of hollowed-out logs in the trees, so the wild bees provide us with honey."

"So you eat well?"

"We do, and tonight it's spit-roasted beef."

James looked around. "Thomas, where does Colonel Tom sleep?"

"He has a hut which is just around the bend in the stream about twenty paces beyond the last shelter. It's quite large and has two rooms."

"And this girl that Colonel Tom has, where did she come from?"

There was a long silence. "Colonel Tom said that if she stayed with me, the men in camp would want her, so he decided that it was better if she stayed with him, as no one would dare to touch her."

James Ngithi was dumbfounded. "You mean she is your *wife*? Didn't she object?"

Thomas shrugged his shoulders. "Here James you obey orders."

James Ngithi thought about his wife. Without his support where could she go? Back to the village?

# CHAPTER NINE

THE JANGLING OF THE TELEPHONE on the bedside table aroused Dundas from a deep, deep sleep. He lifted the mosquito net and fumbled until his left hand made contact with the handset.

Joanne stirred beside him, still heavy with sleep. "What is it darling?"

"No doubt trouble." He lifted the handset. It was the Night Duty Officer.

"Sorry to disturb you Robert, but there's a bit of a flap on. There's been a gang raid on a European farm on the edge of the South Kinankop area. The farmer and his wife are badly shaken up but unharmed. He shot and killed five of the attackers; one of them was the cook. Bill Stewart has been alerted and Superintendent Lewis wants everyone to be armed, so your Browning automatic, with a full clip of ten rounds, will be ready for your signature."

"Thanks, I'll be there in about ten minutes."

Joanne sat up and rubbed her eyes. "Is it serious?"

"Yes. A European farmer and his wife have been attacked in the South Kinankop area. Thank God they are unharmed. Joanne, cover your eyes, I'm about to switch on the bedside light."

"Robert, can I get you anything – a hot drink?"

Dundas shook his head. "Darling, I don't even have time to shave. Cover your eyes."

As the harsh light from the bedside table lamp hurt his eyes, he placed his bare feet onto the cold, polished floor, stood up, stretched and began to quickly dress.

As Dundas descended the steps to his car, the faint moonlight made it easy for him to see the vehicle's door lock and insert the key. Having gained access, he made himself comfortable, put the gear-stick into neutral, released the handbrake and let the slope of the drive provide the initial momentum. Just before the entrance, he turned the key in the ignition and placed the gear-stick into second. The car started and he continued down the hill to the large roundabout. There he turned right and headed into town, passing the usual night-watchmen huddled over their charcoal stoves in the shop doorways. He noted a beat constable chatting to the man in the doorway of the French Bakery. There was not another car on the road. At the traffic lights he ignored the red light, turned left and headed down the road to the Police Station and Provincial Headquarters.

Superintendent Lewis was already there, talking to the Night Duty Officer. He looked up as Dundas approached, then glanced at his watch.

"You've made good time Robert! So, if you can sign for your pistol, we'll be off."

Having taken possession of his Browning automatic, Dundas slipped out the clip of ten 9mm rounds, opened the breech to check that it was clear, then let the action snap back and applied the safety catch. He then reinserted the clip into the butt. He looked up at the Duty Officer. "What about the shoulder holster?"

The Duty Officer nodded. "Here it is." He handed over the holster and pushed the armoury book towards Dundas for signature.

Dundas signed the armoury register and pushed it back across the Charge Office desk.

"Thanks."

As usual, Dundas was sandwiched between Ndibo and Superintendent Lewis. Although this provided a modicum of warmth, having to straddle the gearbox housing was very uncomfortable on any protracted journey.

Ndibo drove up the road from Headquarters, turned right at the traffic lights and headed along the High Street towards Naivasha. Having cleared the township boundary, Dundas glanced at the softly illuminated speedometer. It was hovering around seventy. He wondered if he should remind Ndibo about zebra running across the road at night, then thought better of it.

Superintendent Lewis broke the silence.

"A penny for your thoughts, Robert."

"I was just thinking, Sir, had we attempted to catch the gang who murdered the Blakes, would this latest attack have taken place?"

Before replying, Superintendent Lewis nodded several times.

"The thought I had was, if Mr Myers has killed five, is the Blake's houseboy, who disappeared after their murder, one of them?"

"Sir, these attacks on farms... unless we can achieve rapid arrests and convictions, these gangs of criminals will become bolder and bolder. The next thing will be an attack on a Police Station."

"Hmm... so you still hanker after going into the Aberdare Forest and tracking them down?"

"Yes I do."

"Despite the fact that you are married and have a tiny son?"

Dundas shrugged. "I'm sure that Joanne will understand."

Superintendent Lewis shook his head and made a 'tch' sound.

"Anyway, at this juncture it's merely conjecture. Now let me give you an update on this attack. Evidently, the Myers chief clerk is involved. In order to lure Mr Myers to open the door, he said one of the cows was sick. Two things saved Mr Myers and his wife. He was carrying a .455 Webley revolver, and a member of the gang barged the door when the top bolt was withdrawn, but before he had released the lower bolt and turned the key. He shot three of the gang in the doorway and another one who had smashed the bedroom window. Finally, he shot the cook when he tried to open a door into the dining room."

"So what happened to the chief clerk?"

"He's missing; the assumption is that he escaped with the rest of the gang. One other thing; they slaughtered two cows and have gone off with the carcasses."

Dundas nodded. "Which tends to point to the fact that they need food. Sir, what if the local police set up a series of ambushes on the edges of the forest?"

"Two reasons. Lack of manpower and... where would they ambush? One other thing; let's assume that one night they catch ten men exiting the forest, and let's also assume that they are unarmed, what's the offence?"

"I take your point Sir. But if they can't prove any visible means of support, detain them on a charge of vagrancy. At least it would give us time to check them out."

Superintendent Lewis turned to Ndibo. "Ndibo, as before, turn left just after the Naivasha Hotel, then continue up onto the plateau. After about six miles, the farm's entrance will be on the right."

Ndibo nodded. *"Ndiyo Effendi."*

❖ ❖ ❖

Thirty-five minutes later, the Land Rover headlights picked out two armed constables on the right hand-side of the road. A red glow in the sky had been visible since arriving on the plateau. Now being in close proximity to the farm, the flames leaping into the night sky were clearly visible, and as they watched, a shower of sparks flew up into the night sky.

The Land Rover slowed and Ndibo stopped by the farm's entrance. One of the constables pointed his rifle and the other, holding a large torch, approached very cautiously and challenged, *"Nani wewe?* (who are you)?"

Superintendent Lewis leaned across. "C.I.D. Nakuru."

The Constable's demeanour immediately changed and he saluted.

*"Jambo Effendi.* Be very careful, there are some very bad people about tonight."

The earth track to the farm was about half a mile long. On each side of the track the headlights illuminated acres of ripening maize, then a large paddock fringed with what appeared to be blue gum trees. A small dik-dik ran onto the track and then stopped, transfixed by the headlights. Ndibo slowed down and continued to crawl towards the dik-dik. Suddenly, it darted into the long grass beside the paddock and made off.

Ndibo gestured. *"Nyama mzuri sana Effendi!* (Very good meat Sir)."

Superintendent Lewis grunted. "Hmm... but not tonight!"

In the soft lights of the fascia, Dundas could see Ndibo's grin.

*"Ndiyo Effendi!"*

Having rounded a bend, the yellow lights of the farmhouse could be seen, then, as they drew closer, the usual gaggle of police vehicles and some armed constables. Superintendent Lewis leaned across to Ndibo.

"Pull up behind that other Land Rover."

*"Ndiyo Effendi."*

Ndibo switched off the headlights and the ignition.

"Shall I stay with the vehicle Effendi?"

"No, join the constables by the house and ask the usual questions about thefts from farms bordering onto the forest."

Superintendent Lewis and Dundas set off towards the farmhouse. At the foot of the steps were three bodies. Dundas flicked on his torch. All three were wearing ex-army khaki greatcoats. He shone the light onto their faces – their eyes were partly closed and their mouths open. Superintendent Lewis grunted.

"Hmm... once they have been identified there will have to be an Inquest. As if Mr and Mrs Myers haven't had enough trauma."

Dundas swept the light across the faces again. "Sir, have you noticed their hair? It's long and multi-plaited. And look at this..." He shone the light onto each of the greatcoat lapels. "Each one is wearing a small bunch of feathers. The tall one on the left has two black feathers and one white. The others have two white and one black."

Dundas bent down to take a closer look as the Assistant Superintendent from Naivasha came down the steps and saluted.

"We meet again Sir, but this time in far better circumstances."

Superintendent Lewis nodded.

"Hmm... How are the Myers?"

"Badly shaken, but he's already saying they are not moving off the farm."

"I take it that you haven't mentioned anything about an inquest?"

"No Sir, and I suggest that we leave mentioning it for the time being."

Superintendent Lewis nodded his head. "Agreed. Where are the other two bodies?"

"One is slumped over the bedroom windowsill and the cook is behind the kitchen door that connects to the dining room. We had to move the other three bodies, Sir, as they were in view of the Myers, but a statement is being given by the Inspector from Njabini as to the position of the bodies when he arrived."

Superintendent Lewis turned to Dundas. "When Bill Stewart arrives, I want photographs of any bullet holes or any other damage, and get him to take close-ups of those bunches of feathers." He then turned to the Assistant Superintendent. "Are any members of the labour force missing?"

"At this point in time Sir we know of only one. The head clerk who tried to lure Mr Myers outside."

"And the labour here, are they all Kikuyu?"

"According to Mr Myers, yes."

"It's interesting, Superintendent. At the Blakes' farm the houseboy and the cook were involved. Here it's the head clerk and the cook, and as per the Blakes', the entire labour force is Kikuyu. Do we detect a common thread? The clerk's wife, is she missing?"

"We have yet to establish that Sir. Come first light we can make a thorough check on everyone. Also, as before, I have sent for a tracker dog to be here by dawn. Now Sir if you follow me I'll briefly introduce you to the Myers and then show you the other two bodies."

Mr and Mrs Myers were sat in the lounge before a wood fire. A single Tilley pressure lamp cast dark shadows onto the walls, fragmented by the flickering flames of the log fire. Mr Myers stood up as they entered and held out his hand.

"Phillip Myers." He turned. "And this is my wife Betty."

Superintendent Lewis noted that the grip was firm and the eye contact strong.

"Superintendent Lewis, Provincial C.I.D. Nakuru. And this is Chief Inspector Dundas." They shook hands. Superintendent Lewis continued. "I'm sure that you have answered many questions, so if you'll excuse us we will continue with our work."

The Assistant Superintendent led the way to the dining room. In the light of his torch a ragged hole in the left upper panel of the door leading to the kitchen was clearly visible. The Assistant Superintendent turned to Superintendent Lewis.

"Mr Meyers states that he fired from the cover of the entrance to the dining room. The cook's body is directly behind the door, so in order to view it we will have to go round the outside of the house. Now if you'll follow me, I'll take you to the bedroom."

The body was slumped over the smashed windowsill and in the torchlight, in a pool of blood, was a *simi*. The Assistant Superintendent stepped forward, grabbed the hair and partly lifted the head.

"Most of his face is missing, as it took the full force of the shot.

The Assistant Superintendent gestured. "Sir, when your Scenes of Crime Team have finished their work, we can start to clean up. We've booked Mr and Mrs Meyers into the Brown Trout at Njabini for a couple of days."

Superintendent Lewis turned to Dundas. "Robert, go round and take a good look at the cook's body. In the meantime, I'll discuss with the Assistant Superintendent what statements are required."

Dundas went down the steps, turned left, then left again to the outside kitchen door, which was partly open. Using the torch, he carefully pushed it fully open. There, on its back in a pool of blood, was the cook, his eyes partly open and lifeless. There was a huge wound in the centre of his chest. The shot must have smashed his sternum and impacted onto his spinal column. He would have died instantly.

Dundas shone his torch around the kitchen. It had the usual wood burning stove and there was a faint smell of smoke. Apart from the ragged hole in the wooden door, which clearly showed that the shot had come from the other side, nothing appeared to be disturbed. He shone the light onto the body again. Just to one side of the cook's clenched right hand was a key. Something else for Bill Stewart to photograph. Having scanned the kitchen once more, he exited the kitchen and, as before, used the torch to partly close the door.

Dundas made his way around the outside of the farmhouse, mulling over what appeared to be a common thread with these two attacks on European-owned farms. In both instances, the farm labour were all Kikuyu and household servants were involved. At the foot of the farmhouse steps he paused and shone his torch on the faces of the three bodies. Facially they also appeared to be Kikuyu. The army greatcoats were readily available as ex-War Department surplus stock, so the chance of any lead was very slim. However, when the bodies were fingerprinted, Criminal Records in Nairobi may be able to obtain a match. The bunches of feathers attached to each greatcoat lapel were intriguing – did they represent some form of rank?

He next shone his torch onto their hands. Despite being partly clenched as *rigor mortis* was setting in, it was possible to see the hands were rough and worn, almost like a gardener's hands. So where had these three men come from? It could not be from a nearby farm, as their long multi-plaited hair was very unusual and something that he had never seen before. He switched off the torch, made his way up the steps and entered the French door.

# CHAPTER TEN

THE FIVE BODIES HAD BEEN REMOVED to Naivasha for post-mortems and Superintendent Lewis and Dundas had spent a frustrating day trying to obtain information from the farm's labour-force about the night's events. Their efforts had drawn a blank and they were now on their way back. It was time to return to the farmhouse.

Superintendent Lewis turned to Dundas. "Robert, we have a similar situation here as the Blake's farm. They've clammed up! So what has been going on?"

"There is a definite atmosphere Sir, perhaps when we can trace the head clerk's wife things may change." Dundas glanced at his watch. "It's just turned four o'clock, Sir, the tracker dog party have been away since dawn, so perhaps they can provide a few clues."

Superintendent Lewis stopped by the line of blue gum trees and then sat on the grass that edged the track. "I feel like a pipe. It's time to consider the facts and then to establish what we can do if the Dog Team has not made any arrests."

Superintendent Lewis fumbled in his right-hand jacket pocket and withdrew his pipe. He then went into the pocket again and withdrew his soft, dark brown, leather tobacco pouch and proceeded to fill the pipe's bowl with yellow/brown tobacco. Having tamped it down, he again fumbled in his pocket and produced a chrome-plated lighter. He paused. "Well Robert, we've briefly discussed this before, so let's hear your thoughts."

Dundas waited as his boss drew the flame of the lighter down into the tobacco and blew a plume of blue/grey smoke into the air.

"Well Sir, as we have said before, there is a common thread in these two cases. For some reason these two farms have been attacked and in this latest case there was also a definite intention to kill the Myers. Here a trusted servant was used to lure Mr Myers outside and in the Blake case, it would appear that the houseboy and the cook were involved. In the Blake case, the cook and his wife hanged themselves.

In this current case, the head clerk and his wife have disappeared. In both cases food was taken from the farms. We agreed that at least ten men were involved in the first raid, and here there must have been more. Five were shot and the remainder managed to butcher and walk off with two whole cows. In summary, Sir, I believe that there is a growing criminal gang holed up somewhere in the Aberdare's and unless they can be caught and brought to justice, they will become both more numerous and more daring."

Superintendent Lewis nodded his head several times and looked thoughtful. Then he pointed the stem of his pipe at Dundas.

"So somehow we have to go and get them?"

Dundas gestured. "Can you think of any other way Sir?"

Superintendent Lewis drew on his pipe several times and then removed the stem from his mouth.

"When we get back to base I'll convene a meeting with the Assistant Commissioner and Special Branch. In the meantime, let's get back to the farmhouse and await the outcome of the Dog Team."

With these words, Superintendent Lewis tapped the bowl of his pipe on the heel of his left shoe, stood up, and ground the hot ashes into the red brown earth.

It was close to five o'clock when the Dog Master and the two Constables returned empty-handed. Superintendent Lewis stood on the farmhouse steps awaiting their arrival.

"So why no prisoners?"

The Dog Master saluted. "Sorry Sir. It was going very well until we came to Major Fawcett's farm. We were tracking close to the labour camp when our dog scented a bitch in heat. He refused to go another step, despite dragging him away and trying to pick up the scent by circling around, the bitch's scent was far too strong."

Superintendent Lewis stroked his chin.

"Hmm... Do you think it was deliberate?"

"If it was, Sir, then it was very well planned, as the Major's farm is at least ten miles from here."

Superintendent Lewis posed another question. "And to the edge of the forest?"

"At least another mile Sir."

"So these were heading in the direction of the forest?

"Yes Sir."

Superintendent Lewis turned to Dundas. "Any questions?"

"Yes Sir. During your initial tracking, did you manage to form any opinion as to the number of people that you were following?"

The Dog Master quickly consulted with the two constables. "We estimate at least twelve. They were in two groups and rested several times. We estimated the number by the crushed grass patches."

Superintendent Lewis produced a folded map from his inside jacket pocket and spread it out on the farmhouse steps. He turned to the Dog Master. "Now the scale is quite small. We are here. I want you to show me the route you followed and then whereabouts your dog lost the scent."

The Dog Master studied the map for a few moments. "Right Sir, we went along the road to about here... then headed up this farm road." He studied the map again and pointed. "Then from here we crossed onto a track which is not marked on this map until reaching this rising ground here, which is where the gang first rested. From this point we headed north until reaching Major Fawcett's farm (he pointed again) here. Whilst passing the labour camp it was just about here that the dog lost the scent."

Superintendent Lewis looked intently at the point where the Dog Master had indicated where the track had been lost, then turned to Dundas.

"You're right. There are a bunch of criminals hiding in the forest. Do you recall the wall map in my office and the vectors that crossed about ten miles inside the Aberdares? Now, assuming that this gang of some fifteen men was heading (he pointed at the map) about here, this would lead to an entirely different location. So the question is... has the original gang involved in the Blake's murder moved, or is this another group?"

Dundas studied the distance between the two possible locations.

"Sir, may I make a suggestion? Any group or groups holed up in the Aberdare Range need food and a method to cook it. Is it possible that the Police Air Wing could fly over this sector here looking for smoke rising up through the trees?"

Superintendent Lewis nodded several times and looked very thoughtful. "Assuming that the sight of a plane overhead doesn't make them move, then the suggestion has merit. Something to discuss when we return to HQ."

That night James Ngithi joined the group of men gathered around the fire and, like the others, he chewed his meagre ration of spit-roasted beef. To his right, squatting on his haunches, was his new companion, Thomas. The flickering flames highlighted the cheekbones of the assembled group and reflected off their teeth and eyes as they tore into the meat. James noted that in all, including Colonel Tom and the woman, they totalled twenty-one bodies. Beyond the circle of eating men was the dark of the forest. Hyraxes shrieked in the treetops, almost drowning the noise of the stream as it tumbled over the rocks.

It was the first food that James had eaten since his mid-day meal the day before. He stared into the flames with unseeing eyes and wondered if he would ever see his wife again. His thoughts were disturbed as Thomas placed a hand on his right shoulder.

"James, why are you so quiet?"

James Ngithi shrugged. "I was just thinking."

"About what?"

"My wife and what I've left behind."

"All you've left are two Europeans and, according to Colonel Tom they will not be alive much longer. The bastards killed five of our men, including three junior officers, so he plans to avenge their deaths."

James Ngithi gestured. "But surely the police will be guarding them?"

Thomas spat on the ground. "Piss on the police! At some stage they'll get fed up and leave. That is when we strike!"

James Ngithi again stared into the fire, recalling the three loud bangs, the three men falling and writhing by the doorway, and that he had run away. Was he a coward?

Thomas slapped him on the back. "Cheer up James, you and I will finish them off next time!"

Despite the warmth of the fire, James felt a shiver pass through his body. Here, within this body of men, life was very cheap. He turned and faced Thomas. "Have you ever killed anyone?"

"No, but I let the men in who did the job. The farmer and his wife were having dinner. It was over in seconds. I never realised what a very sharp *simi* could do. We then went to my hut and grabbed everything we could carry, including the stock in my maize store, plus some cabbages, and I joined the other group."

James Ngithi was amazed. "Another group?"

"Yes, it's miles away in that direction." Thomas gestured to the West.

"So how long have you been here?"

Thomas pursed his lips. "About a week. The group I joined was over twenty-five strong and feeding that number every day was proving difficult – so my wife and I were sent here under escort."

James Ngithi was amazed. "So how many groups are there?"

"According to Colonel Tom, over twenty, scattered all over the Aberdares."

"Is anyone in charge?"

Thomas shrugged. "I have no idea and at present I don't care."

❖ ❖ ❖

James had excused himself and, having splashed his face in the fast flowing stream, he cupped his right hand and, kneeling on a small rock, scooped the ice-cold water into his mouth. In the light cast by the fire, he picked his way to his new 'home' and, having rolled himself in his blanket, closed his eyes and listened to the sounds of the forest and of the water in the nearby stream.

In the half light of dawn, James Ngithi hunched his body against the penetrating cold and drew the blanket around his body. Even at this early hour, birds were chirping in the forest canopy, making further sleep impossible. He sat up. Beside him his new companion was fast asleep, his head under the blanket and breathing deeply. It did not seem possible that this man had gloated over the deaths of his European employers and had willingly joined this gang of men. Even more amazing, he had handed over his wife to Colonel Tom! Nature was now pressing. Carefully putting his blanket to one side, he went into the surrounding forest to relieve himself.

Having returned, he made his way to the still smouldering fire and sat close to it, pulling up the collar of his greatcoat against the cold air. He glanced at the wristwatch that Bwana Myers had given him several Christmas's ago. It was almost five-thirty. He wondered what food would be available this morning. His meagre ration of meat from the previous evening had not assuaged his hunger.

At just after 6am, the camp began to stir. Men appeared from their shelters, stretching, coughing, spitting and then wandering off into the forest to relieve themselves. Until now he had almost been ignored. This was about to change!

"You! Don't just sit there, move your backside and get some wood for the fire!" James recognised the voice of the Sergeant and quickly stood up. "Well? Move!"

Having gathered several armfuls of dead branches he was about to return to his shelter when the same voice stopped him again.

"You're down for two jobs. There's been fresh food and *posho* (maize flour) dumped on the edge of the forest. The men leave in about an hour and you'll be with them. Now... tonight. A man has refused to take the oath. Either he takes it or you will kill him."

James Ngithi's blood froze in his veins.

"But I've never killed anyone."

The Sergeant put his face very close and poked him in the chest.

"You have a choice. Either you kill him, or we will kill you."

James Ngithi started to tremble. "But how will I kill him?"

"You'll have a razor-sharp *simi*. All it will take is one blow."

The Sergeant turned on his heel and strode away in the direction of Colonel Tom's hut.

James Ngithi returned to the shelter to find Thomas putting an edge on a *simi*. As he approached Thomas looked up.

"Have you heard the news? We've been selected for a special job tonight!"

James sat down in front of the shelter, feeling sick in his stomach.

"Thomas, I don't know what to do." He shook his head several times and stared at the ground. "I've been ordered to kill someone who has refused to take the oath."

Thomas shrugged his shoulders and spat onto the ground. "So? If the bastard refuses to support us, then we don't want him blabbing to the police. Here, you can use this." Thomas handed over his *simi*. "You can shave with an edge like this!"

James reluctantly held the *simi* by the handle and was surprised by the weight. It was about eighteen inches in length; near the pointed end the blade was about three inches wide, then it tapered to the five inch grip, which was about an inch in diameter and bound with some form of hide.

Thomas gestured at the *simi*. "This is similar to the *simis* used to kill my employers. The heavy end gives you tremendous cutting power. Try it on that log over there."

James handed back the *simi*. "Thanks Thomas but no doubt they will give me one of these for tonight."

James followed the ten-man group making their way to the forest edge. The men were in high spirits and their constant interchanges focused on food and home-brewed beer.

By 10am the overhead canopy started to thin. Suddenly their leader raised his hand. They stopped. James Ngithi could feel his heart thudding in his chest. The only sounds were those of the forest. What was it? Their leader stood still, listening. He raised his hand and signalled for them to move off the game track and raised a finger to his lips for the group to be quiet. James Ngithi felt his level of fear rising as his heart continued thudding in his chest. He strained his ears for the slightest sound. What was it? Their leader slowly returned to the track, looked ahead, then signalled them to come forward. There, some ten yards ahead, on the edge of a small clearing, was a pile of sacks covered with freshly cut foliage.

James Ngithi's heartbeat started to subside. Their leader detailed each man to pick up a sack. From its weight and bulges, James realised that his sack contained cabbages. Having shouldered their loads, the group retraced its steps back into the depths of the forest.

During a brief rest, James spoke to one of the men. "Where does all this food come from?"

The man sat up and spat onto the track. "The women on Major Fawcett's farm. They dump it at dusk and we collect it next morning."

"But surely the Major will find out and tell the police?"

"We've heard he doesn't like the police."

"Why not?"

"The story goes that the police charged him over something to do with his old van."

"So he lets the women provide us with food?"

The man sneered. "Don't be stupid, he's a *Mzungu* (European) farmer and we want his land."

Before James could ask any more questions, they were ordered to shoulder their loads.

That day they ate well. It was the first time since joining the group that James felt replete and with this feeling of contentment, thoughts of the forthcoming night were pushed into the back of his mind. He returned to the shelter and within minutes was fast asleep.

A sharp kick in the ribs roused James Ngithi from a deep sleep. He opened his eyes and sat up with a start.

Looking down at him was the Sergeant.

"On your feet! We leave in under an hour. And you'll need this." The Sergeant dropped a *simi* contained in a skin scabbard onto his lap. "Use the cord to suspend it from your shoulder and underneath your greatcoat."

Within a few seconds, James Ngithi was plunged back into reality and the enormity of the task he had been selected to perform. Perhaps the old man would take the oath. But what if he didn't? In the darkness he could run away, but where? Was it possible that he could make his way to the Kikuyu Reserve and hope that his relatives would hide him. Many thoughts ran through his mind but they all came back to one thing, the oath he had taken and the promises it contained. There was no escape from the oath. He had repeated every word and sipped the chickens' blood. With his brain in turmoil, he made his way down to the stream where, with shaking hands, he cupped several handfuls of the ice-cold water into his mouth.

Colonel Tom stood before the five men and, with narrowed eyes, proceeded to walk up and down before them. He then faced the group.

"Tonight we are going to Major Fawcett's farm to seek out a man who has refused to take the oath to support our cause. He will be offered a final choice. Take the oath or our latest recruit, James Ngithi, will kill him!"

James felt his mouth go very dry and he could not avoid a shudder passing through his body. Colonel Tom continued.

"If he has to be killed, you other four will dump his body down one of the pit latrines and shovel some earth on top. Any questions?"

A tall thin man with long plaited hair stepped forward and saluted.

"Sir, in the dark it will be very difficult to see the blood on the ground. How will we be able to see it without a torch or a lamp?"

The Colonel stopped pacing up and down and faced the group.

"There will not be any blood. The man will be strangled with this."

Colonel Tom thrust his hand into the right hand pocket of his greatcoat and produced a thin plaited cord. James Ngithi broke into a series of shudders and could not conceal it. The Colonel's eyes narrowed even more.

"And if you (pointing a finger at James) refuse to do this, then I will kill you both! We leave in ten minutes. Dismissed!"

James walked back to the shelter. It seemed that at every other step a huge shudder wracked his body. Escape was impossible. Thomas was sitting just in front of their shelter and raised his right hand in greeting.

"So James, tonight will ensure that you become one of us."

James looked down at Thomas who was nonchalantly chewing the end of a thin stick to make a *mswaki* (toothbrush).

"Do you mean that you have killed someone? I thought you said that all you did was to lead the men into the house?"

Thomas didn't look up. He removed the *mswaki* from his mouth.

"I lied. He was an old man. It wasn't easy. But he refused to support our cause."

James squatted down beside Thomas. "And how did you dispose of the body?"

Thomas pointed a finger at the ground. "Down a pit latrine. It's the last place the police will want to look, or think of looking."

James posed another question. "But has the man been missed?"

Thomas shrugged his shoulders. "I have no idea, it's not my problem."

James moved into the shelter, sat heavily onto his folded blanket and stared at his shaking hands.

At 6pm the party of six set off with Colonel Tom at the rear carrying the now familiar shotgun. By seven it was pitch dark, yet the fallen bamboo leaves on the game track were almost luminous and guided their passage. Each step took James closer and closer towards an act that, even at this late hour, he felt he could not perform. Should he try to escape? He had no idea where they were and he was conscious that Colonel Tom was directly behind him. Was it possible? He could hide until it was light, then make his way to the edge of the forest, report to a farm and give himself up. If he told the police about this gang perhaps they would pardon him for assisting the men who tried to kill the Myers? His mind was made up. Suddenly he darted to one side of the track, but due to the surrounding darkness the undergrowth impeded his escape. He heard a loud bang and felt a huge impact between his shoulder blades. All went black and he crashed face down, twitched several times and was still.

Colonel Tom walked forward very carefully, feeling for the body with his feet. Having made contact, he gave the body a hefty kick! There was no movement. He returned to the track and addressed the small group.

"He was a coward who could not face killing a man who has refused to take the oath. We'll leave his body to rot. On our return, we will remove anything of value. Now let's move on, we have a job to do."

Arriving at the Fawcett farm, Colonel Tom led the group to one of the huts in the labour camp and knocked on the door three times.

A male voice responded from inside. "Who is it?"

Colonel Tom placed his face close to the door. "I have four chickens."

The door was slowly opened, allowing a shaft of yellow light from a solitary oil lamp to penetrate the darkness and reflect on the brown faces crowding around the doorway. Colonel Tom stepped inside, followed by the rest of his group. Seated around the walls were ten men who, from their dress, were farm labourers. In their midst was an old man with grey hair, looking very frightened. From the position of his arms, it was evident that his hands were tied behind his back.

Colonel Tom scanned the assembled group and then turned to one of his men. "Close the door." He now addressed the old man. "Come here and kneel before me."

With difficulty, the old man staggered to his feet and knelt before Colonel Tom, who looked down at the prisoner.

"Tonight you have a choice. You can live or you can die! To live, take the oath. The arch of thorns and a chicken can be made ready for you. Refuse and you will die. Make your choice."

In the light from the single oil lamp, the old man looked up into Colonel Tom's impassive face, then at the men within his field of vision. Kneeling before Colonel Tom, the old man tried to control the fear in his voice.

"I have been on this farm for many years. I have seen many of you here grow from *totos* (children) into men. I have no quarrel with any of you. Bwana Fawcett and the Bwana before him have been very good to me. I have never been hungry and have been looked after when sick. Now I am asked to perhaps kill a man who has provided for my needs. Should I not live in peace until *Mungu* (God) calls for me?"

Colonel Tom scowled. "This is your last chance."

The old man remained silent and looked down at the floor. Colonel Tom felt in the pocket of his greatcoat, withdrew the plaited cord and tossed it to the tall thin man who was standing directly behind the prisoner, then clenched his fists and made a jerking movement. There was a pause as the tall thin man placed the cord around the old man's neck and pulled both ends, placing his knee into the old man's upper back. The old man wriggled briefly and made a series of gasping noises, then slumped forward. The cord was released and the old man fell forward onto the floor.

Colonel Tom pointed to two of the farm labourers. "You and you! Take his body and throw it down one of the pit latrines, then shovel some earth on top."

The two men hesitated. Colonel Tom raised his voice. "Do it!"

The men gathered up the old man's body and, as Colonel Tom opened the door, they went out into the night.

Colonel Tom scanned the assembled group. "What you have witnessed tonight is the death of a man who refused to support our cause. If anyone here tells any outsider what they have seen, then we will return to seek vengeance."

With these words, Colonel Tom opened the door and followed by his group was swallowed in the surround darkness.

It was obvious from the strained expressions on the faces of the remaining eight men that the incident had shocked them. What had once been the right thing to do, now left a deep and lasting stain that would be difficult to eradicate.

# CHAPTER ELEVEN

DUNDAS STUDIED THE LENGTHY SIGNAL that he had received from the Inspector at North Kinankop Police Station, listing the map references where produce and livestock had been stolen from farms within his area. He went over to the map on the wall of his office and, holding the signal in his left hand, carefully placed a red map pin at each location. Every one was located within a few miles of the forest edge. He went over to his desk, picked up the handset and dialled a two-digit internal number. There were three buzzes and a click.

*"Stewart, Scenes of Crime."*

"Hi Bill, it's Robert. If you're not busy, can you come round to my office?"

*"Give me five minutes and I'll be with you."*

There was a click and the phone went dead. Dundas replaced the handset into its cradle, then sat in his chair and drummed his fingers on the desk. He still had to interview the two men convicted for sheep theft. Their arrest and conviction was now several months old. He looked at the activity chart on the wall. Tuesday was reasonably clear and the prison was on the outskirts of the township. He went over to the wall chart and, using the chinagraph pencil, on the horizontal column headed TUES he scribed PRISONER VISIT 2PM.

There was a knock on the door.

"Come in!" Dundas turned away from the wall chart as Bill Stewart entered the office. He gestured. "Take a seat Bill. First things first. Can you update me on the Blake's case?"

Bill Stewart grinned. "Robert, you must be a mind reader. I've just received a signal from Criminal Records in Nairobi. Evidently, one of the three men shot by Mr Myers was involved in the attack on the Blakes. His dabs were on the glass fragments of the gun case."

Dundas leaned back in his chair. "Is that it?"

"Apart from the fact that the Blakes' cook and houseboy have no criminal records. However, I am still awaiting additional information."

Dundas nodded. "Thanks for the update. Have you informed Superintendent Lewis?"

"Not as yet; he's in a meeting."

"OK. Now an update on the Myers case."

"One of the men who tried to break in via the French door has previous. He was a nasty piece of work with convictions for theft, assault and robbery with violence. That's all I have to date, except that the prints I lifted from the farm office telephone, which I have to assume belong to the missing clerk James Ngithi, have not been traced by Criminal Records. Incidentally, has the man's wife been traced?"

Dundas shook his head. "Not as yet, but we have discovered that she comes from the Kiambu area. The police there have been alerted." Dundas leaned forward in his chair. "So to date, only two have any previous?" He sat back and drummed his fingers on the desk. "Damn! I was starting to form a theory that a load of 'bad hats' were avoiding arrest and holing up in the Aberdares. But come over to the wall map."

Dundas picked up a pencil from the 'desk tidy' as Bill Stewart joined him at the wall map. He pointed. "These red pins here represent thefts of farm produce, including livestock from farms under the jurisdiction of the Police Station at North Kinankop. Any comments?"

Bill Stewart studied the map for a few moments, then touched one of the pins. "So, apart from this pin here, all the others are within two to three miles of the forest?"

Dundas nodded. "Bill, the question I ask is this. Why would well-fed farm labour want to steal produce and livestock?" He tapped one of the pins. "This one here was where a pig was stolen."

Bill Stewart studied the map again. "On balance, it doesn't make sense, unless, as you have suggested before, a criminal gang is hiding in this area around here and exit the forest from time to time to steal food."

Dundas tapped the map with the pencil. "The boss and I had a similar discussion." He pointed at the map. "Now this is the Blakes' farm here and the Myers' farm here. The tracker dog lost the scent." He pointed. "Here and here. Now, if I pencil in two lines from each farm to where the tracks were lost and if I continue the lines as I'm doing now, they cross *here*. You will note that all the red pins, with the exception of this one here, fall within this segment. Every one is within two miles or so of the forest edge."

Bill Stewart stood before the wall-map, nodding his head. "Have you shown this to the boss?"

"Not yet, as I only received the signal from North Kinankop about half an hour ago. Well... what do you think?"

Bill Stewart looked at the wall-map again, concentrating on the red pins falling within the segment. He turned to Dundas. "Despite the fact that to date only two criminals have been identified, C.R.O. may come up with others. Now, can I go back to my office, as we are developing some mug shots of the bodies taken at the Myers farm?"

Dundas gestured towards the door. "Be my guest... and thanks for your help."

❖ ❖ ❖

With Bill Stewart departed, Dundas returned to his desk and opened the second right-hand drawer and withdrew a ruled foolscap pad. Having placed it onto the desk, he wrote in pencil the figure 15. Out of habit, he ran his fingers through his hair, then looked hard at the figures and drummed his fingers on the desk. "Assuming that a gang of fifteen were hiding in the forest, how much food would be needed to sustain each man per day? He jotted down the following headings:

POSHO – MEAT – VEGETABLES

He looked at the headings again, paused and leaned back in his chair. Placing his hands behind his head, he mulled over the facts.

"Assuming that food was not in plentiful supply, what would be the bare minimum to feed a man for a day? Posho? Say four ounces. And meat the same."

He reached forward and recorded the figure 4 under the first two headings. He thought about the next heading.

"Cabbage is a staple African vegetable which they boil for hours. Hmm... Let's say another four ounces. Now, to feed fifteen to sixteen men for a week? Per day, say four pounds per food item."

Below each of the first three headings he recorded the figure 28 lbs. He picked up the signal from the desk and studied the dates per reported theft, and the quantities, then scribbled a quick calculation on the base of the ruled pad. He studied the figures and his calculations and concluded that either thefts were not being reported, or there was an additional source of supply.

His mind went back to the Blakes' houseboy.

"His maize store had been cleared and, being dried maize cobs, would last for several weeks. Then there was the Myers butchered cattle. A mass of meat that, if cured, could also last for weeks."

He picked up the signal and studied the dates again. Most of the dated preceded the attack on the Blake's farm. He went over to the wall map again and looked at the red map pins within the segment he had pointed out to Bill Stewart, plus the location that his boss had pointed out. Dundas stood there for a few minutes then returned to his desk and picked up the phone.

"It's Chief Inspector Dundas. I need to speak to the Government Doctor." There was a click, the African operator said, "Hold the line Sir and I will try to connect you," followed by a series of clicks.

*"Doctor Lang."*

Dundas leaned back in his chair. "Sorry to disturb you Doctor, it's Robert Dundas C.I.D. Nakuru. Can you spare me just a few moments?"

*"Yes, providing it's quick."*

"Doctor, would four ounces of posho and the same quantities of meat and cabbage per day sustain a man in reasonable health?"

*"A strange question. Well, he certainly wouldn't be overweight! Depending on the type of activity, say digging, walking long distances, or running in some sporting event, then you would need to at least double the posho and vegetables and increase the meat to at least a pound a day. As I've just said, it all depends on the type of activity, but only four*

*ounces per food item is close to starvation rations. Is there anything else?"*

"No. Thank you Doctor, you have answered my query."

Still holding the handset, he went to tap the bar on the phone's cradle with his left hand, but paused and replaced the handset, leaned back in his chair and mentally juggled with the figures.

Dundas gazed out of the window, noting the birds concentrating their efforts around the bases of the small ornamental bushes. No doubt these areas would be moist and therefore the ideal place to find grubs an insects. He mused that it was strange how the human mind worked, as birds made him think about shooting. This line of thought then led him to think about guns. The average farm labourer would not have a clue how to aim and fire a gun. So who would? Ex-army personnel – or ex-police? His mind extended these thoughts to think about army deserters and, in particular, Kikuyu deserters. If such personnel existed. It was worth pursuing. Perhaps his boss could pull a few strings.

Dundas picked up the phone and dialled a two-digit internal number. There was a click and the usual terse response: "Lewis."

"Good morning Sir, it's Robert Dundas."

"Ah, I was about to call you. Can you come round to my office?"

"Yes Sir." Dundas took the familiar ten steps and knocked on his boss's door.

"Come in!"

Dundas pushed open the door to find Superintendent Lewis standing before an identical wall-map. He turned around as Dundas entered the office.

"Come in Robert. I have just returned from a meeting with the Assistant Commissioner and my opposite number from Special Branch. Information is coming in that some secret society is developing within the Kikuyu tribe. We have very few details, but it gels with the item found at the Blake's farm and the cook and his wife taking their own lives. It is suspected that oathing ceremonies are being conducted on a wide scale. However, the purpose of these ceremonies is unclear. Based on the limited number of attacks on European farms, it is possible that these are being used as some form of intimidation. It is also interesting that where Europeans have been killed, their pets have also been strangled, as per the cat on the Blake's farm, or slashed to death. I broached the subject about your suggestion of going into the Aberdare Range at North Kinankop in an attempt to trace the criminals involved and arrest them. There has been lots of umming and ahh-ing, but in summary it has been agreed that we should pursue this course of action. If you wish, Robert, you can lead a small group. I must stress the danger involved and, as you are newly married with a baby son, you do not have to go."

Dundas didn't know what to say in response. Talking about it was one thing but now he was 'on the spot'.

"Sir, I would like to discuss this with Joanne. Is that in order?"

"Of course. One thing that I failed to mention was your comment about equipment. Contact has been made with the Kenya Regiment and they have agreed to let us have any equipment that we need, including special lightweight ration packs. And finally, the Assistant Commissioner wants you to draw up a plan for his consideration, covering the number of men, equipment, types of firearms, the actual area of the operation and its duration."

"Is that required even if I decline to go?"

"Yes, and my next question is; how soon can you have the report come plan for submission?"

Dundas shrugged his shoulders. "Assuming, Sir, that nothing crops up, forty-eight hours. Sir, is it in order to raise another matter?"

Superintendent Lewis gestured. "Of course."

"I have been carrying out some calculations based on a gang of fifteen to sixteen and I have conferred with Doctor Lang. He is of the opinion that each man would require half a pound of posho and vegetables per day and a pound of meat. Calculating this on a weekly consumption, the quantities mentioned in the signal from North

Kinankop would be insufficient to sustain a gang of fifteen to sixteen men."

Superintendent Lewis held up his hand. "Have you overlooked the maize taken from the houseboy's store and the two cattle butchered on the Myers farm?"

"No Sir, I believe that these were 'one offs', as their rations were running low. I have every reason to believe that either thefts of farm produce are not being reported, or food is being delivered by some farm labour and, based on our observations, they are Kikuyu. In my office I have plotted all the map references where thefts have taken place." Dundas stood up, went over to the wall-map and pointed. "In the main, Sir, they are centred around here."

Superintendent Lewis sat nodding his head. "Interesting. That ties in with the vectors that we discussed before. Now Robert, if you'll excuse me I'll study this case file."

"Sir, there is one more thing. I have been thinking about firearms. The average farm labourer wouldn't know one end of a gun from the other. But what about ex-army personnel? Perhaps Kikuyu ex-army personnel who are deserters?"

Superintendent Lewis leaned forward and gestured. "That's damn good thinking! How about the police?"

"Sir, can you short-circuit the system and try to obtain information on these two categories?"

"Leave it with me Robert. If anything positive arises, I'll call you."

Dundas returned to his desk and picking up the ruled foolscap pad, removed his previous calculations, crumpled the page and tossed it into the waste-paper basket.

This assignment? Joanne had to be told and no doubt it would cause tears, but he would need to avoid the fact that they would be pursuing armed criminals. Based on a previous investigation, a tracker was essential.

Dundas sat there toying with a pencil and looking out of the window at the deep shadows directly under the small trees and shrubs that studded the grass outside. The tracker? Who? Where from? A civilian?

There was a Kipsigi constable stationed at Kijabe. He has assisted in the past. Yes, he would be ideal. Now for a good NCO… Sergeant James based in the C.I.D. Section would be ideal and he had been in a 'tight corner' in the past. How many men? He sat drumming the fingers of his left hand on the desk and looking at the wall map, as in his mind's eye he conjured up several scenarios.

Ten men would be ideal, and on balance the addition of a corporal was required, someone who was used to being fired on and returning hostile fire. There was a corporal who had been stationed in the Northern Frontier, who no doubt had been involved in several fire-fights with Shifta bandits during their annual raids across the border. He was a Somali and could be ideal. As to firearms, the constables were accustomed to the Lee Enfield .303 rifle and there was no time to retrain them. The Somali corporal would be used to handling a variety of firearms, so he could carry a twelve-bore Greener riot gun. Sergeant James had been trained to use a revolver, so could carry a .38 Webley and for himself he would carry his 9mm Browning automatic. This would constitute sufficient force to overcome any resistance.

As to duration? Initially three days and, if need be, the exercise could be repeated. Drawing the ruled pad towards him, he began to draft out his action plan under a variety of headings, not forgetting one headed: 'The Legal Use of Firearms'.

It was close to 6pm as Dundas drove into the entrance of their Government bungalow. No doubt hearing the noise of the car, Joanne came down the steps to meet him.

"Darling, I was just about to telephone, as I was fully convinced that you had been called away at short notice."

He held her close and gave her a kiss on the forehead.

"And where is the little terror?"

"Currently sat in front of the bookcase, removing all the books from the lower shelf. Come and take a look."

Dundas slowly peered around the open French door. His baby son was sat before the bookcase, deeply engrossed as he slowly added to the pile of discarded books. Joanne squeezed her husband's hand.

"Obviously he's going to be a bookworm."

They both smiled at each other and entered the French door.

# CHAPTER TWELVE

DUNDAS WAS CONTEMPLATING the best approach to take with Joanne. Should he say that he had been selected to lead a small team to apprehend the persons involved in the Blake's murders, avoiding the details? Or should he say that it would involve entering into the Aberdare forest, but without mentioning that the men involved possessed firearms? The thought that he found difficult to suppress was: should he go at all? His boss was more than sympathetic to the fact that it could be dangerous and as a father of a very young child, he had added responsibilities. However, one thought was more dominant than the rest. He wanted to go!

Two evenings later, with dinner a recent memory and with coffee having been served, he decided to 'bite the bullet'. With Joanne looking very relaxed and deep into her knitting, the moment seemed opportune.

"Joanne, we still haven't caught the people involved in the Blakes' murders."

Joanne ceased knitting and looked up. "Wasn't one of them their houseboy, surely he can be traced?"

"Well, he's not in the Reserve. Then there's the head clerk who worked on the Myers farm. He has also disappeared. I have been having discussions with Superintendent Lewis and it has been suggested that I lead a small specialist team to track them down."

Joanne put her knitting onto her side-table. "Does that mean you'll be away from time to time?"

Dundas nodded. "Yes. I estimate no more than three days at any one time."

Joanne picked up her knitting again, and then paused. "Robert, will it be dangerous?"

Dundas sat forward in his chair, and then shrugged. "Well... there will be ten to twelve of us in the team, so there must be safety in numbers."

Joanne posed the next question. "So it *could* be dangerous?"

Dundas tried to sound casual. "Well... yes."

Joanne continued. "Do you have to lead this team, or is it an option?"

Dundas thought: *So much for my planned approach!*

"Joanne, the longer these people are on the loose will only make them bolder and they may attempt another crime. I want to stop them before they can strike again. Given time and a good team, we'll find them."

Joanne resumed her knitting and did not respond for several seconds. Then she placed her knitting onto the small side-table, came over and sat on her husband's knee. She stroked his hair and gave him a gentle kiss. "Just promise me one thing. That you will not take any risks. I love you very much." Joanne placed her face against his and could not restrain the tears trickling down her cheeks.

The following morning Dundas arrived at his office at precisely one minute to eight. He had just opened the door as the phone rang. He picked up the handset, the voice was unmistakable, it was his boss.

"Morning Robert, I have some news about army deserters. According to the Kings African Rifles' records, there are only two Kikuyu deserters unaccounted for. One is Thomas Githenge, who has been on the run for over a year. The other is Kamau Gitui, who has been on the run for about the same period. Evidently, very few Kikuyu join the K.A.R. – it's the more warlike tribes like the Nandi and Kipsigis that are favoured. We should be receiving fingerprints and mug shots within the next few days."

Dundas felt elated. "That's excellent news Sir!"

"Two other bits of news, Robert. Your requests for selected personnel have been accepted and they will report to you within the next two days. The final thing is about your equipment. Tomorrow a Captain Knowles of the Kenya Regiment will be calling to see you and they have promised their full co-operation."

Dundas replaced the handset. Things were starting to move! Once the team was assembled, the next thing would be to brief them on what was entailed in this operation.

❖ ❖ ❖

IT WAS LATE AFTERNOON; the overhead fan in the Assistant Commissioner's spacious office caused the edges of the papers on the desk to lift slightly in its down draught, the slatted blinds covering the single large window reduced the sun's glare and, as the office was positioned at the rear of the building, away from the car-park, very little noise intruded on the meeting. The Assistant Commissioner was standing before the large wall map of the Rift Valley Province. Superintendent Lewis and Dundas were looking attentive. The A.C.P. continued.

"The operation will be confined to this area here. Any deviation from this area must be notified to Superintendent Lewis." He turned and faced the two men. "The Commissioner wishes to ensure that despite the fact the team will be dressed in army jungle greens, each man will wear a navy blue standard issue police beret, with the Kenya Police badge clearly displayed. The team will be housed in the police lines here in Nakuru. When not on operations they will wear normal police uniform. For security, the team will be transported from here at dusk per three-day operation and picked up at dusk from the drop-off point. The only other personnel who are aware of the forthcoming operation are the Assistant Superintendent at Naivasha and the Inspectors at Njabini and North Kinankop. Finally, it is imperative that you are not seen by the local farm labour, whom we suspect may warn any fugitives hiding in the forest. Any questions? Lewis?"

"No Sir."

"Dundas?"

"No Sir."

"In that case this 'O Group' is finished. And Dundas..."

"Sir."

"Good luck!"

❖ ❖ ❖

DUNDAS DROVE DOWN THE ROAD from Police Headquarters and turned left into the Police Lines, clearly marked by the large white signboard displaying the Kenya Police crest and the whitewashed stones on either side of the entrance; the blue Kenya Police flag, on its thirty-foot white flagpole, was stirring gently in the late afternoon breeze. He drove up one side of the large earth parade-ground and stopped by a large single-storey stone building that was the recreation hall and bar. Standing by the entrance was Sergeant James of the Provincial C.I.D. team, who greeted Dundas with his usual, almost old-fashioned English.

"Good afternoon Sir. All the men are assembled inside ready for your briefing."

"Thank you James, and how are you?"

"I am very well Sir, and your good-self?"

Dundas was always glad that he and his C.I.D. Sergeant were on the same side. At just over six foot and the shoulders of a rugby player, Sergeant James was the ideal man to have around in a 'tight corner'. Physical strength was not his only attribute; he was a very good investigator and always looked happy.

"James, are all the men assembled?"

"Yes Sir, and I'm sure that you will be pleased with Corporal Abikar."

"And why is that?"

"I've been talking to him, Sir, and he has been in many gun battles with the Shifta bandits who carry out raids over the northern border. Also, Sir, he has gained the instant respect of the men."

Dundas gestured. "Right James, let's go and meet the team."

❖ ❖ ❖

On entering the recreation centre there was a sharp word of command "Atten...shun!" The men sprang to their feet as Corporal Abikar delivered a very smart salute.

*Jambo Effendi!*

Dundas liked the look of Corporal Abikar immediately. He was slim, about five nine, wiry, with the high cheekbones that identified him as a Somali. He stood ramrod-straight in his immaculate starched uniform with his hat square on his head. Corporal Abikar was the type of NCO who radiated toughness and discipline.

"Jambo Corporal Abikar." Dundas stepped forward and shook the Corporal's hand. He noted that the grip was firm and the eyes unwavering. "Stand the men at ease Corporal."

Corporal Abikar did a very smart about-turn, stamping his right foot onto the ground as he completed the drill movement. It would not have been out of place on a major parade. This was followed immediately by his next order. "Stand at... ease!"

Corporal Abikar performed another smart about-turn and took up the at ease position. Dundas stepped forward and spoke in Kiswahili.

"I want to tell you why you are here and what we will be doing as a team. First of all, we will be stationed here and during daylight hours we will wear normal police uniforms. From time to time we will leave here at dusk. Each and every one of us will be dressed in army jungle green uniforms."

There was a stirring in the assembled group. Dundas continued.

"The reason for this is that we will be patrolling in the Aberdare forests to hunt down criminals who have committed murder and who so far have managed to evade arrest. To show that we are police and not army, we will wear a standard issue police beret with the Kenya Police badge positioned over the left eye. Each patrol will leave here at dusk and each will last three days. We will be collected at dusk from our drop-off point. The reason for being here rather than nearer the forest edge is to maintain secrecy and to prevent persons who may be assisting these criminals and may warn them of our presence. Tomorrow we will all be on the rifle range for two reasons; one to remind everyone when it is lawful for us to use firearms and two, to obtain some practice. Any questions?"

A hand went up. "Effendi, how many criminals are there hiding in the Aberdares?"

"We estimate ten to fifteen and we are aware that they have a shot-gun and a rifle."

Another hand went up. "Effendi, will we need to bring our blankets and food?"

"No. The Kenya Regiment have supplied our equipment, which includes special blankets and rations. Any more questions?"

No one moved.

"Good. Sergeant James here is with our C.I.D. team and he will join us in this operation. He is responsible for your welfare and accommodation."

Once outside, Dundas spoke to Sergeant James. "James, what tribes do the team come from?"

"Well Sir, as you know Corporal Abikar is a Somali. There are three Wakamba, four with myself, four Kipsigis, including constable Kipchumba from Kijabe, and three Nandi."

"So James, quite a war-party!"

"Indeed Sir, and in particular the Wakamba."

Dundas grinned. "Sergeant James..."

"Sir?"

"Don't forget the *Mzungu* (the European)!"

"As you have said Sir, quite a war-party!"

The phone jangled on the Charge Office desk and it was picked up by the Constable on duty. "Njabini Police Station."

The voice on the other end was that of a European with a limited knowledge of Kiswahili.

*"Wapi Bwana Inspector?"* (Where is the Mr Inspector?)

The constable replied in English. "The Inspector is not available Sir. Can I take a message?"

The caller reverted to his native tongue.

*"My name is Major Fawcett. An old Kikuyu man has lived on this farm for years and he has suddenly disappeared. I thought I should report it."*

"Thank you Sir. How many days has he been missing?"

*"It must be about six days. I've enquired around the farm, but no one has seen him."*

"How about his living quarters; is anything missing?"

*"No everything appears to be there."*

"Thank you for your report Sir and I will inform the Inspector when he returns."

The constable put the phone down and began to make an entry in the Occurrence Book under the heading MISSING PERSON REPORT.

# CHAPTER THIRTEEN

DUNDAS ARRIVED AT THE RIFLE RANGE before 8am to await the arrival of the armourer with the weaponry, the red danger flags, the targets and target markers. He had given considerable thought to the forthcoming practice shoot and had decided that if firearms were to be used, the distances would be way under the usual qualifying standard of two hundred yards. Therefore, he had decided to set the figure targets at a maximum range of 50 yards, and for his 9mm automatic and Sergeant James's .38 revolver, 25 yards.

Some ten minutes later he could hear a vehicle approaching and from around the bend in the track a police three-ton lorry appeared with the team and the armourer sitting beside the driver.

The lorry was parked beside Dundas's car and the team started to de-bus and be formed up in twos by Corporal Abikar. The armourer came over to where Dundas was standing.

"Good morning Chief Inspector, a good day for a shoot! Hardly any breeze and the sun will not be in the men's eyes."

Dundas held out his hand. "Good morning. I want to change the usual range system. I want the figure targets set up at no more than fifty yards. Then, when we switch to the automatic and the revolver, we will move forward to twenty-five yards."

The armourer frowned. "The standard to qualify is two hundred yards."

Dundas nodded his head. "I am aware of this, but I have reasons for this departure from standard practice."

"In that case Chief Inspector, I'll position the danger flags and position the figure targets."

The armourer turned to go as Dundas asked. "How many figure targets do you have?"

"Ten," came the reply.

"In that case, position all ten, grouping two or three close together and the remainder widely spaced."

With the flags and the targets in position, under the 'eagle eye' and sharp commands from Corporal Abikar, the team were formed up at the firing point. Dundas stepped forward.

"Each man will fire a total of fifteen rounds which will be five rounds from each of the following positions: prone, kneeling and standing. Having fired all fifteen rounds, the rifle will be left on the ground with the bolt open. Then, as a team, we will go forward to inspect the targets. The armourer will remain here with the rifles. Any questions?"

No one moved.

"Right, we'll commence with Corporal Abikar and as each man fires I will observe through these binoculars."

Corporal Abikar took up the prone position and loaded the five rounds into the magazine, rammed the bolt forward and applied the safety catch, then glanced at Dundas, who nodded.

"Commence firing."

Corporal Abikar fired the first shot, then quickly rolled to his left and fired again, repeating the exercise until all five rounds were expended. The whole shoot had taken less than ten seconds. Dundas was astounded!

"Corporal Abikar, excellent shooting! Every target hit in the centre of the body! But why roll after each shot?"

Corporal Abikar placed the rifle on the ground stood up and saluted. "Effendi, the 'Shifta' bandits wait to see the muzzle flash and then shoot at it. To stay in the same position would mean instant injury or death."

"And from the other positions?"

"The same Effendi. Go down, roll and reappear and go down again."

During the next ten rounds, Corporal Abikar demonstrated both the system and his prowess with a rifle.

The results from the rest of the team using the rifle, ranged from 'not bad' to 'erratic'. It was obvious that the men were accustomed to shooting from the prone position and taking their time over each shot.

Rapid fire resulted in some of the figure targets being missed altogether.

By mid-afternoon things had improved and Dundas was glad that he still retained the ability to rapidly put nine rounds into a figure target at 25 yards and Sergeant James did not disgrace himself with the Webley.

Dundas thought how strange the men looked in their army jungle greens and blue police berets. His own felt semi-stiff and smelt new. The khaki woollen shirt felt coarse against his skin and the jungle green boots that laced to just below the knee, with their cleated black rubber soles, also felt awkward, but at least the thin canvas material used in their construction was soft and yielding. Perhaps the best thing was the camouflage three-quarter length smock. It was capacious and could be secured at the neck and thighs to retain body heat. Made from a special 'Grenfell' cloth, the fibres were designed to swell when wet and thus become waterproof. The other main items of equipment were a single lightweight jungle-green blanket, plus a matching waterproof poncho that could double as a cape, or when clipped up at the sides, a sleeping bag to contain the blanket. Each man was issued with a small back-pack, a webbing belt and aluminium water bottle. As regards firearms, the constables carried the standard issue .303 rifles, plus ten rounds of ammunition per man. Corporal Abikar had a Greener 12-bore shotgun and ten rounds, Sergeant James a .38 standard issue police Webley revolver and twelve rounds, and Dundas carried his standard issue 9mm Browning automatic with twenty rounds, contained in two clips. Dundas felt confident that, as they would be facing only a shotgun and a rifle, they had more than sufficient firepower to scare the criminals into surrendering.

❖ ❖ ❖

The three-ton truck left the police lines at precisely 6:45pm. It was already dusk and the men were huddled in the rear out of sight, with Dundas and Sergeant James sitting beside the driver. At the 'T' junction, the truck turned right onto the main Nakuru Nairobi road and headed towards Naivasha. The plan, agreed with Superintendent Lewis, was to drop off on the road near the Fawcett farm and make their way under the cover of darkness to the forest edge, there to 'hole up' for the night and to begin checking for tracks soon after dawn.

The truck stopped and the driver doused the lights. As the men debussed, they formed up on the road. Dundas was finding it difficult to see until his eyes adjusted to the starlight. Peering into the gloom, in a quiet voice he addressed the men.

"You all know the plan. Silence is essential. Corporal Abikar will lead and I will be directly behind him. Sergeant James will be at the rear. Keep the man to your front in sight at all times. If we have to stop, I will raise my hand. Each of you will do the same and despite the starlight, the signal will be visible. Remember, silence is essential. Let's move."

Dundas glanced at his luminous watch. It was just after 8.20. With luck, they should be in position in under two hours. By now his eyes had adjusted to the starlight but it was strange to be making their way without lights and Dundas realised what it must have been like for the gang making their way to attack the unsuspecting Blakes. Suddenly Corporal Abikar held up his hand and Dundas repeated the signal. He crept forward, tapped Corporal Abikar on the shoulder and whispered.

"What is it?"

"I've seen a light coming towards us Effendi. It could be a bicycle."

Dundas whispered again. "We'll hide in the long grass on the left. I'll pass the word."

The lonely cyclist passed by, not realising that thirteen armed men were hiding within five feet of his passing. Corporal Abikar went back onto the track, waited a few moments, and then went back down the file, checking that everyone was present before continuing. After some fifteen minutes, muffled voices and laughter could be heard. Again, Corporal Abikar held up his hand, bringing the file of men to a halt, and then carefully made his way back to Dundas.

Keeping his voice to a whisper, he said, "Effendi, we need to be careful. The voices sound to be coming from the labour lines and there are bound to be dogs there. If this track passes close by, then they will sense our presence and raise the alarm."

Dundas nodded. "We'll continue ahead and then try and make our way across a field."

After some fifty yards, Corporal Abikar stopped again.

Dundas went forward. "What is it?"

"Effendi, I can hear cattle breathing over to our right. Perhaps this is where we can leave the track and skirt around the field?"

"OK. If you see a gate we'll climb over, but will we disturb the cattle?"

"Not if we move slowly Effendi."

With Corporal Abikar in the lead, they set off once again, stopping beside a wooden gate only to find a large white cow resting on the ground. The animal got to its feet and placed its head over the gate. Through pursed lips, Corporal Abikar made semi-fast deep breathing noises and slowly approached the cow until his face was no more than a foot from the cow's nostrils. He continued to make deep breathing noises. To Dundas's utter surprise, the cow made similar noises in response, then, after a minute or so, lost interest and ambled off. Dundas made his way forward until he was beside Corporal Abikar.

"Why didn't the cow run off and arouse the others?"

"I made the same noise that cows make to each other, Effendi."

And with these words, he started to quietly clamber over the gate.

Once off the track, making their way in starlight was more difficult. Normal objects such as small bushes took on the shape of crouching men and they constantly stopped until Corporal Abikar was satisfied the way ahead was clear.

By now they had entered the fringe of the forest. Due to the overhead canopy, it was as 'black as pitch' and soon proved to be impossible to continue. Dundas realised they would have to halt and bed down where they were, then move off again at dawn. He passed the word down the line, detailing the six men immediately to his rear to stand guard at one-hour intervals. Dundas was quickly realising that passing words of command in utter and complete darkness and in whispers would prove to be difficult. Not only that, but with thirteen men readying themselves to sleep, arranging unfamiliar blankets and ponchos onto ground they could not see, was both noisy and confusing. Dundas cursed himself for not realising in advance that this apparently simple procedure would prove to be so difficult and create so much noise.

Dundas spent a fitful night. Despite being fully dressed, plus being wrapped in a lightweight blanket and covered by a poncho, he felt cold. The forest, which he had expected to be quiet at night, resounded to the shrieks of hyraxes in the forest canopy. Even before dawn, the forest birds came to life, the numerous and different calls reaching a crescendo by first light.

Dundas sat up and looked at his immediate surroundings, realising that he now needed to answer a call of nature. How far should he go in order to obtain a modicum of privacy? He eased himself out of his blanket and poncho and made for a large tree some ten yards away. On his return, he noted several of the men wandering off to do the same thing. He realised that while living in such close proximity to the men, his British inhibitions would need to be discarded.

Corporal Abikar was oiling his Greener gun and, as Dundas approached, he looked up.

"*Uli lala mzuri Effendi?*" (Did you sleep well Sir?)

Dundas replied in the same tongue.

"*La, ni baridi.*" (No, it was cold).

Dundas walked down the line acknowledging several greetings of "Jambo Effendi" until he came to Sergeant James, who stood up as he approached.

"Good morning Sir, did you sleep well?"

"No James, I was cold and the forest noises kept me awake!"

"Sir, may I ask what are the plans for today?"

"We will patrol just inside the forest edge to see if Constable Kipchumba can find any human tracks. If he does, then we will follow them and hopefully make contact."

"Sir, how soon will we be moving off?"

Dundas glanced at his watch. "It's now 5.27. We move in twenty minutes. Make sure that the men eat. Remember, no fires and any *taka-taka* (rubbish) must be buried off track. Our formation will be the same as last night."

Dundas walked back to his blanket and poncho, then sat down, inspected his special ration pack and opted for the small tin of corned beef, the oatmeal stick and the Mars bar, to be washed down with the icy cold contents of his water bottle. The small packet of hard biscuits and the tiny tin of jam, he would consume later. Looking up, he noted that Corporal Abikar was finding it difficult to open one of the tins with the small folding tin opener and went over to help. He realised yet again that he had failed to anticipate that even opening the ration packs could cause problems. Having assisted Corporal Abikar, he made his way down the line, explaining the pack's contents and demonstrating how to open the tins. As a result, the move off was delayed by twenty minutes.

Dundas decided to stay within the forest fringe and head roughly West. If there were any tracks leading in or out, then Constable Kipchumba would see them. Kipchumba cautiously moved ahead, stopping from time to time to examine the ground and to listen. Dundas was immediately behind him at a distance of no more than three yards, with Corporal Abikar the third in line. As previously agreed, Sergeant James was at the rear of the patrol.

Due to the sparseness of the forestation, moving ahead was not difficult; everyone could walk upright, with the only obstructions being the trees, which they constantly skirted. At 10.00am Dundas called a halt and consulted his map. Having crossed five small streams, he estimated that they had covered no more than eight to nine miles. Having folded his map, he returned it to the right-hand hip pocket of his camouflage smock, then leaned back against a tree, going over in his mind the problems they had encountered. Tonight would be different. They would stop at dusk to ensure that everyone could see what they were doing and he would ensure that the men could identify each type of food contained within the special ration packs. He glanced back down the line. Some of the men were conversing in low voices, whilst others rested against trees. Momentarily, Dundas closed his eyes. The hyraxes were not screaming, but there was bird-life in abundance.

A tap on his left shoulder made him open his eyes. It was Corporal Abikar, who was crouched low and holding his finger to his lips. He then pointed the same finger ahead and slightly to the left of their heading and cupped his right hand to his ear. Dundas strained to catch whatever was producing the sound. What was it? Then he heard it; female voices. Constable Kipchumba was already in a prone position, looking ahead. Dundas watched as Corporal Abikar, crouching low, went down the line to warn the others. Would they be spotted? The voices came closer and stopped within fifty yards. Soon the sound of the shrill voices was joined by the sound of wood being chopped. The patrol stayed low and it was some thirty minutes later that the sound of the female voices began to fade and they were able to proceed along the forest edge.

Dundas looked up through the trees and then, out of habit, glanced at his watch. It was 4.36; in two hours' time he would call a halt and they would bed down for the night. Suddenly, there was a crashing in the undergrowth to their right! Dundas froze in his tracks and reached for his automatic but Constable Kipchumba just turned around and grinned, holding his thumbs and forefingers to his head to represent horns. The patrol continued cautiously ahead.

By now it was dusk and Dundas called a halt beside a small stream. They were still within the forest fringe and the stream would provide clean water for drinking and washing. Dundas decided that everyone should sleep within a circle and that the men detailed for guard duty would sit in the middle during their one hour stint. Dundas opted to take the first 'stint', commencing at 7.00pm.

Having eaten, the patrol settled down for the night and Dundas took up his position in the centre of the circle, tightening the hip and neck cords on his smock to retain body heat. With darkness, the hyraxes began shrieking, their calls echoing all over the forest. He strained his eyes and ears. He held his hand in front of his face at a distance of no more than nine inches. He couldn't see a thing! Suddenly, there was a rustle somewhere behind him, perhaps no more than twenty five yards away. He strained his ears to catch the slightest sound, but the noise had stopped. There it was again! He eased his Browning automatic from its shoulder holster and very carefully and slowly turned around. The rustling had stopped. What was it?

He was answered with a snort and a crashing in the undergrowth, as the inquisitive Bush Buck beat a hasty retreat. Dundas could hear his heart thumping in his chest and breathed a sigh of relief. For the remainder of his hour he had time to mull over the fact that there was a lot to learn about patrolling in the forests of the Aberdares. His mind turned to the men that they hoped to trace and arrest – where were they in this vast expanse of forest?

Having handed over to the next man on guard duty, Dundas slipped gratefully into his blanket and poncho and was asleep in seconds.

The cold water splashing onto his face awoke him with a start. It was raining! He snuggled down into the poncho to keep the rain off his face, only to discover that the rainwater was now pooling behind his neck. It was surprising how the rain falling onto his poncho made so much noise and he realised that it would make it impossible to detect anyone approaching their position. It was proving to be a wet, cold and miserable night.

Dundas was awakened by two things, the dawn chorus and feeling cold. He sat up and looked at the man on guard duty who, upon seeing Dundas, partly raised his hand in greeting, then hunched his body, indicating he was also cold, then grinned. Dundas ran his fingers through his hair. So much for lightweight blankets! The cold was acting on his bladder. With all the men asleep, it seemed an ideal opportunity to 'disappear' behind a tree. A few minutes later, he returned and sat beside the man on guard.

*"Jambo Kipkoske."*

The man grinned. *"Jambo Effendi. Leo tutaa enda wapi?"* (Today where will we go?)

Dundas had already given this some thought. In view of the fact that no tracks had been discovered, they would return to their starting point and head in the opposite direction. Having conveyed this to Kipkoske, he returned to his blanket and poncho and began examining his special ration pack. What should he have for breakfast? He opted for the oatmeal stick, the small tin of meat, to be washed down with icy cold water. He glanced at his watch. Joanne and Ian would be fast asleep, and within the hour Steven would enter the kitchen to commence preparing Dundas's usual breakfast of fresh orange juice, 'Uplands' bacon and egg, toast with local honey... and coffee. Coffee! Dundas momentarily closed his eyes and savoured the memory of that aroma as he poured the first cup of the day. A sound made him open his eyes. It was Sergeant James.

"Good morning Sir, another cold night."

"Agreed James, somehow we need to keep warmer at night."

They discussed the forthcoming plan for the day. Dundas estimated that the return to their starting point would take less than a day, and then they could head in the opposite direction.

"So James, we'll brief the men and move off in thirty minutes."

Constable Kipchumba still headed the patrol, but walked at a much faster pace. By just after three, they had reached their starting point and Dundas called a halt for a brief fifteen-minute rest. He felt into the right hand hip pocket of his smock, withdrew the map and then unfolded it. The pick-up was arranged for ten o'clock the following night, so, based on their first night's experience, they would need to be out of the forest fringe by just after dusk and then retrace their steps past the Fawcett farm to the waiting truck. Dundas estimated that by two o'clock the following day they would need to return to where they were now. It was time to move off.

The pace as per day one was slow, with Constable Kipchumba constantly scanning the ground and stopping from time to time to examine it more closely, with Corporal Abikar looking ahead. Suddenly, Corporal Abikar cupped his right hand to his ear, then, turning his hand palm-down, signalled for everyone to crouch down. What was it? Corporal Abikar moved very slowly and crouched down behind a tree, then pointed with his finger ahead and to their right. Dundas strained his ears to catch the slightest sound. Womens' voices again. Could it be another group gathering firewood? The sound of their chatter was now almost dead ahead and then began moving to the left of their line of advance. Dundas estimated the distance to be no more than 25 yards. Within minutes, the sound of their voices had faded into the distance.

Crouching low, Dundas carefully made his way forward to Corporal Abikar. "Did you see them?"

"No Effendi, but it sounded as if there were at least five women."

Dundas was now faced with three options: follow them and risk discovery; continue ahead as planned or wait until the women returned, then follow their tracks to ascertain if they had deposited any food.

Within minutes the sound of the womens' voices could be heard approaching again. It had to be option three. Dundas waited, crouched beside Corporal Abikar, until the sound of the voices faded into the distance again. Dundas stood up and, looking back down their line of advance, signalled for everyone to gather round, then, speaking very quietly, he addressed the men.

"A group of women crossed our line of advance and have since returned. It is possible that they may have been carrying food to be collected by the criminals hiding in this forest. We will follow their tracks and, if they have dumped food, we will lay an ambush and arrest anyone appearing to collect it."

Dundas could sense the air of excitement.

"Constable Kipchumba will lead, as before. Remember, we must proceed with extreme caution. Constable Kipchumba, Corporal Abikar and I will have our firearms ready, in case we meet any armed criminals. Sergeant James..."

"Sir."

"The remainder of the patrol will load their guns and apply the safety catch. The rifles will be carried across the body, as was demonstrated on the firing range at Nakuru. Now, load carefully and quietly."

The patrol moved ahead, with Constable Kipchumba in the lead, followed by Corporal Abikar and then Dundas. All three had their weapons ready for instant action. Just thirty yards ahead, Constable Kipchumba paused, studied the ground, then turned left and began following the womens' tracks into the forest. Dundas felt a tingle of excitement – would they find where food had been dumped and make an arrest?

Within less than ten minutes, they came to a clearing. Constable Kipchumba held up his hand and motioned Corporal Abikar to come forward, then, by a hand signal, indicated for him to circle the clearing whilst he kept watch. Dundas and the remainder of the patrol waited, with a growing level of expectation. Corporal Abikar disappeared from view. Dundas could feel the tension rising; would he find anything? The minutes ticked by. Suddenly, Corporal Abikar reappeared, his face wearing in a big grin. He gave the thumbs-up sign and came to where Dundas was standing.

"Effendi, there are five sacks of food hidden under bushes to one side of the clearing. From the shapes inside, I would say they contain cabbage and maize cobs."

Dundas patted Corporal Abikar on the shoulder.

"Excellent! Wait here and I'll inform the others."

The news had an immediate impact on the men. This is what they had been waiting for, some action! Dundas conferred with Sergeant James.

"The food may be collected at any time before dark, or early tomorrow morning and we'll ambush and arrest everyone as they arrive to collect it. In order to prevent any escapes, we will position three men just off the track that leads into the clearing and three men on this side of the clearing. Corporal Abikar will be in charge of the first group and you, James, will take charge of the other. The remainder of us will conceal ourselves very close to the sacks. Now we will call the men together and brief them. I want to stress again about the lawful use of firearms."

Dusk came and went, but no one appeared to collect the food, so the ambush party resumed their nightly routine of sleeping in a circle with the man on guard duty sat in the middle. The Hyraxes resumed their shrieking in the tree canopy and it rained heavily, blotting out all sound. Even the Hyraxes became silent as the rain continued. Dundas felt a trickle of water entering his poncho to herald yet another wet and cold night. He had opted for the pre-dawn guard duty as an insurance against the men over-sleeping and being late in taking up their ambush positions. Sleep eluded him as cold rainwater continued to splash onto his face.

❖ ❖ ❖

Dundas stirred, turned over and realised that he must have slept. The hands on his luminous wristwatch read 5.52am. Time to make a move. He slid out of his poncho and blanket, went over to where Sergeant James was sleeping and shook him gently.

"James, time to get the men moving, it will be dawn in less than thirty minutes. The ambush positions will be the same as last night. I'll be back in five minutes."

Dundas moved away from the circle of sleeping men and, as before, found a convenient tree to give him some privacy. On his return, the men were already eating, or wandering a short distance to relieve themselves. Dundas rinsed his hands with his water bottle and once again examined his ration pack. He decided to eat half the oatmeal stick and the Mars bar, a strange breakfast but he had to admit that, despite their lightness, the contents were sustaining.

Everyone was in position and well concealed. All they could do now was wait. The dawn chorus had faded and the Hyraxes were silent. The usual daytime sounds now echoed around the forest. The man beside Dundas tapped his left shoulder. As Dundas carefully turned his head, the man cupped his right hand to his ear and pointed up the track to where Corporal Abikar and his men were secreted. Dundas strained his ears. What was it? He then realised that the bird-life in their immediate vicinity had stopped singing. Did this mean that someone was approaching? He could feel his heart thumping in his chest as his excitement reacted to the expectation of making an arrest. He heard a twig snap! It could not have been more than fifteen yards away. Dundas increased the grip on the butt of his Browning automatic. A few moments later, a solitary figure entered the clearing. His hair was semi-long and multi-plaited, like the dead bodies Dundas had seen at the Myers farm and he wore a khaki, ex-army overcoat. He looked around, then went over to the sacks and prodded them. He looked around again and walked back the way he had come. Dundas realised this was to call the others.

A few moments later, five men appeared, including the man Dundas had first seen. Three of the men had long hair but one had hair of almost normal length. None of the group was armed. For a while they sat on the ground no more than ten paces from where Dundas and his group were secreted in the undergrowth.

It was time to pounce! Dundas carefully reached across to the man on his immediate left, then the man on the right, indicating that they should alert the others, then held up his clenched fist and displayed his thumb. Now the first finger, the second, third, fourth... and finally, the fifth.

As they sprang into action, the five men sat open-mouthed at this totally unexpected attack. Two partly rose to their feet but were knocked down and overpowered. The whole action had taken less than thirty seconds. Now handcuffed, the five men were still looking shocked. When searched, every one of them was carrying a razor sharp *simi* suspended by a thong slung over the left shoulder.

Due to their shocked state, Dundas decided it was an ideal time to commence questioning and, with his team reassembled, each prisoner was questioned alone, then kept apart from the others. The information obtained revealed the following:

They were part of a gang of 21 men and one woman.

Their leader was called Colonel Tom.

Their camp was some five miles away deep in the forest.

The man with normal hair said he would lead them to the camp.

Colonel Tom had a shotgun.

The 'sergeant' known as Simba had a rifle.

Another man they called 'Kenya Bus' had a revolver.

They had come to collect food left by Kikuyu women from Major Fawcett's farm.

Every man admitted to being a Kikuyu.

Dundas now faced a problem. Their pick-up by the police truck was not until dark. If these men did not return it was highly likely that someone would come looking for them. Therefore, it was important to remove the food and the prisoners to another location within the forest. Dundas hoped that this course of action may lead the gang in the forest to think that the five men had absconded and taken the food with them. To attempt to trace the camp and arrest the remainder of the gang could be risky, as it would mean splitting his force. It was very, very tempting to do so, but... Dundas pondered the pros and cons. What if they ambushed the food dump again? This would add to their number of prisoners, however, the non-return of the second group would alert Colonel Tom that something was amiss. On balance, it was best to remove the food, along with the prisoners, to Nakuru, replenish their army ration packs, then return to trace the gang's camp and arrest the lot. Having made this decision, the patrol with the five prisoners and the sacks of food, moved their position to wait for dusk before moving off.

Dundas realised that five prisoners and surrounding darkness was not an ideal combination. In order to improve security, individual handcuffs were removed and Dundas had them handcuffed in pairs, right wrist to right wrist, a trick he had learned many years ago. Running away when handcuffed in this manner was impossible. He also made sure that none of the prisoners was carrying a small piece of soap. All a prisoner had to do was urinate on his wrists, apply the soap and then slide off the handcuffs.

It was now dusk and time to move off. Each pair of prisoners was placed between two constables, the fifth man being handcuffed to Sergeant James. Due to the method employed in handcuffing the prisoners, progress was slow. As per their inward route, the patrol stopped from time to time to listen and observe. The Fawcett labour camp was given a wide berth and, having arrived at their pick-up point, the patrol secreted itself on the side of the road to await the police truck.

The homeward journey was uneventful and laughter coming from the rear of the lorry indicated that the men were in high spirits.

With the five prisoners in custody, Dundas phoned Joanne and then Superintendent Lewis.

"Congratulations Robert! Get a good night's sleep and we can get together tomorrow morning at ten thirty."

Dundas replaced the handset. Suddenly he felt very tired. Three things were uppermost in his mind: a deep hot bath, a hot meal and feeling the warmth of Joanne in his arms.

# CHAPTER FOURTEEN

WITHIN THE CAMP the non-return of the food party was subject to much discussion and conjecture. Everyone had been waiting in anticipation of five sacks of fresh produce. The failure of the five men to return by early afternoon caused Colonel Tom to utter a series of threats that indicated it would be far better if they did not return. Rumours circulated around the camp but the consensus was that the men had fled to avoid the harsh realities of forest living.

By mid-afternoon Sergeant Simba and Kenya Bus were ordered to go and find the food party, with the added directive that if the men were found drunk, they were to be killed. Moving at speed, the two members of the search party arrived just before dusk and went immediately to where the food was normally hidden. The food was missing and there was no sign of the five men. They discovered an area of crushed grass, perhaps where the five men had rested. Or was it? Sergeant Simba thought about it for a moment but reasoned that if the police had ambushed the five men, they would have waited to arrest the search party that was bound to come looking for them. Besides, the police did not patrol in the forest, hence the gang's ability to wander around at will. He concluded that the men had absconded, taking the food with them. In the fading light, Sergeant Simba and his underling retraced their steps into the depths of the forest. Little did he realise that his decision would cost him his life.

For Robert Dundas it was a very unusual start to the working day. He had stayed an extra half hour in bed and had a very casual breakfast; he even had time to spoon cereal into Ian's eager young mouth. The rigours of his brief existence in the Aberdares seemed almost a distant memory. Even driving into town was a new experience. There were more cars and more people around and the shops were open for business. Dundas parked in his usual place, then made his way to the entrance of Headquarters and the Charge Office. Inspector Farrell, the

Duty Officer, was talking to one of the constables. On seeing Dundas, he broke off the conversation and glanced at his watch.

"Morning Robert! Oh to be a member of the C.I.D! Your five 'babes in the wood' slept well and my nose tells me they could do with a shower! As per instructions, they have been kept apart from the other prisoners."

Dundas grinned. "I trust that they have not phoned for room service!"

Dundas made his way to his office and went over to the window. The birds were, as usual, strutting across the grass, pausing to thrust their beaks into the ground, sometimes without a visible result. His mind drifted back to the previous night; evidently, three nights in the forest were not conducive to family planning! His thoughts were disturbed by the telephone. He went over to his desk and picked up the handset.

"Chief Inspector Dundas C.I.D."

"Robert, it's Bill Stewart. I understand that congratulations are in order."

"Good morning Bill. Yes, we arrested five of them and I'm hoping that when you take their fingerprints you can obtain a match."

"So, how was life in the Aberdares?"

Dundas grinned. "In two words, cold and wet."

"Hmm... Rather you than me! I'll be in touch if we obtain any matching fingerprints. Again, congratulations."

Dundas replaced the handset into its cradle, then went over to the map on the wall and looked intently where he believed the remainder of the gang was located. The 'big question' was, with the non-return of the food party, would the gang have moved?

The jangling of the telephone intruded into his thoughts. Once again, he went over to the desk and picked up the handset.

"Chief Inspector Dundas C.I.D."

"Robert, Superintendent Lewis. If you are free, can you come to my office?"

Dundas realised it was an order and not a request.

"Yes Sir, I'm on my way."

As Dundas entered the office, Superintendent Lewis rose from his chair and extended his hand.

"Congratulations on a job well done! The Assistant Commissioner is awaiting your report. However, before we visit his office, Special Branch are very keen to interview your five prisoners. I take it that you have no objections?"

"No Sir, none whatsoever."

"Good. I understand that Bill Stewart will be taking fingerprints this morning and let us hope this will result in someone being charged for the Blakes' murder. Now, before we see the A.C.P., give me a 'thumbnail sketch' of the operation."

The Assistant Commissioner shook Dundas warmly by the hand.

"Congratulations on a job well done!"

"Thank you Sir."

The A.C.P. turned to Superintendent Lewis.

"I'd like Chief Inspector Dundas to point out the actual area of his operation, plus the location where they found the food dump, and made the arrests."

Dundas stood before the wall-map flanked by the two senior officers. "This, Sir, is where we dropped off and made our way towards the forest, skirting Major Fawcett's labour camp about here, then bedded down for the night here. What I had overlooked was how dark it can be once under the forest canopy. It is black as pitch and virtually impossible to see a hand in front of your face. Also, as regards equipment, the single blanket and poncho did not keep out the cold. Day two we went in this direction and turned back about here. Having retraced our steps to our starting point, it was just beyond this that the women from Fawcett's farm dropped off the food. We ambushed the drop off point and made the arrests the following morning. In order not to alert the other gang members, we removed the food and the prisoners to about here. (Dundas pointed) Then went to our RV that night."

"Hmm…" The A.C.P. stroked his chin. "Would it not have been better to continue with the ambush in order to arrest any subsequent search party?"

Dundas shook his head. "In my opinion Sir, had the search party also failed to return, then this would have alerted the gang that something was amiss and they would have moved."

The A.C.P. nodded his head several times. "I see." He studied the map again, then turned and faced Dundas. "I have two questions. One, what lessons if any have you learned? And two, what are you and Superintendent Lewis planning to do about the remainder of the gang?"

"In brief, Sir, to bed down before total darkness sets in. The number of men in the patrol was ideal, although due to the forestation the rear of the patrol was often out of sight. Also, we need to improve our warmth. I plan to contact the Government Doctor to see if he can make any suggestions. As regards your final point, Sir, I have yet to discuss this with Superintendent Lewis."

The A.C.P. nodded. "I understand. Thank you Chief Inspector." He turned to Superintendent Lewis. "Superintendent Lewis…"

"Sir."

"Keep me updated on events and in particular if Scenes of Crime obtain a match."

"Of course, Sir."

Dundas followed Superintendent Lewis down the stairs to ground level. At the foot of the stairs, Superintendent Lewis paused. "Robert, do you really want to finish the job?"

"Yes Sir. I'd like to leave again this evening at dusk."

"You appreciate that if contact is made with the remainder of the gang, there may be an exchange of fire."

"Thank you for your concern, Sir. I plan to be in position just before dawn. I doubt if they post any sentries and therefore we can take them by surprise."

"So you will bed down tonight and then trek into the forest tomorrow?"

"Yes Sir. Hopefully we can locate the gang's camp without being spotted, then bed down close by and hit them at dawn."

Superintendent Lewis nodded several times. "In that case Robert, I'll interview the five men and let you know if they reveal any information. Whatever transpires, I'll see you before you leave." He held out his hand. "Good luck Robert, and no heroics. Never forget, dead heroes are ten a penny. We want you and your team back here safe and sound."

Dundas walked towards his office, realising that he had yet to tell Joanne that he was leaving at dusk for two days and he knew how she would react. He entered his office, sat at his desk, then reached for the telephone and spoke to the police operator.

"I wish to speak to the Government Doctor."

He replaced the handset, then swivelled his chair and looked at the wall-map. Would it be a wasted trip? The phone rang. He picked up the handset. It was the police operator.

"Your call is just going through Sir."

There was a click and a response.

*"Doctor Lang."*

"Good morning Doctor, it's Robert Dundas. Can you spare me a few moments?"

*"As it's you Robert, yes, but be quick!"*

"The reason for my call is that I want to travel light and carry only a lightweight blanket and a poncho for sleeping. Is there anything, apart from the obvious, that I can do to keep warm?"

"Robert, I take it this is a serious question? Wear a sweater and keep your stomach well covered. The ideal thing would be one of your long police puttees. Wind this around your middle and you'll be as warm as toast. It's something I learned in India when in the foothills. Now I must go..."

❖ ❖ ❖

Dundas drove down to the police lines to alert Sergeant James and Corporal Abikar that they were leaving at dusk with the intention of arresting the remainder of the gang. He also issued the instruction that every man was to carry a police sweater and a long puttee, adding that he would return at five thirty to brief the team.

Having reached the roundabout on the Eastern edge of town , he took the first exit road and drove up the hill to their bungalow, parking by the steps leading up to the front door. As he did so, Joanne came around the corner, carrying their baby son Ian on her hip.

On seeing Dundas he held out his arms. "Dada!"

As Joanne passed across her tiny charge, Dundas felt a wave of emotion. Was he mad to put his life at risk, just to satisfy his ego? Joanne kissed him. He held her close, sensing the slimness of her waist and smelling the scent of her bronzed skin, deliciously inter-mixed with her perfume. Again, the thought entered his head, 'Am I crazy to risk all of this just to pursue some criminals in the forest?' It was not as if he was the only police officer capable of the task.

Joanne sensed the tension in his body.

"Darling, what is it? You are not going away again?"

Dundas disentangled Ian's tiny fingers from his hair.

"Yes, we leave again this evening."

Joanne kissed him on the cheek. "Robert, will you be away for long?"

"The estimate is three days."

Joanne kissed him on the cheek again. "I'll go and alert Steven that you require an early dinner."

As Joanne turned away, she could not conceal the tears starting to well in her eyes.

That evening it was with a heavy heart that Dundas started the Morris Oxford and set off down the drive to Police Headquarters.

The men looked expectant as Dundas addressed them.

"We now know the drill, so tonight will be a vast improvement on our previous experiences. As before, we will be dropped off close to Major Fawcett's farm and make our way to the edge of the forest. There we will bed-down. The formation of the patrol will be as before. At dawn we will move off and try to find the gangs' camp. When found, the plan is to bed-down nearby and move in the following morning at dawn. By moving quietly, we will arrest them before they wake up.

We estimate the members of this gang to number about fifteen men. They just outnumber us. However, we will have the element of surprise! Now re-check your equipment. In ten minutes we'll board the truck and collect our weapons from the armoury."

As the truck began its climb from Naivasha, there was a noticeable change in temperature. It was going to be another cold night. The headlights cut into the darkness, highlighting the numerous potholes in the murram surface.

Since leaving Naivasha they had not seen another vehicle or even an African cyclist. It was as if all human life had ceased to exist. The only sign of any life form had been a solitary dik-dik as it darted across the road. Dundas realised how easy it was for gangs of criminals to wander around unhindered at night. It made him realise just how vulnerable European farmers were in their isolated farmhouses and he made a mental note that it would be a very good idea to issue a circular regarding security.

With doused lights, the truck stopped at the previous RV and the men quickly de-bussed and assembled at the roadside. As before, there was only starlight and it took several minutes for their eyes to adjust. Dundas spoke quietly.

"Remember, no noise and be alert for the slightest sound. Finally, keep the man to your front in sight at all times. Right, let's move off."

Dundas had the same eerie feeling as he followed Constable Kip-chumba and Corporal Abikar along the track, and again he realised how easy it was for any criminal gang to roam around at night, unseen and undetected. The patrol quietly continued ahead. Dundas hoped that with luck, they could bring the remaining gang members nocturnal attacks to a halt.

They continued along the farm track and at the now familiar gate carefully climbed over into the field where they had encountered the cattle. Constable Kipchumba held up his hand and motioned them to crouch down. What was it? Dundas strained his ears. Then he heard it again. Voices. The sounds were coming from the farm track and following the same route that they had taken. The voices drew nearer. It was now possible to distinguish that three men were approaching and from the manner of their speech they had been drinking. Arriving opposite the gate, one of the men stopped. Had they been seen? There was a sound of clothing being handled as the man said, "Wait... wait a minute, I must have a pee. It's all that bloody beer!" Less than twelve feet away from where the patrol was concealed, there was a sound of fluid hitting the ground. Then a moment of silence as the man sighed with contentment, then ambled off to join his two companions.

Constable Kipchumba carefully rose to his feet and indicated they should move ahead. As they proceeded, Dundas wondered where the cows were. He did not have long to wait, as several large shapes appeared, breathing heavily through their nostrils. No doubt they had sensed the patrol's presence and, out of curiosity, had come to investigate. Once again, Constable Kipchumba held up his hand and indicated that everyone should stand still. The herd of cattle approached closer. Despite the surrounding darkness, Dundas knew that, as before, Constable Kipchumba and Corporal Abikar would purse their lips and suck their breath in and out, emulating the noise made by the cattle. Hearing this, the herd came closer, then, having stood for a few moments, began eating grass. Once again, the patrol moved off and, following their previous route, reached the edge of the forest without detection.

This time their equipment was familiar and within five minutes the men had clipped their single blanket into their ponchos, donned their sweaters underneath their smocks and wound the long puttees around their stomachs. Dundas took the first watch. He sat in the middle of the circle of sleeping men, straining his ears to catch the slightest sound. Within minutes, the hyraxes began their shrieking in the overhead canopy, being answered in a similar manner by their brethren at least a hundred yards away. Dundas tensed as a bush buck, sensing the patrol's presence, sounded a warning cough that was almost human, then noisily darted away. A raindrop pattered onto his smock, soon followed by many others as the downpour penetrated the forest canopy. It was going to be another wet and cold night!

The rain blanked out all other sound, apart from the Hyraxes, who increased the volume of their shrieking in apparent protest at the downpour. Dundas realised that it would also blanket the sound of their approach to where the gang were camped.

Despite the rain falling onto his Grenfell cloth smock, Doctor Lang's advice had been sound, the sweater, but in particular the long puttee, kept him warm. He held his luminous watch close to his face; just another 28 minutes and he could slide into his blanket and poncho.

Dundas slept fitfully, mainly due to the rain falling onto his poncho and the shrieking Hyraxes. He opened his eyes, with the darkness almost disappeared, and realised that he must have slept. He sat up. Sergeant James, who was on guard duty, raised his hand in greeting and grinned. Dundas ran his fingers through his hair and slipped out of the damp blanket and poncho. Nature was calling. It was time to wander off a short distance and find a suitable tree to provide a modicum of privacy.

Having returned, he rinsed his hands with his water bottle, then opened his pack. He held the tiny tin of corned beef in his right hand and then, delving into the pack again, produced the cellophane wrapped oatmeal stick, peeled back the cover and took a bite. As before, it was tasty but rock hard. Using the very small folding tin-opener, he proceeded to remove the lid of the corned beef. The tiny tin of jam, the small tin of mixed vegetables and some biscuits would provide his evening meal. The Mars bar and the tube of wine-gums, he planned to stuff in the left hip pocket of his smock. He rubbed his hand over his chin. His beard was already making its presence felt and would, after three days, provide a challenge for the Gillette razor blade nestling in the bathroom cabinet at home.

As Dundas stripped open his poncho and blanket, as per their previous patrol, the inside of the poncho was running with trapped perspiration. He shrugged his shoulders. At least it had kept out the rain. He continued to pack.

With the patrol adopting its previous formation, they made their way into the forest with extreme caution. Bearing in mind that some members of the gang would be armed, Dundas had Constable Kipchumba, Corporal Abikar and himself, load their weapons and apply the safety catches. The remainder of the patrol had the magazines of their Lee Enfield rifles loaded; the weapons had not been cocked but could be brought into action at a moment's notice.

It was very slow going. The forestation became denser and, from time to time, they were forced to bend low to follow game tracks. Now and then Constable Kipchumba stopped and bent down to examine the ground, sometimes very quietly conferring with Corporal Abikar, both men perhaps examining the ends of a broken twig. This was something Dundas had seen before. By taking a broken twig, then breaking it again, the colours of the two ends could be compared, and an estimate made as to the amount of time that had elapsed between the two breaks.

Corporal Abikar turned and motioned Dundas to come forward, then whispered, "Effendi, a person has passed this way about five days ago." He pointed to the twig's broken ends and then to an impression in the ground that matched the twig. "He was going in this direction."

Corporal Abikar indicated ahead with a vertical palm gesture of his right hand and continued, "Effendi, stay here. Kipchumba and I will go a few yards ahead to check if there are any more tracks."

Dundas was conscious that his heart rate had increased. He placed his hand inside his smock and touched the butt of his Browning.

Between the birdcalls, there was utter silence. The air felt dank and shafts of morning sunlight penetrated the forest canopy, picking out the slight mist rising from the wet ground. There was also a faint smell, neither pleasant or unpleasant, perhaps caused by the fallen rotting branches. Corporal Abikar appeared on the track ahead, gave Dundas the thumbs-up sign and motioned the patrol to come forward. He whispered, "Effendi, about four or five people have come from over here." He indicated to the left. "And have joined this game track and are heading in this direction." Again he indicated ahead using the vertical palm of his hand.

"Are the tracks fresh?" Dundas studied the ground, although seeing very little.

Corporal Abikar nodded his head and held up two fingers.

"Two days ago?"

"*Ndiyo Effendi.*"

By sign language, Dundas conveyed this information down the line.

The patrol continued to move ahead with extreme caution.

How soon would they bump into 'the gang'?

# CHAPTER FIFTEEN

SERGEANT SIMBA AND KENYA BUS made their way back to camp, fearful of Colonel Tom's reaction when he heard that the food party had absconded and taken their supply of fresh food. Kenya Bus was the first to voice his thoughts.

"We should have made contact with the women at Fawcett's farm to leave more food for collection tomorrow."

"And risk being seen by the European?" Sergeant Simba sneered. "Don't forget, we both have long hair, so we could hardly pass as visiting friends."

They continued ahead in silence. Suddenly Sergeant Simba held up his hand and motioned his colleague to crouch down, then pointed ahead and to the left of their line of advance. There it was again. Voices. Kenya Bus felt his scalp tingle and could hear his heart thumping in his chest. He reached forward, tapped Sergeant Simba on the shoulder and whispered, "How many are they?"

Sergeant Simba looked back and shrugged. "I don't know."

"Could they be from our camp?"

Sergeant Simba shrugged his shoulders, unsheathed his *simi* from its shoulder sling and motioned his colleague to do the same.

"Keep low. We'll creep forward and try to see who they are – and don't tread on any twigs."

After some twenty paces they reached a point where another game track joined theirs. Sergeant Simba pointed to the left, then, with the palm of his left-hand palm down, indicated that they should hide in the undergrowth. By now the voices were within fifteen paces. They both tensed, ready to strike... but suddenly all tension was gone as Sergeant Simba recognised two members of the gang, who were carrying a dead bush-buck.

As the two men joined the track, Sergeant Simba stood up.

"Halt!"

The two men dropped the dead buck and turned to flee, but stopped upon seeing it was their Sergeant, their taught faces turning to smiles. "God, you scared us!"

Sergeant Simba was not amused. "Idiots! Stand to attention when I'm speaking to you!"

The two men looked shocked at this unexpected tirade and stood ramrod stiff. Sergeant Simba placed his face very close to theirs. "What have you always been told not to do?"

"Make a noise Sergeant."

"Had Kenya Bus and I been the police, we could have arrested you with ease."

The very small man called Mafupi spoke up.

"We were excited that we had snared a buck."

Sergeant Simba placed his face about four inches from Mafupi's nose. "So excited that you were prepared to risk our camp being discovered, our gang arrested and those of us who have killed to be hanged?"

"No Sergeant." Mafupi shook his head and avoided Sergeant Simba's eyes.

"Then pick up the buck and let's move off."

As Mafupi bent down to take up his share of the load, Sergeant Simba delivered a huge kick that sent Mafupi sprawling along the track. "In future you obey orders and keep quiet!"

Sergeant Simba strode off ahead, followed by Kenya Bus, with Mafupi and his colleague struggling to keep up.

Arriving at camp, Sergeant Simba turned to the two men.

"You two, skin that buck and chop it up. And you..." pointing to Kenya Bus "are responsible for dressing the skin." With these words he strode off in the direction of Colonel Tom's hut.

On route to make his report Sergeant Simba mulled over in his mind that the three junior officers taking part in the Myers farm raid had been killed. Would this lead to a promotion? Perhaps the rank of Captain? Arriving at the hut, he knocked on the door and waited.

There was a sound of hurried movement inside and Colonel Tom appeared at the door, fastening his trousers. Sergeant Simba greeted him with a smart salute.

"Good evening Sir. I have come to make my report."

Colonel Tom scowled. "Well?"

"The men have absconded and taken the food with them."

Colonel Tom swore. "So what prevented you from obtaining more food?"

"It was possible that we could have been seen by the European farmer, Sir."

"So you made no attempt to obtain any food, not even a chicken?" Colonel Tom's voice rose two octaves. "Not even a bloody chicken!"

Sergeant Simba realised that this was not an ideal time to mention his promotion prospects, but all was not lost.

"Sir, two of the men have snared a large bush-buck and I'm having it prepared now."

"A bush-buck?"

"Yes Sir!"

"Then I expect a portion that reflects my rank. Understood?"

"Yes Sir!"

Sergeant Simba gave another very smart salute. "Will that be all Sir?"

"No, wait by the stream. I'll be out in a few minutes."

The door was closed in his face and he made his way to the nearby stream and sat on a small rock. "Bloody officers!"

But it was not all bad. As the second in command, he would soon receive an excellent cut of bush-buck. On hearing the hut door open, he stood up and stood stiffly to attention, noting that Colonel Tom was now fully dressed and carrying his familiar shotgun.

Sergeant Simba saluted again and awaited the expected haranguing but to his complete surprise Colonel Tom said, "I am about to tell you a secret. You must not tell anyone else. To do so could mean death. Is that understood?"

"Yes Sir."

"Tomorrow before dawn I am leaving to meet with other senior officers. We need more guns and ammunition. Something big is being planned. I will give you the details upon my return. You are in charge until my return in two days' time. Now this woman..."

He jerked his thumb in the direction of the hut.

"If anyone touches her, including you, I will kill them and you without mercy. Understood?"

"Yes Sir!"

Sergeant Simba gave another smart salute as Colonel Tom turned on his heel and made his way back to the hut.

Several miles away Constable Kipchumba had no problems. He was now tracking four men who were making no effort to cover up their tracks. The only thing that slowed the patrol's progress was caution. Everyone was on 'tenterhooks'. Every bend and twist in the game track required a halt to allow Constable Kipchumba and Corporal Abikar to check that it was safe to proceed. Following each brief halt, they reappeared and motion the patrol to follow.

By four o'clock, despite their slow progress, Dundas estimated that they must have covered at least ten miles and from now on extra vigilance was required. He also realised that by 6:30 dusk would make further progress close to impossible. This presented a paradox. Ideally, they needed to locate the gang's position before nightfall, but to press ahead at speed could mean they could be spotted and the whole gang would escape.

To their right, the sound of water could be clearly heard. Dundas consulted his map. He was not completely sure where they were, as there were numerous streams. However, the clear tracks they were following, plus the proximity of water, indicated that such a position was an ideal location for the gang's hideout. He motioned with his right hand to move forward. The surrounding forest had a beauty of its own; the bird calls, the shallow angles of sunlight penetrating the overhead canopy, capturing the rising moisture in its beams, the smell of the forest, the sound of running water. Under other circumstances, Dundas mused, it would be an ideal location to sit below a tree and read a book. His reverie was disturbed as Constable Kipchumba raised his hand again, indicating that they should halt. He bent down and studied the ground, then motioned Corporal Abikar to come forward. Corporal Abikar bent down, studied where Constable Kipchumba was pointing, then, crouching low, made his way back to Dundas and whispered, "Effendi, there are lots of tracks. We believe that we must be very close to the gang's hideout. I suggest that Constable Kipchumba and I go ahead to check."

Dundas weighed the possibilities. It was obvious that they would be cautious and two men would make far less noise than the whole patrol. He gave the thumbs-up sign. Crouching low, Corporal Abikar moved off, removing his police beret, stuffing it into his smock and indicating that Constable Kipchumba should do the same. They then disappeared into the forest.

Dundas passed the word down the line and, in so doing, felt his heartbeat increase. How many were in the gang, and could they avoid a shoot-out? Twenty minutes passed. It seemed like eternity. Another five minutes passed. Dundas glanced at his watch; he was now having second thoughts. What if the gang had detected their presence and grabbed them? Suddenly, Constable Kipchumba and Corporal Abikar appeared on the track. The expressions on their faces revealed that they had located the gang.

Corporal Abikar crouched down beside Dundas. "Effendi, about six hundred paces ahead the gang are camped beside the stream. There are at lease twelve open-fronted shelters and there was no sign of any sentries. They have two fires burning and it looks as if they are preparing an evening meal. We estimate that there are in excess of fifteen men and a woman. Only one was carrying a rifle."

"That's excellent news Corporal Abikar."

Dundas turned around and, by holding three fingers across the sleeve of his smock, used sign language to pass the word for Sergeant James to come forward. Crouching low and moving with extreme caution, Sergeant James came and squatted beside Dundas.

"Yes Sir?"

Dundas kept his voice to a whisper.

"The gang are camped by the stream. Corporal Abikar estimates there are in excess of fifteen men, he hasn't seen any sentries, and only one man was seen with a rifle. My plan is to move off the track. From here, go about a hundred yards and then bed-down for the night. Before first light we can move forward and surprise the gang whilst they are asleep. We will make our final plans when we have de-briefed Corporal Abikar and Constable Kipchumba. Pass the word down the line that we are moving off up the slope to our left. Utter silence is needed. The rising ground will be in our favour."

Adopting the same posture Sergeant James went down the line, pausing by each man to pass on the message. Dundas carefully stood up and indicated that it was time to move.

Avoiding fallen twigs that could break in two and make a noise was not easy. Speed at this juncture was not needed, the criteria was not to reveal their presence. Having gained the high ground, Dundas indicated that the patrol should stop and go to ground. He realised that there was a possibility that the gang could be arranging a night sortie and leave within the next half an hour, or perhaps even less. In view of their lack of security, he was confident that they would detect the noise of their departure and be in a position to follow them and take them by surprise. But what if some of the gang remain in camp? Should he then split his force? Sergeant James could tackle the camp whilst he followed the gang. It was time to de-brief Corporal Abikar and Constable Kipchumba but, before doing so, someone had to be detailed to guard their position.

With the de-brief completed and no auditory evidence of the gang's departure, it was time to brief the patrol on the forthcoming raid on the gang's hideout. Normal speech was not possible and the men gathered very close, crouching down in order to hear the whispered orders. Dundas felt a tinge of excitement as he addressed the men.

"The gang are camped beside the stream some six hundred paces ahead of our position. Corporal Abikar and Constable Kipchumba estimate there are about twenty men and a woman. We know that some of them are armed with a shotgun, a rifle and a revolver stolen from the Blakes' farm. It is important to remember the law governing the use of firearms by police. If anyone is unsure speak up now."

Dundas scanned the group. All he could see were their expectant faces. "We bed-down here for the night and move off just before first light. Before we leave, everyone will have one bullet in the breech of his rifle and the safety catch applied. Carry the rifle across the body at an angle, like this, with the muzzle pointing into the air. We will move down to the stream and proceed in single file. The gang are camped on this side of the stream in a number of bamboo shelters. We plan to surprise them when they are still asleep and arrest them. It is important to have your handcuffs ready in the pocket of your smock. We will position ourselves outside each shelter. I will take the upstream position, Corporal Abikar the mid-position and Sergeant James the first shelter that we encounter. The man in front of Sergeant James will take the second shelter and the man ahead of him the third shelter. Utter silence is essential. No one will make a move until your hear just one blast on my whistle. Make the arrests with the gang still on the ground in their blankets, and then apply the handcuffs. Also remember to attach the handcuffs right wrist to right wrist. This was demonstrated to you back at Nakuru and we know that this method prevents two men being able to run off. Any questions?"

Dundas scanned their expectant faces again.

"No one? Good. Sergeant James will arrange the guard duties for tonight and I will take the last hour. In about an hour it will be dusk. As before, we sleep in a circle with the man on guard sat in the middle.

One final thing. When we move off tomorrow morning, we use only sign language. Now let's eat and bed-down."

Dundas spread his poncho on the ground, inserted the lightweight blanket and then clipped up the side of the poncho to form a sleeping bag. He rummaged through his pack and placed the opened ration pack onto the poncho, then sat down and selected his evening meal. As every ration pack had the same contents choice was not a problem, and he mused what it would be like if Joanne organised the same meal every day? Boring beyond belief! But then again, how come this did not apply to breakfast?

He removed the Browning automatic from its shoulder holster, removed the clip of nine millimetre bullets, quietly worked the action several times, re-inserted the clip and applied the safety catch. He recalled the words of the firearms instructor at the Police Training School, Kiganjo. "If ever you have to shoot to kill, fire twice in quick succession and always aim at the centre of the body." This had been good advice and had saved his life some years earlier when he had been ambushed during a previous investigation.

Sleep did not come easily. This whole operation had taken time, planning and training. In less than twelve hours it would be over. What could go wrong? One of the men accidentally discharging his rifle and alerting the gang? Some of the gang might be awake and they would lose the element of surprise? The gang outnumbered the patrol and could attack a single man trying to effect an arrest? Then there was the problem of making their way back to Fawcett's farm with perhaps twenty prisoners. On route escapes might be attempted. These and many other thoughts passed through his mind. His last recollection was the inevitable shrieking of the Hyraxes and the rain pattering on to his poncho.

He awoke with a start. There was the dark shape of a crouching figure. "Effendi, time for guard duty."

Dundas sat up and ran his fingers through his hair.

"Is it all quiet?"

"All quiet Effendi."

Dundas looked at the luminous dial of his watch, 4:32. It was still as black as pitch. He unzipped his smock, withdrew his automatic, quietly cocked it and applied the safety catch. He then took up his position at the centre of the circle of sleeping men.

It had stopped raining but at this height, of at least ten thousand feet, at night the cold seeped into you. He tightened the draw cords around the neck and the bottom of his smock, then thrust his hands into the deep hip pockets. The Hyraxes were some way off, shrieking, then remaining silent for a few minutes before making their weird call yet again. Apart from this, there was utter silence, so silent you could almost hear it. Surely this was the blood circulating in his ears? There was a slight sound as one of the men turned over in his sleep, grunted twice then resumed his deep breathing.

Dundas's mind drifted back to home and their bed, feeling the warmth of Joanne at his side. Joanne said he snored and sometimes she had to shake his shoulder to stop the noise. Had he been snoring on this patrol? He glanced at his watch again. Just past 5am. In less than fifteen minutes it would be time to wake the men.

There was a series of soft clicks as each man pulled back the bolt of his rifle, fed the live round into the breech and secured the safety catch. A final check of the sleeping area ensured that nothing had been left behind and all ration tins had been quietly crushed and buried. It was time to move off.

The composition of the patrol remained as before but with one minor change; Corporal Abikar took up a position in the centre.

It was only just light enough to see as Constable Kipchumba moved ahead with extreme caution, stopping from time to time to listen. The only sound was the stream some fifty yards below their line of advance and to their right. Each time Constable Kipchumba stopped, Dundas was conscious of his heart thudding in his chest. Slowly but surely, they made their way down to the stream, startling a bush-buck that snorted then sprinted off downstream. Had this noise disturbed the gang? The patrol remained rooted to the spot for several seconds, listening for the slightest sound. All was quiet. Constable Kipchumba moved unerringly but cautiously ahead, then stopped again and made a sniffing noise. Dundas did the same. Woodsmoke.

Within less than five minutes, the first shelter came into view. Constable Kipchumba stopped yet again and indicated by a hand signal that everyone should crouch down. Dundas could feel the tension rising – just a few more minutes...

Satisfied that there was no movement, Constable Kipchumba stood up and signalled to proceed ahead. There was now a modicum of light from the approaching dawn. Passing the first shelter, Dundas was able to discern the shapes of two bodies, both breathing heavily in deep sleep. There was no time to pause. Moving like ghosts, he and Constable Kipchumba passed by the remaining shelters, stopping at the final one. It was empty! Where were the occupants? He signalled to Constable Kipchumba to move back downstream and closed on the penultimate shelter.

The light was improving with every second; it was time to blow his whistle. Clutching his automatic in his right hand, he flicked off the safety catch with his thumb, then, using his left hand, blew one short blast on his police whistle...

All hell broke loose! There were shouts, screams and the sound of a single shot. There was no time to wonder if it was a member of the gang. Dundas shouted at the two men in the shelter.

"Police, don't move or we fire!"

The two men flipped back their blankets and found themselves staring into the muzzles of an automatic pistol and a .303 rifle. They looked sleepy eyed and shocked. Dundas put on a stern voice.

"Roll over onto your stomachs, then stay still."

He placed the muzzle of his automatic into the ear of the man nearest to him.

"Place your right arm over the body of your companion."

He spoke to the other man.

"You! Place your right hand beside your head. Good! Both of you keep still. Constable Kipchumba, apply the handcuffs."

*"Ndiyo Effendi!"*

With the two men secured, Constable Kipchumba stripped back the blankets. There was a stench of warm body odour made even more revolting by the close proximity of the prisoners. Constable Kipchumba searched the prisoners, then the shelter.

"Only these two *simis* Effendi." He held up the two exhibits.

Dundas spoke to the first man. "Where's the woman?"

The prisoner, with his face still facing the ground, muttered, "In Colonel Tom's hut."

"Which is where?"

"Upstream and round the bend."

"Is he armed?"

"Yes, he has a shotgun but he isn't in camp."

Dundas turned to Constable Kipchumba. "Take these two down to Corporal Abikar. I'll go and arrest the woman."

Dundas moved quickly upstream, where the hut, built in typical native style, came into view. The door was closed. Was it possible that the noise of the stream had muted the sounds of their attack? He carefully made his way to the door, then paused to one side, listening for any sounds of life. Nothing. Using his right foot, he carefully tried the door. It wasn't locked. He crouched low and to the left of the door and applied gentle pressure. It started to open.

As he did so, he heard a twig snap behind him. He spun around to see a large man pointing a revolver at him. As Dundas flung himself to the ground and rolled to one side, the man fired. Dundas instinctively fired twice at the centre of the standing figure. The man gave a huge gasp, staggered back half a pace and then crashed face-down onto the ground. He twitched several times and was then still. Dundas remained in his prone position, listening for the slightest sound. All he could hear was sobbing from inside the hut. Was the woman alone? He crawled to one side of the partly-opened door then shouted,

"Police! Come out with your hands on your head!"

The sobbing stopped and a very young frightened Kikuyu woman opened the door and came outside with her hands on her head. Dundas noted that she was trembling.

"Is there anyone else inside?"

The woman looked down at him and shook her head.

"Are you lying?"

The woman shook her head again.

"Who is this?"

Dundas gestured towards the dead body with his automatic.

"It is Sergeant Simba."

"And what was he doing here?"

The woman remained silent. She suddenly glanced to her right. Dundas pointed his automatic in the indicated direction. It was Corporal Abikar. He gave Dundas a smart salute, grinning from ear to ear.

"We have arrested fifteen men Effendi and recovered a rifle. One of the gang was shot when he tried to attack Sergeant James with a *simi*. We heard a shot in this direction Effendi, so I came to check if you were OK."

Dundas stood up and gestured at the dead body.

"He was about to shoot me in the back, but luckily he trod on a twig so I heard him. The woman here says that there is no one else in the hut. Guard her and I'll check inside."

In order not to silhouette himself in the doorway, Dundas shielded his body by crouching to the left of the entrance listening for the slightest sound. The running water in the nearby stream was making it difficult. Was it worth the risk? He fired five quick shots across the width of the hut at knee height. There was no return of fire. Feeling reassured, Dundas stepped inside. His nostrils were assailed by a mixture of woodsmoke and human body odour. Despite the increasing light outside, it took a few moments for his eyes to adjust to the dim interior. Empty sacks, suspended from a crude roof beam, divided the hut in two. On the side where he stood was a small table and two chairs made from bamboo. On the table were two unwashed and badly chipped white enamel plates. On the mud wall to his left was a bush-buck skin which had stiffened with drying. He stepped forward and lifted two of the sacks. Against the wall was a crude bed, made from what had once been green branches. Strips of animal hide stretched across the frame in a square formation had been used to support grass stuffed sacks and, on top of these, were two very dirty blankets. Dundas carefully lifted the blankets, then the sack mattresses. The bed was still warm. Now that his eyes had adjusted to the gloom, under the bed, resting on an old biscuit tin, was what looked like a school exercise book. He bent down, retrieving both the book and the tin. Having glanced around the hut once more, he made his way outside. The woman was sitting on the ground some ten yards to his right, closely guarded by Corporal Abikar.

"Effendi, the woman here said she was sobbing because she thought that Colonel Tom had returned and shot Sergeant Simba for sleeping with her. She was convinced that he would also kill her."

Dundas looked down at the woman.

"Where did Colonel Tom go?"

Still looking at the ground, she replied, "To a special meeting."

"A meeting? Where was this being held?"

The woman wiped her eyes. "A day's walk away."

Dundas gestured. "Here in the forest?"

The woman nodded.

"When will he be back?"

The woman shrugged her shoulders and avoided eye contact.

"Are you his wife?"

The woman shook her head.

"Where do you come from?"

There was a moment of silence.

"Bwana Blake's farm."

Here was a possible witness! Dundas continued.

"How did you come to be here?"

The woman shuffled her feet and looked at the ground.

"I came with my husband. He was the houseboy at Bwana Blake's."

"Is your husband in camp?"

Without lifting her head, the woman nodded.

"Yes, but I have to live with Colonel Tom."

Dundas opened the exercise book. Apart from the names of various farms, the writing was in Kikuyu. He opened the tin. On top of two more books were ten rounds of twelve-bore ammunition. The books contained lists of Kikuyu names and again more writing in Kikuyu. He spoke to the woman again and pointed.

"What can you tell me about these books?"

Still with her eyes cast down, the woman shrugged her shoulders. Dundas continued.

"Some of these books contain the names of local European farms. Do you know why?"

The woman shrugged her shoulders again. Dundas decided it was time to re-join the patrol, but first he retrieved the dead man's revolver and thoroughly searched the body.

As the three of them made their way back, Dundas was not surprised that the man he had killed had not heard the sound of his whistle. Due to the angle of the slope, the stream descended in a series of turbulent mini-waterfalls that then tumbled into a series of pools.

By now, dawn was but a memory. Shafts of sunlight penetrated the overhead canopy and the numerous birdcalls echoed around the forest, to be repeated by some distant bird of the same species. As Dundas recalled later, it was the ideal place to create a fishing camp.

As Dundas approached, the jubilant faces of the patrol were in sharp contrast to the handcuffed gang. Stretched out to one side was the body of a member of the gang, wearing the now familiar ex-army greatcoat and with long plaited hair. Sergeant James detached himself from where he had been crouching beside a member of the gang, came over and saluted.

"Sir I regret to inform you that I had to shoot in self-defence when one of the gang attacked me with a *simi*."

Dundas could see that having to shoot a man had made Sergeant James uncomfortable. "James, I know that you would not infringe the law. I had to do exactly the same thing. All I can say is, thank God he missed me. Now, what can you tell me about this lot?"

Dundas gestured at the squatting line of prisoners.

"Most of the men had *simis* and we have marked each *simi* with the man's name, plus the initials of the man making the arrest and taking possession of the weapon. The man fifth from our right had a rifle and a *simi*. Under his blanket he also had eight rounds of ammunition. Every prisoner has been searched and they have been handcuffed as per your instructions. Also Sir, no one escaped."

"Excellent James, excellent. Have any of the prisoners talked?"

"Yes Sir. One of them has told me that the man known as Colonel Tom shot and killed a member of the gang who refused to kill someone. He says that he can take us to the body."

"Any other information?"

Sergeant James gave a huge grin. "Not as yet Sir, they are still shocked at being arrested in their beds."

Dundas walked over to the line of prisoners to be met with sullen stares. He noted that all the men had bloodshot eyes.

"Sergeant James."

"Sir!"

"Look at their eyes. Has any evidence of *bhang* (hashish) been discovered?"

"No Sir."

"Detail a man to check in the corners of each shelter, just under the banana leaf thatch."

As Sergeant James went to issue his order, Dundas wandered over to the body of the gang member. He also had long plaited hair. The eyes were partly open and blood had trickled from the left hand corner of his mouth onto the ground. Dundas bent down and examined the ingress wound just below the base of the throat. The bullet must have smashed the top of the spinal column, causing instant death. He stood up and suddenly felt very tired. Was it due to lack of sleep, excitement, or both? He went over to the side of the stream and sat on a small rock.

During the planning stage, one thing that he had not fully considered was what to do about the gang's camp. Initially, destruction had been the obvious answer. However, the absence of the so-called Colonel Tom was placing other thoughts into his head. The fact that the gang had not moved showed that their original ruse had worked. If the camp was left intact, minus all moveable objects, was it possible that Colonel Tom would be led to believe that the entire gang had absconded? He called Sergeant James and Corporal Abikar over.

"I want the camp left intact so that when the man Colonel Tom returns, he may be led to believe that all his followers have deserted him. So every moveable object we will take with us. Any items can be bundled into prisoners' blankets. The next thing is we have two bodies to transport. In order to prevent any escapes, the prisoners carrying the bodies will be handcuffed as follows. The man at the feet of the corpse will have a wrist handcuffed to one of the corpse's ankles. The man at the head will have one wrist handcuffed to that of the corpse. It may mean adjusting the bodies on each 'stretcher' in order not to impede carrying. Now for the other prisoners. They stay handcuffed as they are and each pair will carry a bundle. I appreciate that progress will be slow, but at least no one will escape. Any suggestions or ideas?" Yes Corporal Abikar?"

"What about the woman Effendi?"

"She will carry a bundle and be handcuffed to a member of our patrol. As before, Constable Kipchumba will lead. Corporal Abikar, as before you will be in the middle and you Sergeant James at the rear. Now we need to be on the edge of the forest by dusk and at our pick-up point at the usual time. I do not want Major Fawcett's farm people to see us with prisoners. Someone may see our tracks, but all this will do is to point out that a body of people have passed near the farm, and if Colonel Tom enquires, it may help to confuse him. Anything else?"

Yes Sergeant James?"

"Sir, would it not be a good idea to wait in camp and arrest him when he returns?"

Dundas nodded.

"Yes I have considered that. However, one, we do not know when he will return, two, our rations are almost finished and three, what if he returns with some armed men? And we have a witness. One of the prisoners states that he witnessed Colonel Tom shoot one of his followers. If we have managed to confuse him, he may continue to use his hut. At least we will have a starting point in trying to track him down. Now, let's get moving and reach the forest edge before nightfall."

# CHAPTER SIXTEEN

COLONEL TOM HAD BEEN well pleased with the meeting of 'senior officers'. The talk had been of how to obtain more guns and ammunition. General Kargo had said what was needed was to mount a raid on a police station, kill all the men on duty, break into the armoury and seize dozens of rifles and revolvers. Once armed in this manner, other police stations could be attacked and they would become a formidable army. In the meantime, raids were to be stepped up on European farms. When asked, he had pledged two raids within the next three weeks. He had selected the sawmills at Njabini. He planned to set fire to the sawmill, kill the manager and any European or Asian staff and hopefully secure a few more firearms. His next target would be the Fawcett farm. The European was old, lived alone and was known to have at least two rifles, a shotgun and a large revolver. It would be an easy target.

As Colonel Tom made his way through the forest, he had but two prominent thoughts in his mind. The woman and a hot meal. It was no wonder she preferred him to that scrawny houseboy. He was a colonel and issued orders. Men quailed before his gaze, just as he had done a few years previously when standing before that bastard of a Kamba Sergeant Major of the Kings African Rifles. Now he was the boss; men stood to attention when he addressed them and they saluted! He lived in a hut, had a bed and extra rations.

He looked at the angle of the sun's rays penetrating the forest canopy and estimated that it would be just before dusk when he arrived back at camp. From time to time he startled a bushbuck drinking at one of the numerous streams that followed the ridgelines, meeting on route other streams, swelling them and providing a sanctuary for the fish introduced by the *Wazungu* (Europeans) that they called trout. He wondered if their fish traps would provide his supper?

It was almost dusk as he walked down the final ridgeline to the stream and approached his hut. The door was open. Where was she?

He flipped the sacking division to one side. The blankets were missing. The bitch had absconded, no doubt with that scrawny husband of hers. Then he noticed that the biscuit tin was missing. It contained all his spare ammunition and the names of all the Kikuyu on local farms who had taken the oath. No doubt that idle bastard Sergeant Simba had been asleep. Had she taken the money? All those five shillings came to a tidy sum. He quickly went outside. To the left of the entrance was a small sapling. The ground by its root appeared not to have been disturbed. He withdrew his knife from his belt and thrust the point into the ground. There was a reassuring 'clunk' as the tip made contact with metal. He set off round the bend to inspect the camp. The fires were still smouldering, but the whole camp was deserted. He looked into several shelters. Everything had been taken. The bastards had run away.

That night a hungry, angry, cold and womanless Colonel Tom enacted in his mind's eye, exactly what he would do to each man, and in particular Sergeant Simba and that woman...

❖ ❖ ❖

At approximately the time that Colonel Tom had arrived at the deserted hideout, Dundas, with his string of prisoners, plus the two dead bodies, was nearing the forest edge. So far no one had escaped during the return journey. The only problems encountered were the prisoners and in particular the woman needing to be un-handcuffed to answer 'calls of nature'. Even before setting off, Dundas had realised that the whole entourage would exceed the capacity of the three-ton lorry, exacerbated by the space that the two bodies would occupy. The obvious answer was to use the phone at Major Fawcett's farm and request additional transport from Njabini Police Station, or better still, Nakuru. However, two things concerned him: one, not to be seen by Major Fawcett's house servants or any of his farm labour and two, exposing the operation to Major Fawcett. Sometimes people could be indiscreet when meeting other Europeans at the Brown Trout bar or the Naivasha Hotel, telling 'in confidence' what the police had been up to and being overheard by an African barman who spoke English and would very likely be Kikuyu. On balance, Dundas decided to tell Major Fawcett a 'white lie' to explain the presence of a European Police Officer clad in army clothing.

Dundas glanced at the luminous dial of his watch. Just after eight thirty five. It was time to move off. He made his way down the seated line to Corporal Abikar and whispered, "Corporal Abikar..."

"Effendi."

"We need extra transport. Having avoided the labour camp, I will go with Constable Kipchumba to Major Fawcett's house and telephone Nakuru for an extra three-ton lorry. We will hide just off the side of the farm track. I'll now go and tell Sergeant James what I intend to do."

With Constable Kipchumba in the lead, Dundas made his way back up the track to the farmhouse. Again, he realised how easy it was for a bunch of criminals to move around in the dark and how vulnerable isolated farms were.

Only one light was on in what must be the lounge. The main thing was to check the kitchen at the rear of the building. Moving like ghosts, Dundas and Constable Kipchumba skirted the side of the building to where they could observe the kitchen. It was in darkness. Carefully, they retraced their steps to the veranda and looked into the French window. Major Fawcett was alone, reading a book and sprawled in a deep leather armchair. Beside him on a small round table was a Tilley pressure lamp and a glass containing what was probably whisky. Dundas tapped gently on the French window. Major Fawcett looked up but did not move. Dundas tapped again. The Major stood up, crossed the room and then peered through the glass. Seeing a European face, he bent down, released the bottom bolt, then the upper bolt and unlocked the door.

"Yes, what is it?"

"Chief Inspector Dundas, Sir, of the Kenya Police. I wonder if I may use your phone?"

Major Fawcett looked suspicious. "So why are you in army uniform?"

"We are trying to catch people stealing farm produce and livestock. The normal pale khaki police uniform is easily seen in the dark, hence the smock and jungle greens."

Major Fawcett grunted. "Hmm... about time something was done instead of checking on motorists. Well, have you caught anyone?"

"Not as yet, Sir. Tonight is a test. Based on your experience, Sir, I am sure that you realise the problems of controlling men in the dark."

Still holding the door, Major Fawcett gestured with his free hand.

"So, how many men have you?"

"Just five at this stage... now, may I use your 'phone?"

Major Fawcett glanced over his shoulder.

"Of course. It's through that door in the hallway. Care for a drop of Scotch?"

"That's very kind of you, Sir, but we are not permitted to drink whilst on duty."

Dundas followed Major Fawcett into the room, who slumped into his chair, picked up his glass and stared thoughtfully into the log fire.

Having made his 'phone call Dundas returned to the lounge.

"Thank you Sir."

Major Fawcett looked up. "Chief Inspector. Before you go, an old chap who has been on this farm for years and years suddenly disappeared without even saying goodbye, which I find difficult to understand. I reported it to Njabini Police Station. I don't suppose that you have heard anything?"

Dundas shook his head. "I'm afraid not Sir. However, I will follow this up with the Inspector there to check if they have made any progress. I take it that you have questioned your farm labour?"

"Yes I have, but no one seems to know where he's gone."

Dundas gestured. "Did you check his hut?"

Major Fawcett slowly shook his head. "No, I left this task to my chief clerk. All he could tell me was that everything had been taken."

"Hmm... it does seem odd that he suddenly took off. Anyway Sir, as promised I will check with the Inspector at Njabini. Now, if you will excuse me..."

Placing his glass of whisky onto the small side table, Major Fawcett stood up. "I'll accompany you to the door."

At the door, Dundas turned and shook Major Fawcett's hand.

"Once again, Major, thank you for your co-operation."

Major Fawcett raised a slight grin. "Let us hope, Chief Inspector, that next time you catch someone red-handed."

As Dundas and Constable Kipchumba made their way down the steps there was a distinct 'clunk-clunk' as Major Fawcett re-bolted the French window.

For a few moments they paused to let their eyes adjust to the surrounding darkness, then, moving cautiously and quietly, they made their way down the farm track to the patrol and the prisoners.

# CHAPTER SEVENTEEN

DUNDAS GLANCED AT HIS WATCH, almost 10AM and time to set off for Police Headquarters. It had been a long night! The two three-ton lorries had arrived on time and none of the prisoners had escaped. They had arrived at Nakuru close to midnight where, having booked the prisoners into cells, the final act had been to deposit the two dead bodies at the mortuary. It had been nearly 2am before he headed for home, a hot bath, a warm bed and a good night's sleep.

It was almost 9am before he stirred and awoke to find himself alone in bed. Having been revived with a pot of tea, an invigorating shower and his usual substantial breakfast, he felt replete and refreshed. After subsisting on ration packs, the aromas of fresh coffee and frying bacon wafting in from the kitchen and the spluttering sound of frying eggs were a treat for the senses! It seemed strange to be wearing his usual C.I.D. garb of linen jacket, grey lightweight trousers, white shirt and tie, but as he gave Joanne and his tiny son a parting kiss he reflected that it was good to be back to a semblance of normality.

The objective of tracking down the gang responsible for the Blakes' murders and the other attacks had been achieved. All that remained was the painstaking task of the actual investigation.

On entering the Police Station, Dundas was greeted by the Duty Officer, Inspector Farrell.

"Morning Robert! I understand that you are the man responsible for cluttering up my pristine cell block with a mass of long-haired, evil smelling, humanity!"

Dundas grinned. "I'll purchase a bottle of disinfectant on pay day!"

Inspector Farell held up his hand. "On a serious note. Before you go, Superintendent Lewis wants you to call him a.s.a.p."

Dundas made his way to his office and sat in his familiar chair, placed his hands behind his head and looked out of the window. The birds were, as usual, strutting across on the grass outside, placing their heads to one side before making a jump and plunging their beaks into the ground. Nothing had changed. The birds, the musty smell of his office when he opened the door. Yes, it was good to be back! He reached across the desk for the 'phone and dialled an internal two digit number to be greeted by the usual terse response.

"Lewis."

"Good morning Sir, I have been asked to call you."

"Robert, welcome back and congratulations to you and your team! So you got the lot?"

"No Sir, one man was missing, a so-called Colonel Tom. We did not destroy the gang's camp but we did carry away all removable items. My hope is to make this man believe that he has been deserted by the gang."

"Hmm... anyway, well done! Bill Stewart has some good news for you. From the original five arrests, he has obtained two positive matches aligned to the Blakes' murders. One a different note, the Assistant Commissioner wants to see you at 2pm. So, assuming that you are free, come round to my office and give me your verbal report."

Dundas leaned back in his chair. "Right Sir, I'm on my way."

Dundas exited his office, turned left and took the usual ten paces down the highly polished corridor to Superintendent Lewis's office, to find the door open and Superintendent Lewis studying his wall map. On hearing the knock he turned around.

"Come in Robert and take a seat." Superintendent Lewis turned away from the map and returned to his desk. "So Robert, apart from this self-styled Colonel Tom, you bagged the lot! Special Branch are very interested in these new arrests, but before we do anything else, what charges can we levy against them?"

"I've given this some thought Sir. Every one of them was carrying a *simi*, so my initial thought to obtain their remand is being in unlawful possession of an offensive weapon. And one of them was in possession of a stolen rifle and eight rounds of ammunition, so in addition he can be nailed for theft and the unlawful possession of a firearm."

Superintendent Lewis nodded then leaned back in his chair.

"And what about the woman?"

"I thought, 'consorting with known criminals' or 'aiding and abetting'."

"Hmm..." Superintendent Lewis placed his hands behind his head, then changed his mind and placed his forearms onto the desk.

"Before she is placed before the court, I suggest that we have a meeting with Crown Counsel. There is no offence for living in the forest, but she was living with illegally armed men. I'd feel a lot happier if we sought legal advice on this one. Now, the two dead men. Is Bill Stewart aware of the need to take their fingerprints?"

"Not as yet Sir, but he's my next contact."

"That leaves us with two major tasks. One, their inquests and two, questioning your latest prisoners. You have a lot on your plate, so I suggest that I obtain the statements from your men, the woman and yourself. Relating to the two deaths, I'll arrange with the Government Doctor to carry out post-mortems. This will relieve you to liaise with Bill Stewart and, with the help of Sergeant James, to question the prisoners."

"Thank you Sir, that will be a tremendous help."

Superintendent Lewis leaned forward. "Now, before you give me all the details, there is something else. Don't forget, the Assistant Commissioner wants to see you at two o'clock. Come over to the map and brief me on the whole operation." Superintendent Lewis started to push back his chair. Dundas remained seated.

"Sir there is something else. In the hut of this self-styled colonel, I found an old biscuit tin containing what you and I would call school exercise books, containing the names of European farms in the area, and listing Kikuyu names. I suspect that these refer to each labour force. There is also lots of writing in Kikuyu. With your permission I would like to hand these over to Special Branch for translation."

Superintendent Lewis frowned and leaned forward in his chair.

"We've had this conversation before. Why only Kikuyu names?" He nodded. "Something is going on that could have very sinister dimensions. The Blake's dead cat. The cook and his wife preferring suicide to assisting us with our investigations. Now these lists you have mentioned..." Superintendent Lewis slowly nodded his head several times. "No, I don't like it one little bit. So in answer to your question, Robert, the sooner we have these translations the better." He pushed back his chair and stood up. "Now, let's have a look at the map."

Dundas and Superintendent Lewis were seated before the Assistant Commissioner's desk. The slatted blinds kept at bay the strong afternoon sunlight and the slowly turning overhead fan provided a gentle cooling airflow. On the wall to Dundas's left was a large-scale map of the Rift Valley Province covered in acetate, with numerous coloured pins denoting Divisional Headquarters, Police Stations and Police Posts. To Dundas, the serenity of this office was far removed from days and nights in the Aberdare forest, and the day to day ups and downs of normal police duties. The Assistant Commissioner, as befitted his rank, wore a tailored, pale khaki, lightweight uniform, set off to perfection with a crisp, white shirt and a black tie. Dundas placed his age as mid-fifties. His auburn hair failed to hide the tinges of grey at his temples. From his build, Dundas imagined that in his youth he must have played rugby, perhaps a 'winger'. An outstanding feature of his appearance were his piercing blue eyes. The Assistant Commissioner stood up and held out his hand.

"Chief Inspector, congratulations on the success of your operation. Well done! Superintendent Lewis has informed me that apart from one man, all the gang has been accounted for – and I understand that a number of documents have been recovered and handed to Special Branch. No doubt the Blake's murders and the attack on the Myers can be cleared up, and these documents could lead to more arrests. I am putting your name forward for a commendation."

"Thank you Sir, but it was a team effort and it would not have been possible without the sharp eyes of Constable Kipchumba and the support of my two NCOs."

The Assistant Commissioner nodded. "Well said. Discuss this with Superintendent Lewis and let him have your recommendations."

❖ ❖ ❖

Dundas glanced at his watch. Almost four o'clock. He pushed his completed statement to one side and looked out of the window at the lengthening shadows outside. Yes, it was good to be back! Soon the team would be disbanded and the uniforms and equipment handed back to the Kenya Regiment. Colonel Tom could be left to the police at Njabini. Perhaps the answer was to issue a reward for information leading to his arrest. He would discuss this with Superintendent Lewis. His thoughts were disturbed by the telephone. He reached across and picked up the handset.

"Chief Inspector Dundas C.I.D."

"Superintendent Lewis. Robert, I've just had Special Branch on the 'phone. The exercise books that you recovered evidently refer to people on the local farms in the Kinankop area who have taken an oath. What the oath is, they have yet to discover, however, it also lists the names of people who refused to take the oath and they are very few and far between. The list for Fawcett's farm is interesting, as only one man refused. He's the old man that Major Fawcett reported to Njabini Police Station as missing."

"Very interesting, Sir. So he may have been *removed*?"

"That's exactly my thinking, so it is highly probable that some of your prisoners may have information that could lead to an arrest. Now for some more news. One of your prisoners has told Special Branch that there are other gangs similar in size to the one headed by the man who calls himself Colonel Tom and that these gangs are scattered across the Aberdare Forest. It would appear that you have uncovered something very sinister. As you can imagine, the lines have been buzzing between here and Nairobi. So, in summary, this oathing is widespread and far greater than you or I could ever have imagined. I'll keep you updated on any future developments."

Dundas looked pensive as he said "Thank you Sir" and replaced the handset into its cradle. There was a click and the line went dead.

Dundas leaned back in his chair, staring outside with unseeing eyes. The number of gangs hiding in the forest was an unknown quantity but, based on recent examples, it pointed to the possibility of more attacks on European farms bordering onto the Kikuyu Reserve. If this was so, it was bigger than the C.I.D. could handle, or come to that, the normal Police Force. The army would need to become involved. His thoughts were once again disturbed by the telephone. He leaned across the desk and picked up the handset.

"Chief Inspector Dundas C.I.D."

"Robert, it's Joanne. Is there any chance of you being home at a reasonable time?"

Dundas grinned at the familiar question. "Yes, I'll be home in time for tea."

There was a pause. "Is that a promise, as you have said this before?"

He looked at the lengthening shadows outside.

"It's a promise."

The following morning Dundas awoke at his usual time as Steven arrived with the tray of tea. Having showered, he consumed his usual breakfast and, having kissed Joanne and his baby son goodbye, started the car and set off for Headquarters. It was the usual beautiful Kenya morning. As he drove along the High Street, past the bakery and the Nakuru Hotel, he mused how far removed this was from the dank forests of the Aberdares. With the arrests of the gang, his role was finished, apart from sifting through the evidence and hopefully being in a position to clear up the Blake murders and the attack on the Myers farm.

He entered his office and paused for a few moments to watch the industrious actions of the birds as they scurried across the grass, then out of habit, Dundas glanced at his watch. Almost two minutes to eight. Provided that nothing else cropped up, he would liaise with

Special Branch regarding any information of a criminal nature that had come to light and then, along with Sergeant James, commence interviewing the prisoners.

There was a knock on the door. Dundas turned away from the window and called "Come in."

The door opened to reveal the familiar face of Bill Stewart.

"Morning Robert! Can you spare a few minutes?"

Dundas indicated the vacant chair. "So what's the good news?"

"We have identified the man that you shot. He's Kikuyu and a deserter from the King's African Rifles who has been on the run for over a year. All your prisoners have been fingerprinted and the results sent off to C.R.O. in Nairobi, together with the prints of the man shot by Sergeant James."

Dundas leaned back in his chair and gestured. "So, assuming that some of them were involved, we may be in a position to clear up the Blake murders?"

Bill Stewart pushed back his chair and stood up. "Here's hoping Robert, I'll be in touch."

❖ ❖ ❖

During the next few days, interviewing the prisoners revealed that the Blake's houseboy had led the murderers into the dining room and that his wife was the woman living with the man who called himself Colonel Tom. The houseboy, no doubt wishing to save his own skin, had named two members of the gang who were involved in the attack and the murders. Two other members of the gang stated that they had witnessed Colonel Tom shoot and kill a man who had joined the gang from the Myers' farm. Now armed with the location of the body, or what remained of it, this information was passed to Njabini Police Station to carry out the recovery. All in all, Dundas was well pleased with the progress that had been made. No doubt when the reports from Criminal Records Department Nairobi came to hand, he was confident that fingerprints found at the Myers farm would provide a match that would result in several formal charges for murder being levied against members of the gang. It had also come to light that one member of the gang alleged that he had witnessed the strangulation of an old man employed on the farm of Major Fawcett.

Overshadowing all this success were two facts. One, the oathing of most of the farm labour within the area of the North and South Kinankop and two, the reports from Special Branch that there were other gangs of Kikuyu hiding within the Aberdares was disturbing. It was these two thoughts that dominated his mind as he drove down the High Street on his way home.

With dinner a very recent memory and with the coffee served, Dundas stretched out in his favourite armchair to listen to the evening news. He glanced across at Joanne, who was deeply engrossed in studying a knitting pattern and asked, "Is it complicated?"

Joanne looked up, still frowning. "Very. It's cable stitch, something I have never done before."

Dundas grinned. "So who is the lucky person?"

Joanne bent down, poked a loose strand of grey wool into its paper bag, then resumed looking at the pattern book. "It's a surprise."

The grin on Dundas's face increased. "So it's for me?"

Joanne continued studying the pattern. "I refuse to discuss it."

At this juncture all conversation ceased as the radio announcer said: *"This is the nine o'clock news from Nairobi, read by Michael Owen..."*

The news contained little of real interest, so after a few minutes Dundas rose from his chair, went over to the bookcase and switched off the radio. He then bent down, withdrew a book and flicked through its pages. Joanne looked up from her pattern.

"Robert, obviously you are bored. How about planning our next home leave?" Dundas continued to scan the various books, pausing from time to time to flip through the pages. Joanne looked up from her knitting.

"You haven't answered my question."

Dundas turned around. "It's over a year away and at this stage it's a pointless exercise.. Anyway, we haven't any brochures."

Joanne placed her knitting onto the small side table. "But at least we can talk about what we would like to do."

Dundas realised it was going to be *one of those* evenings!

The jangling of the bedside telephone roused Dundas from a deep sleep. He instinctively lifted the mosquito net and fumbled on the small bedside table until his fingers made contact, then sat up and placed the phone against his right ear. The voice was unmistakable and the tone meant trouble.

"Robert, get down here right away! Naivasha Police Station and Divisional Headquarters has been raided by a large armed gang. Most of the night duty staff have been killed and the armoury has been broken into and every firearm and round of ammunition taken. Every Police Station and Police Post is now on full alert and all staff have been armed."

Dundas was staggered by the information. An armed raid on Naivasha Police Station and Divisional Headquarters? All he managed to reply was, "Right Sir, I'll be there in less than ten minutes."

Dundas ran his fingers through his hair and flipped back the mosquito net. Shaving was out of the question. He went into the bathroom, splashed cold water onto his face, then hurriedly dressed.

Joanne stirred and sat up. "Darling, is everything all right?"

Dundas continued to tie the laces on his left shoe. "There's been an incident at Naivasha, I'll call you as soon as I can."

He went over to the bed, gave Joanne a kiss on her forehead, then turned and made for the bedroom door.

At Headquarters, armed Constables were patrolling the perimeter; he was stopped by the Court building before being allowed to proceed. Having parked, he entered the Charge Office, to be met by Superintendent Lewis.

"Robert, sign for your automatic and we'll be off. Evidently Naivasha Police Station has been ransacked and looks more like a slaughterhouse. Every firearm has been stolen. It's a bad business and a first in the history of this Colony."

"Sir, have we any idea of the number of police killed?"

"The initial reports stated at least eight, there could be more."

"And the size of the gang Sir?"

"The reports vary, but the best estimate is at least sixty, some of whom were armed. I'll brief you on route to Naivasha. One other thing, you and I will also carry a 'Sten Gun' and two full clips of ammunition. I've already signed on your behalf."

The Land Rover sped along the familiar tarmac surface that led to Naivasha. Dundas glanced at the speedometer, the needle was hovering around eighty and he hoped that a herd of zebra, attracted by their headlights would not try to dash across their path. The headlights stabbed into the darkness and at this high speed the tyre noise and the flapping of the canvas covering the rear section of the vehicle became onerous. Each man was alone with his thoughts.

Superintendent Lewis broke the silence.

"The lines between H.Q. and Nairobi have been red hot. The belief is that the Governor will declare a State of Emergency in the morning. The effect of this will be that all army and police reservists will be called up for active duty. It is also highly likely that the Aberdares will be declared a prohibited area."

"Sir, it's possible the gang we arrested could have knowledge regarding the planning of this attack? It's a line of enquiry that we could pursue. The main thrust of our enquiry has been directed at trying to solve the Blake murders. Yet we knew there were other small gangs hiding in the Aberdares, little did we realise the significance of this information."

Superintendent Lewis grunted. "With hindsight, Robert, a State of Emergency should have been declared weeks ago. But who was to know or even think that an armed gang would attack a Police Station and Divisional Headquarters? Now we have at least sixty criminals armed to the teeth, with a capability to carry out another raid."

Having passed the Naivasha Hotel, the Land Rover turned left, making its way up the rise before turning first right towards the Police Station and Divisional Headquarters. Armed police were everywhere and they were immediately stopped by two constables, who levelled their rifles at the Land Rover. Superintendent Lewis turned to Dundas.

"Get out very slowly and immediately make sure that they know you are a European. They are bound to be trigger happy, so don't move towards them until they tell you to do so."

As Dundas eased the door of the Land Rover open, he was aware of a tingling at the back of his scalp. He stepped onto the road and spoke in English. "Chief Inspector Dundas from Provincial Headquarters at Nakuru."

He stood stock still. One of the constables spoke in Kiswahili.

"Put your hands on your head and stand in front of the Land Rover."

Dundas moved slowly and stood in the glare of the headlights. One of the constables approached, still pointing his rifle. Then, having satisfied himself that all was well, he saluted.

"Sorry Effendi, but we were ordered to stop any vehicle or persons trying to enter the Police Station."

Dundas lapsed into Kiswahili. "Is the Bwana Assistant Superintendent here?"

"Ndiyo Effendi, he was in his office." The constable saluted again and Dundas returned to the Land Rover.

Dundas spoke to Superintendent Lewis. "The Assistant Superintendent is here, Sir, so no doubt we can obtain a full report."

The Land Rover stopped outside the Divisional office and Dundas and Superintendent Lewis clambered out.

"Robert, you have a look around and I'll see the A.S.P."

Dundas made his way to the Charge Office. Several bodies were covered in blankets and from the protruding shiny black boots it was obvious they were police. Blood was everywhere and from the position of the bodies they had been taken completely by surprise. He went outside. Two more bodies, also covered in blankets, were face down in the dust and within yards of the Charge Office. It appeared that they had been struck down whilst trying to escape. As reported, the place had been ransacked. He turned and made his way to the armoury. The steel door was wide open, showing very clearly the marks of a forced entry. Every rifle rack was empty, the only signs of anything connected with firearms were several loose rounds of .303 ammunition scattered across the concrete floor.

At this late hour he had seen enough, no doubt the morning light would reveal the true extent of the raid in all its gruesome reality. He turned and made his way back to the Land Rover.

# CHAPTER EIGHTEEN

TWO DAYS HAD PASSED following the raid on Naivasha Police Station and Divisional Headquarters. Despite the enormity of the crime the main people involved were 'Scenes of Crime', smothering all possible surfaces in fingerprint powder and taking photographs. The tasks of obtaining and eliminating lawful access prints, which included all the police killed in the raid, would prove to be a daunting task. All other prints would be shipped to Criminal Records in Nairobi for checking. Very few statements had been obtained and contained nothing concrete apart from how they managed to escape from the carnage. All the firearms' serial numbers had been circulated. A major worry was that both 9mm and .303 automatic weapons had been stolen along with some grenades, and flare-firing pistols. The various types of ammunition amounted to several thousand rounds.

Now back in Nakuru, Dundas sat at his desk looking out of the window watching the labourers from the 'Public Works Department' digging holes and then inserting ten foot blue gum poles before attaching multiple strands of barbed wire. Such activity was taking place at all police locations within the White Highlands and the Kikuyu Reserve. There was an almost siege mentality. As expected, the Colony's Governor had declared a State of Emergency and army and police reservists were in the process of being mobilised. Dundas now carried his Browning 9mm automatic even when off duty and the European population within the affected areas had been warned regarding the safekeeping of firearms; the penalty for their unaccountable loss was increased to automatic imprisonment.

The investigation into the Blake murders was proceeding. Bill Stewart's efforts had resulted in three members of the gang being identified by C.R.O. and several were keen to betray their colleagues. The remains near the Fawcett farm had been recovered by police from Njabini and, despite decomposition, identification had been achieved. With the gang now on remand, information was coming in of statements being made to other remand prisoners that if proven could clinch a number of convictions. One rumour of extreme interest was that some of the persons residing on Fawcett farm had been involved in the murder of an old man.

Dundas resumed working on the case file on his desk. If the evidence held up in court, then this one was 'for the chop' regarding the murder of Mr Blake. Dundas glanced at his watch as the 'phone rang. He reached across the desk and picked up the handset.

"Chief Inspector Dundas C.I.D."

There was no mistaking the voice. "Chief Inspector, I'm speaking from the Assistant Commissioner's office. Can you come up right away." The unusual formality and the tone of voice, made Dundas realise it was not a question, but an order.

There was only one possible reply. "Yes Sir."

Dundas knocked on the A.C.P.'s door and, having been told to enter, pushed it open. Superintendent Lewis was seated to the left of the A.C.P's desk. As usual, the capacious office exuded an air of orderly calm. The only noise to intrude was the soft hum of the large ceiling fan. The A.C.P. looked up.

"Come in Chief Inspector." He indicated the chair beside Superintendent Lewis. The A.C.P. continued. "The reason for calling you here is to ask you a very personal and important question." The A.C.P. paused and looked keenly at Dundas. "Chief Inspector, how would a change of job appeal to you?"

Dundas's immediate thought was promotion but his reply was guarded. "It would depend on the job Sir."

The A.C.P. nodded. "Quite."

The A.C.P. placed the tips of his fingers together. "You have recently been engaged in two unusual and successful operations. Superintendent Lewis has informed me that although investigations are ongoing, at least two men will be charged with murder. Currently you and your team are the only people with some experience of operating within the Aberdare Range. We now know that there are other gangs of an unknown size, perhaps poised to attack both Police Stations and outlying European farms. What we do not know is where they are and their numbers. Let us take a look at the map..."

The A.C.P. rose from his leather chair and, followed by Dundas and Superintendent Lewis, stood before the large map of the Rift Valley that dominated one wall. He picked up a pointer in his right hand.

"The army will be at full stretch. As a result, Nairobi H.Q. wants us to be responsible for this area here..." He pointed to the area of the North Kinankop. He continued, "You will note that it covers a depth of approximately twenty miles, but initially covers an area which is familiar to you." He turned and looked at Dundas. "As army units will be operating within the Aberdares, it is very important not to stray outside our designated boundaries. I must stress again, this is an intelligence gathering operation. It will be dangerous, but whoever undertakes this task will have a high degree of protection. The Aberdare Range is now a prohibited area, therefore the normal rules governing police use of firearms do not apply. I am not suggesting that it is a shoot-on-sight policy but we will not be restricted to the usual rules. So, Chief Inspector, I now come to the personal part of my question. I realise that you are married and have a young son. Let me also stress that we wish to give you time to consider my proposal, which is... will you take on this task? Let me also stress that the duration is unknown and it could also involve passing on your recently gained knowledge to others. Finally, whatever decision you come to, should you accept this task, then when things return to normal you will return to your duties with the C.I.D."

The outcome of this unexpected interview was not what Dundas had envisaged. He could understand why he had been selected. Before replying, he paused and looked once again at the wall map.

"Sir, how long do I have to decide?"

The A.C.P. pointed at the wall-map. "Ideally, we want someone in there within the next forty eight hours."

"Sir, I think that it is only fair that I discuss this with my wife. May I ask two questions?"

The A.C.P. gestured with his right hand. "Of course."

"First, what is the proposed duration of each mission? And second, between each operation, will I be based away from home?"

The A.C.P. nodded. "In answer to your first question, the proposed duration will be from three to five days, but basically such decisions will be made by the man on the ground. Regarding your final question, it is proposed that between each sortie, you will return home. One final thing. Superintendent Lewis will take over the current investigations, so between each sortie you will not be responsible for any other police duties. Do you have any further questions?"

"No Sir."

"Then, Chief Inspector, I will await your decision."

Having exited the A.C.P's office, Dundas followed Superintendent Lewis down the stairs to the ground floor where Superintendent Lewis paused.

"Robert, you must have very mixed feelings at the moment."

"I certainly have Sir. It is asking a lot of Joanne and I have yet to speak to my team. It has come rather like a bolt out of the blue. To switch from being a member of the C.I.D. to a semi-military role was totally unexpected. It is not the danger, Sir. It's just that currently I am doing a job that I enjoy..."

Before Dundas could continue Superintendent Lewis interjected.

"I do not want to influence you in any way. Only you can decide what to do. All I will say is this, no one will think any the less of you if you say 'no'. Mull it over and discuss it with Joanne, then let me know of your decision first thing tomorrow morning."

With these words, Superintendent Lewis made his way towards his office.

Dundas sat at his desk, looking at the Incident Chart with unseeing eyes. His mind bounced between Joanne, his tiny son and the comforts of home, to the dank forests of the Aberdares. In theory, the choice was easy; turn down the offer. But this thought was pushed to one side by the scenes he had witnessed at the Blakes' farm and at Naivasha. He reached down, opened the lower right hand drawer of his desk and withdrew a ruled, foolscap pad with the intention of drawing up a pros and cons list, then decided against it and pushed the pad to one side. What to do? As a single man, he would have jumped at the chance, but he was married now and directly responsible for two other lives. He looked out of the window into the bright sunlight, noting the usual blue starlings scurrying about. Their world was a simple one; it consisted of shelter and finding food. He turned and looked at the ruled pad again, then reached for the phone, dialled an internal number and awaited the click.

"Duty Officer speaking."

"John, it's Robert Dundas. I'll be out of the office for about thirty minutes. Pass any calls to my office to Superintendent Lewis."

He replaced the handset into its cradle, pushed back his chair and made for the door. He needed a different scene – the café just up the road from Police Headquarters.

Dundas had ordered a second cup of coffee, which was now just warm. The change of scene had done nothing to assist with his decision-making. It was time to return to Headquarters. He pushed the tepid coffee to one side, picked up the bill and made his way to the cash desk.

❖ ❖ ❖

It was just three minutes past five as Dundas drove into the driveway of his Government bungalow, stopping just before the steps leading up to the small veranda and front entrance. On hearing the car, Joanne came down the steps to greet him, with Ian in her arms.

"Darling, give me a kiss. You are just in time for tea and Steven has produced one of your favourite fruit cakes!"

Dundas encircled them both with his arms, detecting the scent of Joanne's skin as he nuzzled into her neck. Joanne sensed his tension.

"Robert, something is troubling you, what is it?"

He held them both very close in reaction to his emotion. He shook his head very slowly. "Let's have some tea and I'll tell you all about it?"

Joanne's reaction was immediate. "Is it bad news?"

Dundas stood back and shrugged his shoulders. "Not really, but I need to make a decision by tomorrow morning."

Joanne looked up at her husband's face, noting his serious expression and deeply furrowed brow. "Is it a possible posting Robert?"

Dundas continued to shake his head and gave Joanne a hug. "No, we will still be living here in Nakuru. Let's have some tea and a slice of Steven's cake..."

Following tea Dundas explained his dilemma. He had expected tears and questions such as "Why you?" but Joanne's words made up his mind. "Robert, when we married I realised that from time to time you would be away. I also realised that as a Police Officer you had a job that would not follow the usual nine to five routine. If you accept this task, all I ask is, don't take any unwarranted risks. You must do what you believe to be right." Dundas noted the tears welling in her eyes. He went over to her chair, took her in his arms and again held her close, smelling the scent of her warm skin and hair. Joanne leaned back and looked into his eyes. "Darling, please promise that you will be careful. I love you." With these words Joanne buried her face into her husband's shoulder and burst into tears.

With the memory of Joanne's tearful goodbye, it was with a heavy heart that next morning Dundas drove through the gates of the now barbed wired and guarded enclosure of Provincial Headquarters. He entered his office to find a note on his desk. It read: *"Call me a.s.a.p. Supt. Lewis."* Dundas picked up the phone and dialled the internal two digit number. There was the usual click and terse response.

"Lewis."

"I'm responding to your note Sir."

There was a brief pause. "Have you come to a decision Robert?"

"I have Sir, I'm accepting the task."

"Excellent! I knew you would. Now I have been talking to my wife. She has agreed to visit Joanne every day or have her over to our place for lunch, so I hope that this will put your mind at rest?"

"Thank you Sir, that is very good of you and please thank your wife for me."

"Robert, one other thing. I want you to carry an automatic weapon as well as your Browning pistol. Also, Sergeant James should replace his .38 revolver and carry one of the new Winchester pump-action shotguns. This also applies to Corporal Abikar."

"Sir, I have yet to discuss this new task with the team."

"I can assure you that they are raring to go! We had to have a fall-back position just in case you decided to opt out. So I spoke to the team yesterday, and to a man they want you to lead the patrol. Also to put your mind and theirs at rest, the Police Lines are now surrounded by barbed wire and the Police Station is providing a twenty-four hour armed guard. At nine o'clock Sergeant James and Corporal Abikar will be at the range trying out their new weapons. I suggest that you join them."

❖ ❖ ❖

Even before Dundas stopped the car, the sound of rapid firing could be clearly heard. He walked over to where the Firearms Officer was standing behind Sergeant James and Corporal Abikar. At a range of twenty yards were six human figure targets. The Firearms Officer issued an order.

"Stay facing to the front! Clear your weapon! Check that the breech is empty! Point your weapon at the ground two paces to your front and pull the trigger! Place your weapon onto the ground with the muzzle pointing to your front! Stand at ease!"

He turned and faced Dundas.

"Good morning Chief Inspector. I understand that you are the patrol leader?"

Dundas nodded. "Yes, we leave this evening."

"Have you ever used a Winchester pump-action?"

Dundas shook his head. "No never."

"Then let me demonstrate." The Firearms Officer stepped forward, picked up one of the weapons and turned it over.

"Five twelve-bore rounds are fed in here like this. This is the safety catch, which I have now placed in the on position. The advantage of this weapon is that it can be used for rapid fire. Let me demonstrate. Take off the safety catch. As soon as I pull the trigger the first round will fire. If I keep my finger on the trigger and work the pump action, I can produce rapid fire – like this…"

There were five rapid reports and Dundas could see lumps flying off one of the targets. The firearms Officer went through the usual safety drill, then placed the weapon onto the ground and turned to face Dundas. "Well… what do you think?"

"Very impressive!" Dundas turned to Sergeant James and Corporal Abikar and lapsed into Kiswahili. "What do *you* think?"

Sergeant James expression said it all. "Very good Sir, and ideal in the forest."

❖ ❖ ❖

Once again Dundas was in the Assistant Commissioner's office, with Superintendent Lewis to his left, gathered before the wall-map. The Assistant Commissioner pointed to a red map pin that indicated the position of Njabini Police Station.

"This will be your starting and finishing point. The Njabini sawmill is here. Just to its right is a stream. The plan is to follow this until its junction here, then take the left tributary. Then continue ahead, looking for any signs of terrorist activity. If you do find anything, follow their tracks and pinpoint their camp. Then return to Njabini and we will organise an air-strike using the two Harvards based at Nairobi. The key to this operation is to see but not be seen. Your recent experience will stand you in good stead. Any questions?"

"Yes Sir. We are carrying army field dressings but if anyone is wounded we do not have any morphine. Can this be remedied?"

The Assistant Commissioner turned to Superintendent Lewis.

"It's a fair point Lewis, see what can be done?" He turned to Dundas. "Any other questions or comments?"

"Yes Sir. I understand that we will not have a radio set. Is there any indication when these will be available?"

"The estimate is about four to six weeks. I agree that it is not ideal but, as you are aware, events have overtaken us. Anything else?"

"No Sir."

"In that case Chief Inspector I will wish you good luck and a safe return for you and your team." He shook Dundas's hand and then added. "Again, to the safe return of you and your team."

# CHAPTER NINETEEN

IT WAS JUST PAST 4PM as the police truck carrying Dundas and his team entered the gates of the now fortified Njabini Police Station. Having greeted the Inspector in Charge, Dundas was looking in the direction of his intended route. The Inspector was pointing out various features.

"Over to our left is Fey's Peak and in the same direction is the rounded promontory you can see, is known locally as The Elephant. The forestation stretches as far as the eye can see. Looking directly ahead, which is the direction that you will be taking, the land rises to over eleven thousand feet. If you consult your map..." the Inspector pointed. "...this is the track up to the sawmill, which is run by a European manager who employs Kikuyu labour. Being almost within the forest, it could be an ideal food source for any gang."

Dundas nodded. "More than likely. You have had thefts from local farms, anything in the way of bulk?"

The Inspector shook his head. "Not of late, just the odd sack of maize cobs, some cabbages and a few chickens. No arrests were made and it was assumed that it was local farm labour. I understand that North Kinankop has had more thefts in their area and a sheep was stolen. I seem to recall this resulted in an arrest."

Dundas pointed to the map. "Yes, my Sergeant visited them in prison but they were not giving any information. Most of the thefts took place in this area. This is why we came to patrol the forest edge that led to the arrest of the gang. Now our plan is to leave here just after dark and make our way past the sawmill. We will bed-down just inside the forest and move off again about dawn. Dundas pointed. "That far ridge line, looking at the map, it must be about ten miles away. Have you ever been into the area?"

The Inspector shook his head. "Never. All I have ever done is to fish for trout in the stream here." He pointed to the map. "From a police point of view, there has never been cause to patrol in the forest."

Dundas folded the map and placed it in the inside pocket of his smock. "Now, if you will excuse me, I'll brief my men."

Since it was possible that the patrol could bump into an armed gang, as a precaution Dundas had decided during daylight hours to extend the distance between each man to at least eight paces. During their previous sorties into the forest, he had become acutely aware of how difficult it could be controlling a large number of men who would be in an extended single file formation when making their way along narrow game tracks. By placing Sergeant James at the rear, with himself and Corporal Abikar immediately behind Constable Kipchumba, he considered the make-up of this patrol would be ideal.

With the men fully briefed, every item of equipment and every weapon checked, the patrol set off as planned. They had passed by the sawmill, the only negative being the manager's dog, which had sensed their presence. Its initial growls erupted into barking but as it was inside the house, it did not cause any problems. For a while, due to a modicum of moonlight filtering through the trees, it was possible to make unimpeded progress, but after a further twenty minutes, due to the increasing density of the overhead foliage, visibility became very limited, so Dundas decided to call a halt.

As usual, he opted to take the first hour's guard duty. Sitting on his poncho, hunched into his smock, he was thankful for the warmth of the long puttee wound around his middle. As usual, the hyraxes began their shrieking in the overhead canopy, to be answered by other hyraxes in the far distance. At night the amount and variety of sound was amazing. The almost human warning cough of a bushbuck, the noise of some unidentified animal, the soft hissing as the rain hit the overhead foliage, to fall in large drops onto the ground below. Dundas peered at his immediate surroundings. Due to the darkness, all he could discern were the vague dark shapes of the sleeping men nearest to him. His thoughts turned to Joanne, who now would be fast asleep. He recalled their night together, the warmth of her body, the scent of her skin and hair. Was he mad to have volunteered to search for armed gangs in the depths of the Aberdare forest? A noise disturbed his thoughts as one on the men grunted and turned over.

Dundas held his luminous watch within a foot of his face. Just another eighteen minutes and he could wriggle down into his poncho and lightweight blanket. The hyraxes continued to shriek and their nearby neighbours continued to respond. Come to think of it, he had no idea what a hyrax looked like. Light rain started to patter onto his poncho and as it increased in intensity it drowned out all other sound. Then, as suddenly as it had started, it eased, leaving just the drips falling from the trees. The rain had caused the scents and smells of the forest to heighten. The normal dank smell was now mixed with the faint scent of pine and some other scent that he could not place. The air temperature had fallen and he hunched his shoulders against the pervading cold night air.

His thoughts turned to the attack on Naivasha Police Station and Headquarters. The armoury had been ransacked. Did they know how to use these stolen weapons and, even more important, could they shoot straight? This thought led to gun-shot wounds. Every member of the patrol carried an army field dressing but the morphine had not materialised. He looked at his watch again – just another five minutes and he could hand over to Corporal Abikar.

❖ ❖ ❖

Dundas stirred in his sleep. In his semi-comatose state, he became aware of the cold seeping into his body. He turned over but the cold persisted, causing him to hunch inside his lightweight blanket. He slowly opened his eyes and then sat up. In the dim light of dawn, he could make out the shape of the man on guard duty and raised his right hand as a gesture of recognition. The crouching figure of Constable Kipchumba gestured in return. Dundas ran his fingers through his hair and then rubbed the palm of his right hand over his cheeks and chin. Oh, for a shave and a hot shower! The cold was acting on his bladder; it was time to make a move. He unclipped the poncho, noting the condensation on the inside of its waterproof cover, reached for his dew covered Sten Gun, then made his way to behind a nearby tree.

The dawn light had now increased and it was time to rouse the men and prepare for the day ahead. He made his way to where Sergeant James was positioned within the circle of waking men.

He kept his voice low. "Good morning James, another cold night?"

"Wet and cold Sir."

"James, we move in twenty minutes. Make sure the men eat and that any rubbish is buried and carefully concealed. All weapons to be checked, loaded and safety catches applied. One final thing. Everyone will carry their weapon across their body with the muzzle pointing just above the left shoulder. I know we say this every day, but let's make sure there are no accidents."

Sergeant James saluted. "Yes Sir."

❖ ❖ ❖

Dundas returned to his poncho and sat down to rummage through his small backpack for his rations. What to eat this morning? He opted, without much enthusiasm, for the biscuits and the minute tin of jam. He placed the Mars bar and the oatmeal stick into the left-hand hip pocket of his smock for later consumption, then reached for his water bottle, unscrewed the cap and took a sip. The water was ice cold and tasted refreshing, an ideal combination with the hard-tack biscuits and jam. Having eaten, he checked his Sten gun. He removed the magazine, checked the movement of the breech-block, then reinserted the magazine, cocked the weapon and applied the safety catch. It was time to move off.

With Constable Kipchumba in the lead, the patrol began to penetrate deeper into the forest in an extended formation. The hyrax were now silent, their place being taken by numerous birdcalls. From time to time, between these calls, there was an eerie silence, almost as if every bird had paused to draw breath. Once again, Dundas was aware of the dank smell of the forest, mixed with the scent of pine. From time to time the overhead canopy thinned, permitting shafts of sunlight to penetrate and illuminate the moisture rising from the ground. Kipchumba avoided these areas and hugged the shadows.

By now, the noise of a stream could be heard on their right. It was time to move closer to its course. Kipchumba stopped from time to time, signalling his intention by raising his left hand, then kneeling down and indicating to the patrol to do likewise, by making two slow patting motions. Why had Kipchumba stopped? Each time Dundas could feel his heart thudding in his chest. Each time Kipchumba would stand up, motion the patrol to move forward and the tension would ease. Due to these frequent stops, progress was slow, but the caution was essential and Dundas had stressed to his team the need 'to see but not be seen'.

From the noise, Dundas estimated that they were about one hundred yards from the stream and it was now time to move closer, but not so close that the noise of the water would blanket all other sound. Suddenly, there was a cough as a startled bushbuck ran off to their right. Kipchumba had frozen in his tracks but he now turned and gave a huge grin before moving forward once again.

By mid-day Dundas estimated that they had covered no more than five miles. It was time to call a halt and consult his map. The patrol, now kneeling down, faced outwards in a defensive 'string', with Constable Kipchumba facing to the front and Sergeant James to the rear. Dundas removed the folded map from the inside pocket of his smock and unfolded it. It would appear that it was at least another four miles to the stream's junction and at their current rate of progress it would be dusk before they arrived. He glanced at his watch – at this juncture it was a good time to have a ten-minute break and consume some food. The word was passed. "Eat, but stay alert and keep facing to your front."

Dundas withdrew the oatmeal stick from his pocket and peeled back the paper wrapper. It was only about one inch square and about four and a half inches long, very tough to chew but surprisingly filling. He decided to eat half and to follow it with his Mars bar. He unscrewed the cap of his water bottle and took a few sips to help him swallow the sawdust-dry oatmeal stick and, having consumed half, returned it to his pocket and took a bite of the Mars bar. The chocolate coating was discoloured but it tasted OK. With the whole bar consumed, he looked at his watch. It was time to move off.

It was just after 5pm when they reached the fork in the stream and it was now time to follow the left source. There was a distinct chill in the air and from here on the ground rose at a steeper angle and the altitude of over ten thousand feet made their breath rasp in their throats. The only thing to impede their cautious progress was not the density of the forestation, but the gradient. Dundas decided to reduce fatigue by zigzagging, realising that if they came under attack most of his men would be exposed to enemy fire. After fifteen minutes the gradient dramatically reduced. From the sound of the rushing water to the right of their advance, Dundas estimated the stream was now some one hundred yards away.

The light was now failing, and it was time to call a halt. On a hand signal every man knelt on the ground and faced outwards in a defensive ring. Bending low, Dundas moved forward to Corporal Abikar and knelt down beside him.

"We will keep moving forward until dusk. We will then eat and just before dark, in case we have been seen, move without noise to another position and bed down for the night. Tell Kipchumba and I'll pass the word down the line."

Keeping low and moving with extreme caution, he made his way down the line to Sergeant James and repeated the message. Sergeant James raised his right hand in acknowledgement then whispered, "Sir, it is possible that members of the gang could see our tracks and start to follow us then attack us from the rear? I believe that we should defend our line of advance every hour or so." Dundas cursed himself for failing to realise the obvious. His thoughts had been concentrating on their enemy being to their front, but if a gang stumbled across their tracks, then to estimate the strength of the police patrol would not be difficult. The gang could follow up and attack or keep the patrol under observation and attack at dusk when the patrol would be least alert.

"James, that's an excellent idea. I'll brief the men when we next stop and we'll take up ambush positions."

Again crouching low, Dundas made his way back up the line to Corporal Abikar to convey Sergeant James's suggestion. Dundas noted that Corporal Abikar never once looked at him, always keeping his eyes to his front and nodding his head in understanding.

It was now dusk and time to implement Sergeant James's suggestion. Dundas placed the patrol some ten yards off their line of advance, each man some six feet apart, strung out in a single line in a prone position, with two members of the patrol facing to their rear. All they could do now was to wait.

As the light continued to fade, the hyrax began their nocturnal cacophony, their calls echoing throughout the forest. At a distance that Dundas estimated to be less than twenty yards, there was a sound of rustling to their front moving from left to right. What was it? Dundas noted that his heartbeat had increased and he placed the fore-finger of his right hand alongside the trigger guard of his Sten gun. Suddenly, and without warning, there was an almost human cough as a lone bushbuck sensed their presence and made off into the surrounding darkness.

Another thirty minutes passed and apart from the hyrax augmented with a strange cry that Dundas did not recognise, the forest enveloped them in darkness. Dundas decided to make a move. However, it was now pitch dark and to keep noise to a minimum would be difficult. He moved very carefully to his left, tapped Corporal Abikar on the shoulder and whispered: "We will stay as we are. Kipchumba will take the first watch, you the second and I'll take the third. I'll pass the word down the line."

Having contacted the man to his right, Dundas, now guided only by touch, proceeded to carefully unpack his poncho and lightweight blanket, then fumbled in his pack for his nightly meal. He realised that he had miscalculated the amount of time available to set up an ambush and then secure a 'safe' position for the patrol. Bedding-down had not been a problem before, but now there was a gang roaming around in the forest, armed with automatic weapons and even grenades. He hunched his shoulders against the cold night air, and then fumbled once again into his pack until his fingers encountered the coarse wool of the long puttee. Having wound this around his middle, and making as little noise as possible, he wriggled into his poncho and lightweight blanket. He lay on his back, making sure that his Sten gun was within easy reach. He looked up into the overhead canopy. There was nothing but blackness.

His thoughts turned to Joanne and their tiny son Ian. What would they be doing at this hour? Overhead there was a faint sound of hissing. Rain. As the downpour increased, large drops of rain started to patter onto his face and poncho. It was going to be another wet and cold night. He turned onto his right side, hunching his body against the penetrating cold, listening to the rain now falling freely onto his poncho. He pulled the top of his poncho as high as possible, and despite the rain, the cold and their situation, went to sleep.

Something was shoving his shoulder. He awoke with a start and recognised the whispered voice of Corporal Abikar.

"*Effendi, Effendi!*"

Dundas sat up and out of habit ran his fingers through his hair. Corporal Abikar whispered again.

"*Hakuna matata, Effendi, na hakuna mvua.*" (There is no trouble and no rain).

Dundas held his luminous watch close to his face – just after 11pm. He carefully eased himself from the poncho and squatted on it, grasping his Sten gun and resting it across his lap. Apart from the water dripping off the trees and the murmur of the stream some hundred yards away, all was quiet. Even the hyrax had been subdued by the recent downpour. He strained his eyes, trying to penetrate the darkness, then failing this, gazed skywards – nothing. His thoughts turned to Joanne and the warmth of her body. What was he doing here? He must have been mad to volunteer! His thoughts were disturbed as one of the men grunted in his sleep, then noisily turned over. Hell, it was cold. He thrust his hands deep into the hip pockets of his smock, then withdrew his left hand and glanced at his watch again. Had it only been twelve minutes since relieving Corporal Abikar? His mind churned over the day's events, settling on the possibility of someone being shot. They were miles from any help and all they had were army field dressings and no morphine. In his mind's eye he pictured the scene, two of his men seriously wounded, bullets cracking ad splintering the bushes and tree trunks. How would they cope? He recalled the A.C.P's words. "To see but not be seen." Easily said when you were seated in an office in Nakuru – but what if the enemy saw them first?

The night passed without incident. Dundas awoke just after 6am. The rain had stopped, but the ground was soaked as was the outside of his poncho. He unclipped the sides. As usual, due to condensation, the inside was almost as wet as the outside. He sat up and acknowledged the raised hand of the man on guard duty. All was quiet; the only sounds were the raindrops falling to the ground from the overhead foliage. He carefully stood up, walked a short distance away and went behind a tree to perform his bodily functions. On his return he rinsed his hands with his water bottle and dried them on his jungle green trousers. It was time to rouse the men and have breakfast... At 6.30, in the now familiar formation, the patrol moved off, keeping the stream to their right.

It was now just after 10. As before, Constable Kipchumba kept to the shadows, stopping from time to time and then signalling with his right hand for the patrol to continue. Shafts of sunlight penetrated the overhead canopy, highlighting the rising vapour from the rain-soaked ground. With the numerous birdcalls, the scent of pine and other forest smells, it was almost impossible to realise that at any moment this tranquillity could be shattered by gunfire. It was time to call a halt. The patrol adopted its usual defensive ring. Crouching low, Dundas made his way down the line to Sergeant James who raised his hand in a silent hello. Dundas squatted down beside Sergeant James and kept his voice very low.

"According to my estimate, we must be within an hour of arriving at the point where Superintendent Lewis estimated we would find a camp. If his estimate is correct, we may be about to encounter a well-armed gang. We will move forward with extreme caution and it is important that the men stay well spread out. If we come under fire, make sure the men are in the prone position and heads well down. They will only shoot when they can see a target. You brief the six men in front of you and I'll brief the rest. We move off in ten minutes."

The patrol moved forward with extreme caution. Constable Kipchumba stopped from time to time, going down on one knee and studying the terrain ahead. Every time he stopped, Dundas could feel his heart thudding in his chest. Would they stumble across an armed gang? Birdcalls echoed around the forest, nearly blanketing the sounds of the nearby stream. The early morning sun's warmth was welcoming, casting deep shadows, which were ideal to assist in concealing their presence. The shafts of sunlight and the moisture rising from the forest floor made it seem unreal. Yet at any moment, violent death could eradicate a human life. He motioned for the patrol to continue. On route they would ambush the track.

Some hours later and having carried out two ambushes, the patrol reached a plateau. Dundas decided to call another halt. Each man crouched low in what was now the normal defensive formation. Dundas looking to his front and supporting his Sten gun with his left hand, felt for the oatmeal stick in the right-hand pocket of his smock.

His fingers grasped its square shape and he started to withdraw it from his pocket when suddenly there were a series of very loud cracks. Dundas heard Corporal Abikar's pump- action Remington fire twice in rapid succession. There was a crashing in the foliage ahead and as Dundas turned in the direction of the two shots, he caught the sight of a body falling to the ground with a loud thud! Then all hell broke loose! Some distance ahead there were a series of bugle calls, lots of shouting, guns being fired in their direction, the bullets passing overhead in a series of loud cracks, causing leaves and twigs to shower down. Dundas could feel his heart thudding in his chest and his mouth had gone dry. He called out, "Stay down and take cover!"

His voice sounded as if it belonged to someone else. Hugging the ground, Dundas crawled towards Corporal Abikar. Suddenly Constable Kipchumba opened fire, quickly joined by Corporal Abikar, the Remington making a distinctive sound against the sharp bang of Constable Kipchumba's .303 rifle. The bugle calls continued and the firing in their direction became more intense. Despite scanning from left to right, Dundas still had not seen any targets. Then he saw a figure to his left, dressed in an army greatcoat. He aimed the Sten gun and gave a very short burst. He saw chips of bark fly off a tree – damn, he'd missed! The figure, still crouching low, was obviously intent on getting behind them. At a distance of some thirty yards, the crouching figure appeared again. This time Dundas aimed just an inch ahead of the swiftly moving gang member and squeezed the trigger – the Sten gun juddered against his shoulder and in the sights he saw the man pause and fall face down to the ground. Got him!

He heard Constable Kipchumba's rifle fire again and heard a scream. There was lots of yelling from the direction of the enemy. The firing continued but it was wild and inaccurate. Seeing no other movement, Dundas quickly crawled to where Corporal Abikar was prone beside a sapling.

"Corporal Abikar are you OK?"

Corporal Abikar kept his eyes to his front. "*Ndiyo Effendi*, they had a sentry up that tree and he shot at me but missed. That's his body about twenty-five paces ahead. What were you shooting at Effendi?"

"A man with a revolver was running towards our rear, I hit him with the second burst. I'll go forward to Constable Kipchumba."

"Stay low Effendi."

Dundas crawled the seven or so yards to Constable Kipchumba's side. The shooting was still wild and the bugle had been replaced by what sounded to be blasts on police whistles.

"Are you OK?"

"*Ndiyo Effendi,* I hit one as I heard him scream."

Dundas noticed that Constable Kipchumba was sweating, no doubt with excitement. Apart from this, he appeared to be as cool as a cucumber.

Suddenly all firing ceased. There was only a deathly silence. No bird calls – nothing! What was happening? Dundas strained his ears for the slightest sound. All he could hear and feel was his heart thudding in his chest. He lay there hugging the ground within a yard of Constable Kipchumba, his eyes scanning the forest ahead for the slightest movement. Nothing stirred. It occurred to him that apart from himself, Corporal Abikar and Constable Kipchumba, the rest of the patrol had not opened fire. No doubt they had formed their well rehearsed defensive position, but at this point in time, the other members of the patrol would be totally unaware of the forward situation.

Dundas crawled the one yard over to Constable Kipchumba and whispered, "I'll keep watch. You crawl back to Corporal Abikar and then cover me as I crawl back. Then I can inform the rest of the patrol what is going on."

Constable Kipchumba nodded his head and, still facing his front, began to crawl backwards towards Corporal Abikar. Dundas continued to scan the forest. One of the gang had tried to reach the rear of the patrol, would others try to do the same thing? No doubt they wished to assess their strength. There was a faint whistle behind him. Dundas carefully turned his head. Corporal Abikar was motioning him to join them. Crawling backwards was more difficult than he had realised and it took him several minutes to reach their position. Still keeping his head low, he turned his face towards Corporal Abikar.

"What do you think is happening?"

Corporal Abikar's eyes continued to scan ahead. His reply was barely audible.

"They may have fled Effendi... or like the Shifta bandits in the Northern Frontier, they are trying to cut off our line of retreat and will try to ambush us."

These thoughts coincided with his own. However, the first thing was to inform the remainder of the patrol of their current situation. He whispered to Corporal Abikar.

"You two stay here; I'll go back and inform the others what is going on and then return."

To reach Sergeant James there was some fifty yards to cover. Should he crawl or crouch low? The firing had ceased and up to now had been wild and mainly overhead. He'd crawl to the first man, and then crouch the rest of the way. Their training had stood them in good stead. Every man was in a defensive position to the left and right of the advance. Heads low and scanning the forest ahead, only turning their heads when they heard his approach. He quickly briefed each man, finally arriving at Sergeant James, who completed the defensive 'ring' by facing to his rear. Dundas crawled the last few yards.

"Have you seen or heard anything?"

Sergeant James shook his head and kept his voice low.

"No Sir, just the firing up ahead. Is everyone OK?"

"Yes, thank God. Corporal Abikar shot and killed a man who was a sentry. Constable Kipchumba has definitely hit one of the gang, and I hit one whom I believe is dead."

"Has the gang run away Sir?"

Dundas shrugged. "That I do not know and we do not know. We will remain as we are for another five minutes and then move forward. Keep a sharp lookout as they may try to go to our rear. I'll now return to Corporal Abikar."

Crouching low, Dundas made his way to the front of the patrol, crawling the final few yards to Corporal Abikar's side.

"Any sound or movement?"

Corporal Abikar shook his head and continued to keep his eyes to his front.

Three minutes passed. Dundas continued to strain his ears for the slightest sound – it was as if nothing had happened. Could it be that the gang were waiting for them to make the first move? Dundas weighed up the situation. The choice was very basic: advance or retreat. However, of the two, the former carried the greatest risk. But what if the gang had fled? The answer was to use the trees as cover and move forward in a series of 'leap-frogging' movements. His mind was made up. It was time to pass the word down the line. There was, however, a snag. This type of movement had not been covered in their brief training sessions, and how could he ensure that each man would convey the correct message? He crawled closer to Corporal Abikar and conveyed how they would move forward. He then crawled back down the line to give the same message to the next man in the patrol and hoped that the same message would eventually reach Sergeant James. He returned to Corporal Abikar and Constable Kipchumba. He kept his voice low.

"We move in four minutes. I'll go first to that tree directly ahead, then you two follow and I'll move forward again."

As Dundas crawled forward, he could feel the tension and again he was conscious of his heart thudding in his chest and his dry mouth. Expecting at any moment to be shot at, he used his elbows to assist him and keep the Sten gun pointing to his front. He arrived at the tree. All was quiet. He signalled Corporal Abikar and Constable Kipchumba to join him. Again, all was quiet although the birds, emboldened by the silence, began their varied calls. With the three of them using the tree as cover, Dundas rolled to one side and, keeping his head low, peered cautiously around the trunk. He could see the body some twenty yards ahead and to its side what appeared to be a rifle. All was quiet and in the middle distance the bird calls continued. Had the gang fled? It was time to find out.

On the third move forward, Dundas arrived just to the left of the body. The rifle was now clearly visible. It was a standard issue .303 Lee Enfield', which could have been one of the many weapons stolen during the raid on Naivasha. Having been joined by Corporal Abikar and Constable Kipchumba, it was time to move forward again. Just five yards ahead, slumped behind a tree, the head to one side the eyes partly closed, was the body of another member of the gang. No doubt the man shot by Constable Kipchumba. At first the corpse had taken Dundas by surprise and his first reaction was an ambush but the position of the body made him realise that the man was dead. As per the other body, the hair was long and multi-plaited.

By this time they had moved forward some thirty yards. There were no sounds or movement. Was it now time to move forward more quickly? Dundas briefed his two-man team and then, crouching low, they moved forward, dodging from tree to tree. Through the trees and to their right, Dundas spotted a line of shelters very similar to the camp where they had captured all those prisoners.

By hand signals, Dundas indicated his find. There was no sign of movement. Smoke from a solitary fire rose into the overhead foliage. Apart from this, the camp appeared to be deserted.

Having been joined by the rest of the patrol, Dundas placed sentries at the four points of the compass and then began to search the camp. Based on the number of shelters, it would appear that they had housed some twenty to twenty five men. Signs of a rapid departure were evident. The cooking fire was still burning, complete with a very blackened cooking pot and its contents. There were blankets still in some of the shelters, foodstuffs, and one bandolier of .303 ammunition, but no firearms. Dundas decided to destroy the camp by fire and ordered the cooking pot to be smashed into small pieces. It was now time to check the three bodies.

Together with Sergeant James, Dundas retraced his steps to the body by the tree. There was evidence of heavy bleeding on the clothing above the waist, which on closer examination revealed that he had been shot in the stomach. Dundas stood up.

"James, this one was shot by Kipchumba. He must have crawled to this tree and then died."

A search of the man's pockets revealed only two pieces of leather about two inches square, stitched together with something inside. Dundas showed it to Sergeant James.

"If this was to ward off evil spirits, then it didn't do him much good."

Dundas picked up the rifle and opened the bolt. The magazine still contained three rounds of ammunition. Smelling the breech indicated that it had been fired. Taking the rifle with them they made their way to the body shot by Corporal Abikar. The man was face down in a crumpled heap. With the assistance of Sergeant James, Dundas turned the body over. Dundas pointed to the tree overhead.

"He was on sentry duty and fired at Corporal Abikar. So James, you can now see how effective a Remington' pump- action shotgun can be. Let's search his pockets."

Nothing was found. Having recovered the second rifle they made for the third body. It was sprawled face down and beside the man's right hand was a .455 Webley revolver. Dundas picked it up and opened it. Three of the six rounds had been fired. Dundas then examined the body. Two of his 9mm bullets had entered the man's left side, exited on the right, and must have hit his heart, or very close to it. The second shot could have hit the spinal column. Dundas reached down and turned the body over. It had the usual long multi-plaited hair, the eyes were partly open and there was blood on the teeth and partly opened mouth. Dundas looked at the face, it seemed very familiar. He looked again – despite the long hair, he recognised his former gardener, Kamau, who had left without any explanation. Dundas continued to look in almost disbelief.

Sergeant James interrupted his thoughts.

"Is anything the matter Sir?"

Dundas pointed. "James, this man was employed by me as a gardener and left without any explanation. He was always cheerful, polite and used to greet me each morning before I left home."

Dundas continued to stare at the body. Joanne must never know about this.

"Sir, he had a revolver and it has been fired. He would have killed you or one of us."

Dundas looked down at the body, slowly shaking his head. "It has just been a shock to realise that I have killed a man I once knew."

"Can I suggest, Sir, that I search his pockets?"

Dundas nodded.

Sergeant James completed his search and looked up.

"This is all I've found Sir." He held up a grubby piece of paper that had been folded in four and opened it.

"I think you should read this Sir."

Dundas took the proffered piece of paper. It was headed, in Kiswahili, DEATH LIST. Heading the list of eleven people were three names:

*Bwana Dundas*
*Memsahib Dundas*
*Mtoto (baby) Dundas*

Back at the campsite, Dundas went to the stream and washed his hands in the icy cold water, turning over in his mind the words on the piece of paper now in the pocket of his smock. What type of evil would make a man want to kill an innocent woman and her child? He had already witnessed the power that an oathing ceremony could have on the Kikuyu. His mind went back to the Blakes' farm and the Meyer's. Suddenly hatred had been kindled where before the oathing no hatred had existed. Had this been the same with Kamau?

Dundas retraced his steps to the camp. Its destruction was almost complete. Corporal Abikar came up and saluted.

"Effendi, the four sentries have been changed and what do you want us to do about the bodies?"

The bodies! They would need to be identified. Bodies had not come into his thoughts of the equipment to be carried by the patrol. Had he thought about it, then the inclusion of some fingerprint ink, a roller and fingerprint pad, plus a number of fingerprint forms would have solved the problem. Now he was faced with a decision. Bury the bodies, or convey them back to Njabini Police Station? It would be a task that would not be popular with the men. Corporal Abikar stood, awaiting his orders.

"Thank you for reminding me Corporal Abikar, but first I need to consult with Sergeant James."

Corporal Abikar gave another smart salute, then, carrying out an about-turn in parade ground fashion, returned to supervise the final destruction of the camp.

With the camp totally destroyed, only one thing remained, the three bodies. To remove them to Njabini Police Station would be both arduous and unpleasant and the patrol could be attacked at any time.

Dundas weighed up the pros and cons but there was no escaping it – the bodies would have to be carried.

# CHAPTER TWENTY

SOME THIRTY MILES AWAY from where Dundas and his patrol had shot three members of the gang, Colonel Tom had returned to the now deserted camp. The cowards had taken every vestige of food. Not even a blanket remained! He sat beside the stream staring at the water bubbling over the rocks. What was it that had triggered this mass desertion? He recalled that the Sergeant had requested promotion. Could it be that he had promoted himself to Colonel and then had taken the gang to another part of the forest? That was it! At a stroke, he had been stripped of his command! That bastard Sergeant also had his woman! If ever they met up again, he'd shoot him in the stomach and, with pleasure, watch him scream in agony until he died!

Colonel Tom sat there, clutching his shotgun, realising that he was now completely alone and very hungry. What was he to do? He could try to shoot a bushbuck but the noise would travel a very long way, so he decided against it. He had another thought. Was it possible that the women who supplied food from Fawcett's farm were not aware that things had changed? Failing this, he could visit Fawcett's farm under the cover of darkness and obtain food and shelter – also it may be possible to recruit some new followers. All the Kikuyu men on the farm had taken the oath. The men who had arrested the old man who had refused to take the oath and had witnessed his execution could be coerced to join him.

His anger started to subside and his spirits lifted. He still had this camp deep in the forest. The food supply, if it had ceased, could be quickly reinstated – all he needed were men. Once organised, they could raid some European farms, kill the owners and seize their fire-arms. Within weeks, he could be in charge of a new and well-armed gang...

Colonel Tom made his way down the familiar route towards the Fawcett farm, his shotgun slung over his shoulder and deep in thought. With the amount of daylight remaining, he would arrive on the edge of the farm soon after dark. He could then make his way to the hut where the old man had been executed and arrange a meeting. He wondered if, with his new recruits, he should attack the European farmer and, having killed him, seize his firearms and ammunition, plus anything else of value, such as blankets and warm clothing? There was livestock that could be butchered and stored maize too... As he proceeded through the fading daylight, his plans became ever more grandiose. But, having walked several more paces, caution made him think again. If the European was killed, what would the police do? Unlike the other farm, this farm was situated on the forest edge. The police had tracker dogs and were well armed – it was possible they would attempt to enter the forest and track them down. They hadn't done so to date, but then the two farms that had been attacked were miles away from the forest, so their lack of activity was hardly surprising.

On balance, he decided to recruit some new followers, obtain food and other supplies and then take them back to his camp. In the safety of the camp, he could train them and then attack other farms such as the previous two. This would not jeopardise his food supplies or motivate the police to enter the forest. Colonel Tom's hunger confirmed that food was of paramount importance. Yes, it was a good plan. He continued towards the forest edge, well satisfied with his ability to choose the correct course of action.

By now it was dusk. He cautiously made his way to where the women normally left sacks of food. What would he find? Despite the gloom, the three sacks were in their normal position. He felt the exteriors. The large bulges within the first sack could only be cabbages. The second must be dried maize cobs. The third and final sack felt soft to the touch – could it be blankets and clothing? This was not the time to investigate, he had supplies and, before the night was out, he would have a new army befitting his rank of colonel.

As he approached the labour camp, a dog detected his presence and began to bark. For a brief moment a hut door was flung open and a stab of soft yellow light penetrated the darkness. There was a shout in Kikuyu, then a yelp from the dog. The hut door closed and all was silent once again. The dog still sensed his presence and began emitting a series of growls from deep within its throat that increased in volume as he drew closer. Once again the hut door was opened, the male occupant being silhouetted by the light from within. The man stood there for a few moments, then suddenly the dog erupted into a frenzy of barking and ran towards the intruder. It was time to make his presence known. Colonel Tom tried to make himself heard above the dog's barking.

"I'm a man of the forest and have taken the oath..."

A hut door to his immediate left opened but, on seeing the stranger, was immediately slammed shut. Colonel Tom continued towards the man in the doorway who now shouted at the dog to be quiet. Still growling, it slunk away out of sight. The man in the doorway was peering out into the darkness but as yet could not see this stranger.

He asked, "Where are you from and what is your name?"

Colonel Tom moved closer. "I am with the Freedom Army and my name is Colonel Tom."

The man was still suspicious. "Come into the light where I can see you."

Colonel Tom stepped forward, his right hand clutching the sling of his shotgun, which was slung over his right shoulder. He paused in the light of the open door.

"Well, do you believe me?"

The man still hesitated. "Are you alone?"

"Yes, and I need food and shelter from a man who has taken the oath."

The man stepped forward from the doorway and held out his hand.

"Welcome brother." He clasped Colonel Tom around the shoulders. "You are welcome here. What we have is yours."

Colonel Tom thankfully entered the warmth of the hut, noting the sleeping child and the strained face of the man's wife, her smile of welcome doing nothing to hide her fear of the intrusion of the longhaired, unkempt stranger. She bent down placing more wood onto the open fire, then went to one side of the hut and returned with a blackened straight-sided *sufaria* (cooking pot), poured in some water, then turned away to find other foodstuffs. Colonel Tom noted her high cheekbones and comely figure and was conscious that it was some time since he had had a woman. Placing his shotgun against the wall of the hut, he removed his ex-army greatcoat and squatted beside the open fire.

By now the wood had ignited, the flames casting long flickering shadows onto the hut's mud walls. The man broke the silence.

"So, what news do you bring about our army?"

Colonel Tom continued to stare into the fire and at first did not answer. What should he say? "We are doing well and our numbers continue to grow."

The woman knelt beside the fire, placing cabbage into the now simmering water and he found it difficult to take his eyes away from the well-filled bodice of her dress. The woman, sensing his gaze, looked up and he noted the glint in her eyes and her demure expression. He looked into the fire again.

"A few days ago I attended a secret meeting of our leaders to discuss our future plans to drive the *Wazungu* off our land."

He listened to his own voice, realising how important he would appear in the eyes of his hosts.

"When there, I met a great leader called General Kargo, who has an army of over one hundred and fifty men. They are well armed with many guns and have attacked Police Posts and farms, killing both Police and Europeans."

The man squatted on the opposite side of the fire, nodding his head and feeling honoured that this armed man was sharing these secrets with him. He looked up and spat into the fire.

"So brother, what brings you here?"

Colonel Tom warmed his hands by the crackling fire, smelling the aroma of the boiling cabbage.

"Our army needs more men, men like yourself to join in our fight. As a colonel I need to call a meeting to address the men here. Ideally tonight, or tomorrow night."

His host looked startled. "How many men do you want?"

Colonel Tom noted the man's expression. "At least fifteen to twenty. Men who are not chickens and who will not run and hide at the slightest danger – and we need a woman to cook and care for the men."

The impact of this request was evident in the whining tone of the man's voice. "Fifteen men would halve the labour force of this farm. The men here have wives, children and without the wages how will these women and children fare? Every other day the women carry supplies to the forest edge, but without money and work this would no longer be possible."

Colonel Tom could not disguise his sneering tone. "Are you telling me that the men on this farm are no better than skulking farm dogs! Having taken the sacred oath they will not support our cause?"

Before the man could reply, his wife interjected. "Colonel, your food is now ready."

She removed the boiling cabbage from the fire and, turning away, began to spoon the hot cabbage and other food onto an enamel plate. Colonel Tom found it difficult to hide his hunger and noisily finished off the remnants on his plate, wiping it clean with a ball of posho dough and gratefully accepting the steaming mug of tea from this comely woman. He turned to his hosts.

"I will stay here tonight. Tomorrow you will spread the word that there is a special meeting being called by a colonel who is recruiting men to fight for the cause."

His host looked strained. "Will you be leaving here at dawn?"

Colonel Tom shook his head. "No, I will stay hidden in this hut, but no one is to know that I'm here. Is this agreed?"

His host nodded his head.

The crowing of the cockerels heralded the approach of a new day. Colonel Tom stirred underneath his solitary blanket and watched the woman rekindle the fire and place a blackened kettle onto the flames. The pressure in his bladder reminded him it was time to go outside and in order not to be seen, urinate behind the hut. Having returned, he squatted beside the open fire, watching the smoke from the newly ignited wood rise and seep into the thatched roof. The woman knelt beside the fire and gave him a shy glance before pouring the scalding water into a mug of tealeaves, adding sugar and handing it to her guest. The tea was strong, hot, sweet and satisfying. He went over and sat on his blanket, watching the woman as she busied herself about the hut.

His host dressed and, having eaten, made his way to the door. Colonel Tom's voice stopped him at the doorway.

"Remember, no one is to know that I am here. Call the meeting for ten o'clock tonight."

The man said nothing, left the hut and closed the door behind him.

Colonel Tom turned to the woman. "How old is your child?"

The woman looked down and avoided his eyes. "Almost two".

"Can she speak?"

The woman shook her head. "Only a few words".

The woman made for the doorway. As she did so, Colonel Tom grasped her right wrist, then pulled her towards him, looking down into her eyes and frightened face.

"Go and rearrange the bed, you and I have work to do."

The numerous oil lamps cast long black shadows onto the surrounding walls of the barn, their light picking out the faces and eyes of the assembled men squatting on the floor. Standing at their head was Colonel Tom, shotgun slung over his right shoulder, the bunch of three feathers on his ex-army greatcoat clearly visible. His eyes scanned the assembly and from time to time, rested on one particular man. The effect of this was immediately to cause a silence to descend upon the assembled gathering. He did this several times. Several of the men present had witnessed the death of the old man and felt a deep unease as they looked at this longhaired, unkempt figure. There was something sinister about his appearance. Why had this meeting been called? They were about to find out. Colonel Tom removed the shotgun from his shoulder and held it with both hands across his chest. As he did so, all muttering ceased and there was utter silence. He paused for a brief moment and then spoke.

"My name is Colonel Tom. The last time I visited this farm was to order the execution of a man who had refused to take our sacred oath. Some of you arrested this man and witnessed his death."

He paused again and scanned the gathering, noting that the men he could identify avoided his eyes. He continued, "A few days ago I attended a special meeting of our leaders. We have decided to call our organisation Mau-Mau. This name will be recognised by the *Wazungu* farmers to mean either flee or remain and be killed! Some have already met their deaths, which will act as a warning to others, causing them to heed our warning and leave their farms to us. Soon this farm will be yours!"

This final statement caused a stir in the assembled workers. For effect, he paused again for a few moments.

"Hands-up any man who does not want a share of this farm."

Not a hand was raised. He slowly scanned the men again.

"Everything has its price. If you go to the *duka* (shop) to buy sugar you have to pay for it. If you want a wife, then you have to pay her father bride price. But I am not here to ask for your money. What I want will cost you nothing. Does this appeal to you?"

There were numerous nods from the gathering and some expressions of relief. Colonel Tom paused again, and then continued.

"All I am asking is for some of you to join me in the forest to help carry our fight to every *Wazungu* farmer and his wife who refuse to heed our warning. So, how many here wish to join me?"

He scanned the men one by one. No one moved. Colonel Tom scanned the men again. Every man avoided his eyes.

"No one? Is every man here a coward, content to sit back with his full belly and a warm hut, leaving me and my men to fight for you?"

No one moved and the silence told its own story. Colonel Tom looked down at a man in the front of the gathering.

"Are you a cowardly dog or a man? Well?"

Due to a dry mouth, the man had difficulty in speaking. "I and every man here has a wife and children. If we join you, who will provide the money to feed them?"

Colonel Tom stepped forward and delivered a vicious slap across the man's face. "You are only fit for dog meat! In our army we shoot cowards like you!" He placed the muzzle of the shotgun against the man's forehead. "Open your mouth!"

The man was trembling and made a series of whimpering noises as the muzzle was thrust into his mouth. Colonel Tom scanned the scared faces before him. "Is a dog like this fit to live?"

No one moved or said a word. The gun's muzzle was withdrawn and a hefty kick sent the man sprawling onto his back, causing two of the squatting men behind him lose their balance. Every man's face was etched with fear.

Colonel Tom was enjoying the feeling of power he had over these men. He looked at another man squatting to the left of his previous victim. The man averted his eyes and looked down at the floor of the barn. "Look at me!" Colonel Tom went and stood before the cowed figure, then placed the muzzle of the shotgun underneath the man's chin. "I said look at me."

A series of tremors ran through the man's body and he slowly raised his head as Colonel Tom looked down into his face with narrowed eyes. "And you, have you taken the sacred oath?"

The man nodded his head.

"So you support our cause?"

The man nodded again and tried to look down, but the barrel of the shotgun didn't budge.

The man looked up at this bearded, longhaired, menacing figure.

"My family and I grow extra food for your men and my wife helps to carry this food to the forest edge."

There was a long pause as Colonel Tom again scanned the frightened faces gathered before him, then placed the shotgun over his right shoulder. There was an audible sigh of relief. He continued and pointed. "This man is a true supporter! How many of you also supply food to my men?"

Every hand was raised. Colonel Tom now walked down the left side of the men and stood behind them. Several of the men turned their heads to look in his direction. There was no mistaking the menace in the command: "Did I tell you to look at me? All I want is five, just five of you to join me in our fight against these *Wazungu* farmers. So who will join me?"

No one moved.

"No one? Is everyone here a coward? I will count up to ten. If five men have not raised their hands, I will start to shoot each and every one of you!"

The fact that any noise of shooting would arouse the farmer to telephone the police had not entered the minds of the threatened assembly. Colonel Tom began to count.

"One, two, three, four, five... Just five more to go and I will commence to shoot. Six..."

The whole of the back row raised their hands, including the original victim and two other men squatting in the centre.

"So, we have eleven brave men. The men who have joined my army, go to your huts and collect food and blankets, then join me outside this barn. You have ten minutes. Go!"

The eleven men scrambled to their feet and made for the door. Colonel Tom addressed the remaining men.

"You cowardly dogs will continue to supply us with food and you will support the wives and children of these new soldiers. Now go to your homes!"

With everyone gone, Colonel Tom made his way to the outside of the barn and squatted beside the double doors, resting his shotgun across his knees. He felt well satisfied with his visit to this *Mzungu* farm. He had been well fed, had had a woman, obtained some recruits and kept his supply lines open.

The minutes ticked by and, one by one, his new recruits appeared out of the darkness. At first three, then just one more, each man laden with a blanket and a bundle. Another five minutes passed. Where were the others? Colonel Tom rose to his feet.

"Where are the others?"

No one replied. "I said, where are the others?"

The man nearest to him replied. "I don't know Sir."

Colonel Tom poked the man in the chest with his shotgun.

"Then go and find out!"

The man ran off into the darkness. The waiting continued. Finally, the man returned, panting.

"I have checked their huts Sir, but they are not there and their wives have not seen them."

"Bastards! One night we will return and kill every one of them! Now follow me."

At 10.32 the following morning, Major Fawcett telephoned Njabini Police Station to report that one of his tractor drivers, a clerk and two other workers had disappeared from his farm and no one knew where they had gone.

# CHAPTER TWENTY ONE

DUNDAS AND HIS PATROL, having arrived at the forest edge, were within five hundred yards of the sawmill. In order not to be seen by the workforce, they waited until well past dusk before proceeding to Njabini Police Station under the cover of darkness.

Carrying the three bodies on improvised stretchers had been slow, difficult and at times, due to the terrain, noisier than Dundas would have wished.

The patrol's departure for Nakuru had been arranged quickly and on arrival the three bodies had been deposited in the mortuary, the men's weapons secured in the armoury, and the patrol's return logged in the Police Station O.B. (diary). It was just after 2am as Dundas stopped his Morris Oxford outside his bungalow and thankfully walked up the steps to the entrance.

The brilliant sunlight streaming through a chink in the bedroom curtains woke Dundas from a deep sleep. He slowly opened his eyes, looking up at the apex of the mosquito net suspended above the bed. Stretching made him realise that he felt stiff and tired. He ran his fingers through his hair, stretched again and then sat up. In doing so, he was conscious of his aching shoulder muscles as he recalled the effort and difficulty of carrying the bodies.

Joanne had greeted him with a mixture of kisses and tears, had made him a hot drink and then run his bath. On returning to the bedroom, his only recollection was his head touching the pillow. What was the time? He lifted the mosquito net and picked up his wristwatch. It was almost 11am. For a few moments he lay back on the bed, thinking of what needed to be done during the next few hours. He then sat up and placed his bare feet onto the cool floor. It was time to make a move.

Dundas slipped on his dressing gown and made his way towards the kitchen, rubbing his right hand over the bristles on his chin and face. Steven turned around from the wood-burning stove and greeted him with a broad smile.

"Jambo Effendi! You slept well?"

Dundas yawned and nodded. "Very well Steven. Where's Memsahib?"

"In the garden Effendi. I didn't bring you any tea as Memsahib said I was not to disturb you. Would you like some tea now?"

"Steven, a pot of coffee sounds better. I'll have it on the veranda."

Dundas made his way down the short passage to the lounge, passing through the open French doors onto the veranda. He stood there for a few moments, looking down at the neatly trimmed grass and the pale cream flowers of the frangipani bushes that lined the drive, noting the sharp contrast against the deep red blooms of the hibiscus that framed the entrance to the bungalow. To his right and in the distance he could make out the radio masts of Provincial Headquarters and hear the faint hum of traffic. Had it really been only yesterday that he was in the dank stillness of the Aberdares? His shoulders still ached and, turning, he made the three painful steps and sat heavily into the cane chair. He reached for the steaming pot of coffee on the side table, savouring its aroma and stretched out his six-foot frame, resting his head on the back of the cane chair. He briefly closed his eyes – it was good to be home again!

Following a leisurely if belated breakfast there had been time to spend with Joanne and baby Ian. Now, some two hours later, following a light lunch, Dundas glanced at his watch – almost 2.35 – it was time to depart for Headquarters. As he walked towards the entrance to the Police Station, he mused that it was like having two lives: one fraught with danger, the other, harmonious domesticity.

As he entered the Charge Office he was greeted by the familiar voice of Inspector Farrell, the Duty Officer.

"Robert, everybody wants you. Your boss said to call him the moment you arrived and Bill Stewart has left exactly the same message."

Dundas stopped and leaned on the front of the Charge Office counter. "The joys of being popular!"

Inspector Farrell grinned. "So Robert, how was your fishing trip in the Aberdares?"

Dundas straightened up and stifled a yawn. "We caught three."

"Only three?"

Dundas shook his head several times and stifled another yawn. "It was enough for one day."

Dundas made his way down the highly polished corridor leading from the Charge Office and opened his office door. It was all so familiar, yet he felt as if he had been absent for weeks. He went over to his desk and sat heavily into his chair. As he reached for the phone, he was conscious of the ache in his shoulders. He dialled a two digit internal number and was greeted with the usual terse response.

"Lewis."

"Good afternoon Sir, it's Robert Dundas."

"Robert, congratulations on the success of your patrol! How are you feeling?"

"In a word Sir, tired. Carrying bodies for over ten or so miles over difficult terrain wasn't easy."

"Hmm... As soon as you are free come round to my office, there's a lot to discuss."

There was the usual click and the line went dead. Had he been expecting a sympathetic response but it was obviously not forthcoming. Having replaced the phone into its cradle, he yawned, stretched, then looked out of the window, screwing up his eyes against the bright sunlight. Yes, it was good to be back to normality. He sat there, savouring the thought of being with Joanne and Ian, sleeping in a normal bed, and consuming decent food in place of those Kenya Regiment ration packs. It was time to see his boss. As he stood up, yet again he was conscious of his aching shoulders.

He knocked on Superintendent Lewis's door and, upon receiving the usual "Come" he entered and sat in the left-hand chair facing the desk, noting that the window was open and the pipe was resting in the ash tray. Superintendent Lewis was in an expansive mood.

"So Robert, you managed to clobber three of the gang?"

Realising this was a statement rather than a question, Dundas replied "Yes Sir" and continued. "Sir, I wish to raise a very important point regarding the recovery of the bodies. If we carried fingerprint equipment, we could fingerprint the bodies instead of carrying them all the way back for post-mortems and eventual burial."

Superintendent Lewis leaned back in his chair. "So you propose to bury them where they fell?"

Dundas shook his head. "No Sir, it may sound callous, but once they have been fingerprinted, leave them."

There was a stunned silence. "We can't leave unburied bodies!"

"Sir, we need to consider the practicalities. What if we had killed ten members of the gang? It would have been impossible to carry all of them. And what if two of our men had been wounded and couldn't walk?"

Superintendent Lewis nodded several times and pursed his lips as he contemplated the statement. "Robert, I take your point, but, I cannot see the A.C.P. agreeing to this." He slowly shook his head. "I don't think that I can even put such an idea forward."

Dundas interjected. "Sir, I know it sounds callous and something that the Kenya Police has never ever done in the past, but how else can we deal with this problem? I helped carry out those three bodies along game tracks, down slippery slopes and across difficult terrain. It was arduous and exhausting work. There is one other point I wish to add. Due to the amount of noise created, the patrol could have been ambushed."

Superintendent Lewis nodded but did not give the response that Dundas wanted to hear. "Leave it with me and I'll give it some thought. Now to other business... Our investigations will secure convictions in connection with the Blake and Myers incidents. The next piece of news is that the Government has decided that the Kenya Police needs to expand and currently they are launching a recruiting drive in the UK for six hundred recruits. The initial echelon will be arriving by the end of the month. You look surprised?"

"Not at the news, Sir, but the numbers. Six hundred! Will they have police experience?"

"In the main, no. The idea is we train them here, in situ. A special training school is being set up at Gilgil. Now I'm due to see the A.C.P. in under an hour, so can we go over your report and point out on the wall-map where you encountered the gang."

❖ ❖ ❖

The following morning having been ordered to rest, Dundas was enjoying a leisurely breakfast. The phone rang.

Joanne called from the lounge, "I'll answer it darling."

There was lots of disjointed conversation followed by, "No, he's only having breakfast..." immediately followed by, "Darling, it's Superintendent Lewis. He wishes to speak to you."

Dundas made his way to the lounge, stepped over Ian's large coloured ball and picked up the phone.

"Good morning Sir."

"Robert, sorry to disturb you when you are off duty, but something has cropped up. Njabini Police Station have just reported that Major Fawcett has telephoned, saying that four of his work force have disappeared. Having visited the farm and made enquiries, it appears that they were recruited by a terrorist armed with a shotgun. The description ties in with that given by some of the men you captured. If it is the same man, he calls himself Colonel Tom. A visit to Fawcett's farm may provide us with some valuable leads."

Normally Dundas would have enthused, but he still felt tired and his shoulder muscles still ached. "Sir, may I be honest?"

"Of course."

"Is it possible to put this off until tomorrow morning?"

"So, you are still feeling tired?"

"Bushed is how I would describe myself!"

There was a brief pause. "OK Robert. It is not overly urgent and I'm sure that you need to rest, so let's leave it until tomorrow. Incidentally, what do you think about the latest news?"

Despite holding the phone, Dundas shrugged his shoulders and grunted as his aching muscles reacted. About what Sir?"

"Obviously you didn't listen to the nine o'clock news last night. An armed gang attacked a Kikuyu village at Lari – everything on two legs and four have been butchered. The body count is estimated to be in excess of one hundred and fifty, including children and babies."

Dundas was stunned. "Good God! Over a hundred and fifty?"

"Yes, it's mass murder. Evidently, the Chief had advised his people not to take the oath. It's a bad business. We'll meet tomorrow morning."

Dundas put down the phone. Over one hundred and fifty innocent men, women and children slaughtered! He sat down in his favourite armchair. He still felt shattered and was still conscious of his aches and pains. Slogging along at around eleven thousand feet, carrying a small pack, rations, ammunition, a poncho and blanket, an automatic weapon, plus lack of sound sleep and helping to carry the dead bodies on improvised stretchers had been more draining than he had realised.

❖ ❖ ❖

It was exactly 8.06am as their Land Rover, with Ndibo at the wheel, passed through the fortified entrance of Provincial Headquarters. Ndibo drove up to the main road, turned right along the High Street and headed towards Naivasha. As usual, Dundas was sandwiched between Ndibo and Superintendent Lewis, his legs straddling the gearbox housing. At this time of the year, it was a beautiful, warm sunny morning. Dundas stared at the unfolding landscape, deep in thought. Superintendent Lewis's words brought him back to reality.

"The Inspector from Njabini will be meeting us at Fawcett's and he's bringing a Corporal from his Crime Branch Section who speaks Kikuyu. He has been in touch with Major Fawcett, who reports that some of the farm labour have the hunted look, so one or two of them may wish to give us some information. Evidently, this man Colonel Tom led the gang that you arrested, so you must have missed him by a whisker. According to some of your prisoners, he was responsible for the death of an old man who had been on Fawcett's farm for years. He was killed because he refused to take the oath. They have also told us that this so-called Colonel Tom also shot and killed the head clerk from the Myers farm when he tried to escape from the gang."

Dundas nodded several times. "It's all coming together. But wasn't it assumed that having failed to lure Mr Myers outside, he had joined the gang of his own free will?"

"We think so, but the main reason for his murder, so we've been told, was that he had been selected to kill the old man on Fawcett's farm. On the way to the farm he tried to make a run for it and whereupon the so-called colonel shot him in the back."

"Sir, is he the main gang leader in the Kinankop area?"

Superintendent Lewis shrugged his shoulders. "That we do not know, but he certainly headed up *your* gang. As yet, Special Branch do not have any additional information."

For a few moments, Dundas lapsed back into thought.

"Sir, this oath that the Kikuyu have been taking... What if someone can be offered immunity from prosecution and then used to identify the Mau-Mau ringleaders on each farm? We have the exercise books with lists of names."

Superintendent Lewis shook his head. "If his identity became known, he wouldn't last five minutes."

"I agree Sir, but what if the person was disguised? For example, covered by a sack with slits for the eyes and mouth. He would be seated in a police vehicle simply nodding. This way his identity would be safe.

Or perhaps we could use the woman we captured to identify the ring-leaders."

Superintendent Lewis looked pensive. "I suspect that the woman will have limited knowledge. It would have to be one of your arrested gang members. I would suggest the Blakes' former houseboy. On balance it sounds to be a good idea. I'll discuss it with Special Branch. Hmm... it could work. Good thinking Robert. It will mean obtaining immunity from prosecution, so Crown Counsel will need to be involved. Yes, it's worth a try..."

❖ ❖ ❖

The Land Rover turned off the murram surface and headed down the dirt road to the Fawcett farm, coming to rest outside the farmhouse entrance. Ndibo switched off the engine. Superintendent Lewis opened the passenger door and climbed out, quickly followed by Dundas. As they did so, the French door opened to reveal Major Fawcett, dressed in a blue check, short-sleeved shirt, baggy khaki shorts and long khaki stockings, set off with a pair of highly polished brown brogue shoes. Dundas noted that he had a pipe tucked into the top of his right stocking. Superintendent Lewis raised his hand in greeting.

"Good morning Major Fawcett." He stepped forward and held out his hand. "Superintendent Lewis, Provincial C.I.D. Nakuru. You have met Chief Inspector Dundas before."

Major Fawcett looked keenly at Dundas. "So, why no uniform?"

Dundas smiled. "Sir, this time I am not on special duties."

Major Fawcett seemed to be in a hurry. "Right, you chaps carry on, I'm off to Naivasha. If you need anything, ask the cook."

With these words, he stepped past them and made his way towards an old Ford van, started the engine and headed for the exit.

Superintendent Lewis grunted. "Hmm... not a very effusive greeting,"

"Evidently, Sir, he doesn't like the police."

Superintendent Lewis turned and looked at the disappearing vehicle. "So Robert, where is the Inspector from Njabini? In the meantime, as suggested, let's start with the cook."

The cook was in the kitchen preparing a curry. He looked up as Superintendent Lewis and Dundas appeared at the open exterior door. *"Jambo Bwana."*

Superintendent Lewis sniffed appreciatively. "Chicken curry?"

The cook visibly relaxed. *"Ndiyo Bwana."*

Superintendent Lewis stepped through the open doorway and stood beside the cook. "What has happened to the missing men?"

The cook put his knife down onto the bench, wiped his hands on his white apron and looked stressed. Superintendent Lewis continued.

"Have they joined a Mau-Mau gang?"

The cook had difficulty in replying. "I don't know Bwana."

Superintendent Lewis's next question caused the cook to start trembling. "What can you tell me about a man who calls himself Colonel Tom? He has long hair and a shotgun." Superintendent Lewis paused. "Why are you trembling?"

The cook continued to avoid eye contact. "I'm not well Bwana."

"Rubbish!" Superintendent Lewis thumped his fist onto the wooden kitchen table, causing the knife to jump. "You know that they have joined this man Colonel Tom, don't you?"

The cook wiped his hands on his apron again and stared at the floor. Superintendent Lewis repeated his question. There was a long silence and a series of shivers wracked the cook's body. He went as if to speak but his mouth was too dry. He tried again. "Bwana police, if I speak he will kill me, just as he killed the old man the other night."

"Killed? How do you know this?"

Another shiver wracked the cook's body. "Colonel Tom made us watch."

Superintendent Lewis looked keenly at the cook. "Who did he kill?"

The cook could not control his trembling limbs. "The man who refused to take part in a special meeting. He had him killed. We had to watch."

Superintendent Lewis turned to Dundas. "This is incredible! And they are too bloody scared to report it!" He turned to the cook again. "How many men saw this man die and where was he killed?"

"Ten Bwana. He was strangled." The cook shivered again and looked at the floor.

Superintendent Lewis gestured. "Where is the body?"

"They put the old man down a pit latrine."

"They? Do you mean Colonel Tom's men or men from this farm?"

The cook shook his head and was almost cringing with fear. "Bwana police, if I tell you any more he will kill me, my wife and my children."

Superintendent Lewis looked towards the doorway. "Robert, it sounds like a Land Rover, it could be the Inspector from Njabini. Go and take a look."

Dundas went outside to observe a police Land Rover coming down towards the farm, leaving a cloud of red dust in its wake. It stopped beside their vehicle. As the European officer alighted, Dundas recognised the Inspector from Njabini. The Inspector came over and saluted.

"Sorry I'm late Sir, there was a report of two Mau-Mau seen in the area, although it proved to be a false alarm."

Purely out of habit, Dundas glanced at his watch. "Superintendent Lewis is in the kitchen questioning the cook. He has told us that the old man reported as missing was strangled and his body dumped down a latrine. I want you to round up all the farm labour and bring them here."

"Are they all involved?"

"No, but according to the cook some of them were involved and ten men were made to witness the old man being killed."

The Inspector saluted and hurried away as Dundas returned to the kitchen.

The cook was now seated on a stool, holding his head in his hands and trembling. On hearing Dundas approach, Superintendent Lewis turned towards the doorway. "Well?"

"It was the Inspector from Njabini Sir. I've sent him to round up the farm labour."

Superintendent Lewis nodded. "Excellent! I've discovered this so called meeting was an oathing ceremony and the cook, having told me this, is now convinced that the oath will kill him. As we have already lost one cook I have placed him under arrest and cautioned him."

Superintendent Lewis placed his hand on the cook's shoulder.

"We are calling everyone together. Leave the cooking and sit on the grass with the others. Robert, keep an eye on him."

In twos and threes, the farm labour started to gather. Their expressions ranged from fear to sullenness. When the last man was seated on the grass, Superintendent Lewis addressed them.

"I have a book. In it the man who calls himself Colonel Tom has listed all your names and the five shillings that each of you have paid to help the Mau-Mau." He paused and scanned the group, as he studied their shocked faces, then continued. "Under duress, four men from this farm joined a Mau-Mau gang and are now hiding in the forest. We also know that ten of you witnessed an old man being killed." The men's expressions now registered complete and utter shock, then fear. Superintendent Lewis continued. "What had the old man done? He had refused to take the Mau-Mau oath and pay five shillings." He paused and scanned the group again. Every man avoided his eyes.

He pointed to a man in the front row. "Did you see him killed?"

The man shook his head and stared at the ground.

Superintendent Lewis pointed to another man. "How about you?"

The man remained silent and like his colleague stared at the ground. Superintendent Lewis scanned the men again.

"I want you to listen very carefully. Any man here involved in this old man's death in any way whatsoever, as from now will not sleep soundly in their beds. Why do I say this? Because we will find out who you are. Every time you see a policeman or someone knocks on your door at night, your stomachs will be gripped with fear. Before you took this Mau-Mau oath and paid your five shillings, you were happy with your lot. Now I can see that no one here smiles; it is a place of fear."

The men continued to stare at the ground; some could not control their trembling hands.

Superintendent Lewis then addressed the Inspector from Njabini.

"Inspector, take these men to their pit latrines, where they are going to retrieve the body of the old man... and take your armed constables with you."

As the men walked away, Superintendent Lewis turned to Dundas.

"Don't be surprised if someone wants to confess. The thought of seeing the old man's body may be more than they can stomach. If someone does crack, it's ten to one he'll shop the others."

Superintendent Lewis sat down on the farmhouse steps, fumbled in his right-hand jacket pocket, withdrew his pipe and tobacco pouch, then proceeded to fill the bowl. Using his chrome plated lighter, he drew the flame down into the tobacco, sucked several times and then blew a plume of blue grey smoke into the air.

"Robert, what they don't know is that we know about the food being dumped daily on the forest edge. Assuming that this man Colonel Tom believed your ruse that he has been deserted by his men, then ambushing the food dump could nobble him and his four recruits. How soon can you organise this?"

"If we are back at base by this evening, we could leave the following evening at dusk. So we could be in position by dawn the following morning."

The noisy approach of an old Ford van with its attendant cloud of red dust made Superintendent Lewis look up.

"I have reason to believe that the arrest of his cook will not be well received by Major Fawcett. Add to this the fact his chicken curry will not now materialise. We have the ideal mixture for apoplexy!"

The van stopped beside the steps, whereupon the Major clambered out and greeted them with a cheery, "You chaps being looked after?" quickly followed by, "Care to join me for lunch? It's chicken curry."

Superintendent Lewis stood up. "I'm sorry Sir, that will not be possible. Your cook is under arrest."

The Major's geniality vanished in an instant. "You've arrested my cook! So how the hell am I going to eat? You tell me that!" He went very red in the face, breathing heavily.

Superintendent Lewis chose his words very carefully.

"The reason for his arrest is that he is implicated in the murder of the old man, whose body is currently being retrieved from one of the pit latrines in your labour lines. The other information we have for you is that the four men missing from your farm have joined a Mau-Mau gang who are now hiding in the forest. We also have documentary evidence that your entire Kikuyu male labour force have taken the Mau-Mau oath, part of which includes a pledge to kill Europeans. There was only one exception. The old man refused to become involved and that is why he was killed."

Major Fawcett looked shocked. Superintendent Lewis continued.

"I suggest that henceforth you secure all your doors and windows before dusk. Do not open the door to anyone unless you hear a European voice and keep your firearms and ammunition beside you at all times. One other thing; after dusk, keep your curtains drawn."

Major Fawcett was visibly shaken. "My God! Some of these men have grown up on this farm and their parents are still in my employ."

Superintendent Lewis turned to Dundas. "We had better go and see how the recovery of the old man's body is progressing." He turned to Major Fawcett. "Before we go, do not mention to anyone on this farm that you are aware of their lack of loyalty. Now, if you will excuse me..."

When they were out of earshot, Superintendent Lewis remarked, "Hopefully, what will ensure his safety is the food supply to our friend Colonel Tom. The labour force does not know that we are aware of its existence and neither does Major Fawcett."

# CHAPTER TWENTY TWO

COLONEL TOM, WITH HIS NOW DEPLETED band of just four men, was not in a good mood. His new recruits had not taken kindly to life in the forest. Their expressions constantly registered dejection and despite his pep-talk, followed by a threat to shoot anyone who tried to desert, their mood had not changed. What would dispel their apathy? Perhaps what they needed was a taste of action and the subsequent spoils. The nearest and most obvious target was the *mzungu* farm where his four recruits had been employed. There would be firearms and his men could kill the *mzungu*. Colonel Tom sat beside the stream, contemplating this idea, but he soon realised that killing the *mzungu* would result in the farm swarming with police and put an end to his food supply. Perhaps a better plan would be to go to the farm at night, select one of the men who had failed to join him, strangle the man in front of his colleagues, then have his body thrown down a pit latrine. This seemed a better idea and could result in several more recruits joining him. The death of the old man had not resulted in any police activity and their refuge in the forest had not been disturbed. His thoughts turned to that slimy bastard Sergeant Simba. Where was he now? No doubt strutting around with his self-imposed rank of colonel. He had taken his men and his woman but fortunately not the buried oathing money. Murderous thoughts ran through his mind as he pictured the cringing sergeant pleading for his life. He savoured the thought of pulling the trigger.

❖ ❖ ❖

At Major Fawcett's farm, the gruesome task of recovering the old man's partly decomposed body had been completed. The sight and the stench had resulted in many of the men, including the police, gagging and retching. It had also reminded those who had witnessed the killing and the dumping of the body, of the enormity of their crime.

The police had been on the farm all day, asking questions and searching their huts. Nothing had been found and no one had talked. Only Bwana Fawcett's cook had been arrested and taken away. The men wondered if he would keep his mouth shut. They remembered the words of the Bwana Police with grey hair and the strain was evident in their faces.

It was past midnight as each man made his way to the barn, the faint moonlight casting soft shadows. A dog started to bark. There was a muffled shout followed by a whimper. Then all was quiet again. Within the barn oil lamps were burning, casting black shadows onto the walls, the light picking out the brown skins of the four squatting men. At first no one spoke, each man alone with his own thoughts. The silence was broken by the *shamba*-boy (gardener).

"We need to discuss what we should do. Should we run away and join the others in the forest? What if the cook has talked?"

Another man spoke. "He may give our names and then the police could arrive at any time to arrest us."

Squatting in a circle, with the light from their oil lanterns casting flickering shadows onto the surrounding walls, gave the scene an eerie appearance. Peter, a tractor driver, spoke up.

"What the Bwana police said is true. We now live in fear of discovery and arrest. We should flee into the forest to join the others. If we stay here we may be arrested and hanged." There were several nods of agreement. He continued, "We have taken the oath. One day this farm will be ours and then we can return here without fear of arrest."

One of the men looked doubtful. "But how will we know where they are?"

Peter the tractor driver spoke again. "Our women take food into the forest almost daily. All we have to do is to wait there beside the sacks."

A man named Wynyna nodded his head, spat onto the floor and then looked at the other three men. "So are we agreed, it is best to flee?"

The other three nodded in agreement.

The man Peter spoke again. "These are brave words, but when do we flee? Tonight? Or do we take a risk and do so tomorrow at dusk? If we see the police coming tomorrow, providing our blankets and some possessions are ready, it will not be difficult to evade arrest."

❖ ❖ ❖

Very early the following day, Dundas was in Superintendent Lewis's office studying the wall map.

Superintendent Lewis leaned back in his chair and stretched.

"So Robert, what do you suggest?"

Dundas was still looking intently at the wall-map.

"I was contemplating where to look if Colonel Tom has moved his camp."

Superintendent Lewis grunted. "We know that the four missing men from Fawcett's farm have joined him. Don't forget that we have an ace up our sleeve; neither he nor the Kikuyu on the farm know that we are aware of the food dump. Because of this, I believe the gang will not move. We, or should I say *you*, have the ideal opportunity to arrest this man Colonel Tom, together with the remnants of his gang. For any group of men, food is imperative, so I do not believe that our activity at Fawcett's has caused him to move."

Dundas nodded. "Sir, I agree. Whatever their situation, they will continue to need food. As previously discussed, we will lay an ambush at the food dump tonight. If they fail to appear, we will remain for a further 48 hours."

Superintendent Lewis nodded. "Agreed. Are there any points that you wish to raise?"

"Yes Sir. Until now, no one in my team has been wounded. Have you any news about my request for morphine? The other question is about the non-recovery of any bodies."

Superintendent Lewis nodded his head. "I understand the need Robert, but on the morphia question, to date I do not have any infor-mation. As regards bodies, I have discussed this with the A.C.P. He is of the opinion that all bodies should be recovered and, in the case of this being difficult or impossible, then the regular police will carry out this task, using a map reference supplied by your patrol. Any other questions?"

"Yes Sir. When is it planned that I return to C.I.D. duties?"

Superintendent Lewis smiled. "I have also discussed this with the A.C.P. As soon as the man Colonel Tom is in custody, you and I will finalise the cases stemming from all the arrests that you have made. No doubt Joanne will be delighted to have you back on normal duties."

"I must admit, Sir, that it has been a strain. Joanne has been wonderful and very supportive, but there have been tears each time I go away."

Superintendent Lewis joined Dundas at the wall-map and held out his hand.

"Robert, let's hope this whole case can be finalised and you can return to normal duties. Good luck – and don't take any undue risks."

Several score miles away, Colonel Tom had made up his mind – he would make an example of one of the men on the *mzungu* farm and as a result, on the return journey back to their hideout, he would have at least two or more recruits. And maybe, witnessing what happened to anyone who had taken the oath but refused or avoided their duty to the cause, would produce even more 'volunteers' in future. He stood up and sauntered down to the two shelters being used by his men. As he approached, they all stood up. He stopped and examined their faces. There was no change. He prodded one of the men in the chest.

"You!" The man looked apprehensive. "Have you ever killed anyone?"

"No Sir."

Colonel Tom placed his face inches away. "You are now a soldier and your duty is to kill! Understand?"

The man started to tremble and nodded his head. Colonel Tom's voice conveyed menace. "I said *understand*?"

Due to a dry mouth the man had difficulty in replying. "Yes Sir."

Colonel Tom stood back and scanned the four men.

"Tonight we are going to the *mzungu's* farm to arrest the men who failed to join us. One of them will be killed as an example to the others. One of you will use *this*." He held up a thin, plaited cord.

"Having completed our task, on the return journey we will be carrying the food left at the usual place by the womenfolk. Any questions?"

The man who had been poked in the chest, despite his dry mouth, managed to speak. "Sir, who will kill this man?"

Colonel Tom scowled and looked each man in the face. "I will decide that tonight." With these words, he turned on his heels and made his way back to his hut.

Once he was out of sight, the four recruits looked at each other with one thought in mind. Who would be selected?

Later that night, Dundas and his team de-bussed very close to the dirt road leading to Fawcett's farm. All was quiet. He looked at his luminous wristwatch – almost nine thirty. There was only starlight and it took some minutes for his eyes to adjust. As the lorry quietly drove off with doused lights, Dundas formed his team up on the side of the road. He kept his voice to a whisper.

"As we discussed this afternoon, we will use the usual patrol formation and we will use our previous route. Let's move."

Now that his eyes had adjusted to the starlight Dundas found that he could see Kipchumba's outline quite clearly and had no difficulty in seeing his hand signals. Kipchumba stopped from time to time, then motioned them forward.

By now they were very close to the gate that led into the field holding the cattle. Some distance ahead a dog barked and there was a stab of light as a hut door opened. A man's voice was heard shouting, followed by the noise of a door closing and the distant light was extinguished. Kipchumba raised his right hand, then, placing his outstretched arm palm down, made several up and down motions, indicated for the patrol crouch down. Dundas carefully made his way forward and whispered, "What is it?"

"Something must have disturbed the dog Effendi."

"Hyena?"

Before Kipchumba could whisper a reply, the dog started barking again. Another hut door opened and a man's voice could be heard shouting at the dog. For a few moments all was quiet, then the dog started barking again.

Kipchumba pointed ahead. "*Ni watu* (it's people) *Effendi*."

As Dundas strained his eyes to look ahead, another hut door opened. Kipchumba lightly tapped Dundas on the arm.

"Effendi, a man has just left that hut. I believe that there was another man outside."

The dog began barking again and was joined by two others. Some moments later, the barking ceased. Dundas considered the situation. It could be just one or two men sharing a beer. The important thing was to be in position without being discovered and to ambush the food dump from first light. He decided to follow their usual route to just inside the forest edge and then bed-down for the night.

He tapped Kipchumba on the shoulder. "Let's move off."

Having negotiated the farm gate without incident, they cautiously made their way across the field containing the cattle, Kipchumba stopping from time to time and then motioning them forward. Dundas held his luminous wristwatch close to his face. They would be at the forest edge in less than 25 minutes.

Suddenly there was the sound of a shot about half a mile away and slightly to their right. It was quickly followed by another. What was going on? The two shots sounded hollow, unlike the distinctive *crack* of a rifle. Surely, the police from Njabini were not in the area?

Dundas moved forward to Kipchumba. "It sounded like a shotgun. Stay down and I'll go back to Corporal Abikar and the others."

Corporal Abikar was facing to his front. Dundas knelt down beside him. "I think the shots were made by a shotgun and they came from the direction of the forest. We will need to go and investigate. I'll go back and speak to the others."

Dundas finally knelt down beside Sergeant James. "Those shots sounded like a shotgun, we will need to go forward to investigate, but we will need to be very cautious, for all we know it could be the police from Njabini. I will pass the word down the line."

With Dundas back in position, the patrol moved forward, making every effort not to make the slightest sound. The tension mounted every time Kipchumba stopped and crouched down. Dundas could feel his heart rate increasing. Any moment they could be fired on. Kipchumba stopped again and motioned Dundas forward. He pointed ahead and slightly to their right, then cupped his hand behind his right ear. Dundas strained to catch the slightest sound.

"What is it?" He whispered.

"It sounds like someone in pain Effendi."

"How far away?"

"About a hundred or more paces Effendi."

Dundas listened again. Nothing. Then he heard it. It sounded like a faint groan. This posed a problem. As there was only starlight, it was dangerous to split the patrol. When men are tense, anything can happen. He tapped Kipchumba on the shoulder.

"We will continue moving forward. Go very, very slowly."

Suddenly, there was the sound of people running almost towards them. Dundas felt his heart rate increase even more. At a distance that he estimated to be no more than 25 yards, he shouted out in Kiswahili.

"Halt! Police!"

Being crouched down, he could now make out two figures running away and to their left. He shouted again. "Police... halt or we fire!"

The two figures were almost out of sight as Dundas raised the Sten-gun to his shoulder and, aiming low, pulled the trigger.

The Sten juddered against his right shoulder as twelve 9mm bullets thudded into the fleeing figures and they crashed to the ground. Dundas stayed in his crouched position. The only sounds were the loud groans coming from the two figures. Had he done the right thing? Now it was important to establish who they were. Crouching low, Dundas went back to Corporal Abikar.

"Pass the word down the line. Speak to each man personally. Kipchumba and I will go and investigate."

With Corporal Abikar's return, Dundas felt into his camouflage smock for his pencil torch and then he and Kipchumba, guns at the ready, moved towards the two groaning figures. Dundas knelt down beside them and switched on his torch. The two men were unarmed and did not have long plaited hair. One had stopped groaning and was apparently dead. Dundas shone his torch onto the face of the second man.

"Who are you and where are you from?"

The man groaned again with pain and opened his eyes.

"I drive Bwana Fawcett's tractor..." His voice tailed off and he groaned again. Dundas shone his torch on the man's body. Blood was oozing from both legs. Dundas spoke to Kipchumba.

"Go and bring the patrol here – but make sure they know it's you."

He opened the left hip pocket of his smock and removed the small brown cotton covered pack marked 'Field Dressing.' He turned to the man again and, with the pencil torch in his mouth, began to rip open the man's trouser legs to expose the wounds.

"Why didn't you stop when I shouted?"

The man opened his eyes and grimaced with pain.

"We thought that you had come to arrest us."

"What had you done?"

The man remained silent as Dundas applied the large wound dressing to the man's left leg. The exit wounds were in the front of the leg below the knee – he would need more 'Field Dressings' and to stem the bleeding he would have to apply pressure above the wounds. He needed help! He shouted for Sergeant James.

"Sir!"

"I need you to assist me to save this man from bleeding to death!"

He turned to the man again. "We heard two shots. Was it you?"

The man groaned with pain as Dundas tightened the wound dressing, shook his head and...

"The other two are dead."

"So there were four of you. What were you doing?"

The man closed his eyes and was silent.

❖ ❖ ❖

Earlier that same day, Colonel Tom, having had his meal brought to him by one of his new recruits, was sitting outside his hut cleaning his shotgun. He thought about the forthcoming evening. His four men were without any form of weapon, not even a *panga*.

The group of five men set off about an hour before sundown. As the light began to fade, the birdcalls became less and less and the hyrax began their nocturnal screeching. Colonel Tom had made a great show of loading both barrels of his shotgun, snapping it closed and applying the safety catch. Now in the lead and despite having only four unarmed men, it gave him a sense of power.

It was now dark, yet the fallen bamboo leaves on the game tracks highlighted their route, which when they were close to the forest edge would take them very close to where the food was secreted. They continued ahead, each of the four men deep in thought about the night ahead.

Suddenly, Colonel Tom had the shock of his life. In the dim light, two figures were directly in his path and only yards away. Police! He fired both barrels, turned and fled back down the track, all bravado having disappeared in an instant. He soon ran into the other members of his gang and managed to avoid two men but in his haste his left shoulder came into violent contact with a third man, sending him sprawling into the undergrowth. Moving at speed was difficult and it was some quarter of a mile later that he stopped to catch his breath. Where were the others? Still panting, he felt into the right hand pocket of his ex-army greatcoat and, with shaking hands, withdrew two more 12-bore cartridges and inserted them into his shotgun. His fear was tempered with pride. He had shot and possibly killed two policemen! Later that night, it dawned on him that the police may have found his food source – and if so, someone must have talked.

His four recruits had been stunned by the rapid change of events. There had been two loud explosions and stabs of flame from their leader's gun – in the confusion he had barged past knocking two of them to the ground and had deserted them. Their only course of action was to follow his example and flee.

Panting with fear and exhaustion, they stumbled their way back along the game track towards their camp.

As the four men stumbled towards their camp there was no question of stopping, fear of the police, who no doubt, were 'close on their heels' kept their levels of adrenalin coursing through their bodies. Suddenly, from the direction of the farm there was the sound of distant rapid gunfire. There was no time to pause for breath! In their panic to flee, they ran into several low-hanging branches. Oblivious to the pain, sometimes on their hands and knees, they stumbled and scrambled as they nosily made their escape deeper into the forest.

❖ ❖ ❖

The noise of the two shots, followed in minutes by the burst of fire from Dundas's Sten gun, had alerted Major Fawcett, who, having doused his solitary Tilley lamp, picked up his .455 Webley revolver and made his way to the telephone to call the police at Njabini.

Just a few hundred yards of the farmhouse, with the help of Sergeant James, the wounded man's bleeding had been stemmed and, between groans and grimaces, the story had started to emerge. Four of the farm workers, in order to avoid arrest, had decided to join Colonel Tom. After waiting by the food dump, on hearing someone approaching they had stepped out onto the track but had immediately been fired on. Their attacker had fled back into the forest. Two of them had been seriously wounded, so the remaining two had stayed with the men until they died. They had decided to continue into the forest was dangerous, therefore they decided to return to their homes.

Dundas considered the facts. No doubt Colonel Tom, or some other members of his Mau-Mau gang, had killed the two men. Their bodies could be retrieved later. However, he now had to consider their own situation. If he knocked on Major Fawcett's door, despite making it known he was a European, there was a risk of being shot at. Although the Inspector at Njabini knew they were in the area, Major Fawcett must have phoned them and they would be on their way in force. The safest thing was to make their way back to the dirt road leading to the farmhouse and wait. On seeing the headlights of the police vehicle, he would uncover his arms, remove his beret and stand in the middle of the road. The wounded man would have to be carried. His dead companion would be left until later.

The patrol reached the dirt road without incident. Within minutes, headlights could be seen approaching at speed. It was time to make a move. Dundas removed his beret and smock, rolled up the sleeves of his khaki woollen shirt and stood alone in the centre of the farmhouse road.

The Land Rover stopped about nine feet away. A door opened and slammed shut. In the glare of the headlights, Dundas could see that it was the Inspector from Njabini. The Inspector stepped forward.

"Are you OK Sir? The Major reported hearing automatic fire."

Dundas held out his hand. "Yes we're OK. We have a wounded man here who is from this farm. There's a dead man about half a mile from here and evidently two more dead men, who are also from this farm, shot by Mau-Mau. I suggest that you go and calm down Major Fawcett. We will await here for your return.

The Inspector saluted and returned to his vehicle.

Some ten minutes later, the Inspector was back.

"Right Sir, what can we do to help?"

"We need to recover all three bodies. I will come with you. Sergeant James…"

"Sir."

"You are in charge until I return. Keep the patrol here."

When the bodies were recovered, scattered beside the game track were four bundles of personal items wrapped in blankets. It was obvious what had happened and confirmed the wounded man's story.

Back at the roadside, Dundas decided that it was time to make a move. Using a page from his police notebook, he quickly drafted a message.

"Inspector."

"Sir."

"Upon your return to Njabini, I want you to send this message to Superintendent Lewis, Provincial C.I.D. Nakuru. It covers what has happened here and our immediate intentions."

With the departure of the Inspector and his men, Dundas gathered the patrol around him.

"Tonight we will camp just inside the forest edge. Then, soon after first light, we will attempt to track down and arrest the man or men who shot the two farm workers."

❖ ❖ ❖

# CHAPTER TWENTY THREE

THE PATROL HAD CAMPED just inside the forest edge, adopting their usual circular formation. Dundas considered the chance of a surprise attack to be very slight, so he had opted to take the pre-dawn guard duty.

Sleep had not come very easily. The hyrax emitted their usual screams and despite his sweater and the long puttee wound round his middle, he was cold. What kept running through his mind was shooting the two men. He had shouted twice, little realising that this had made them veer away and run even faster. How would this be viewed at the Inquest?

Someone was shaking his shoulder.

"Effendi, Effendi. Time to take over."

Dundas sat up and rubbed his eyes, then glanced at his luminous wristwatch. Almost four thirty and it was as black as pitch. Thank goodness it wasn't raining. The usual forest noises were there but the hyrax were silent. He carefully made his way to the centre of the sleeping men and then squatted down in the same posture as per his team when they were on guard duty. Surprisingly, it was very comfortable, once your muscles had adjusted to the unusual strains. What would daylight bring? In the far distance, a hyrax emitted its strange cry. Within seconds, another hyrax responded. Soon the whole forest was echoing with strange screams. Only the first light of dawn would once again bring silence.

As usual, the dawn chorus heralded the start to the new day and the hyrax, one by one, fell silent. It was time to wake the men.

The patrol members were now old hands at breaking camp. In just fifteen minutes they were ready. They moved off, stopping at the food dump to destroy, as best they could, the maize meal and cabbages. While they did so, Kipchumba and Corporal Abikar searched for tracks. Within less than ten minutes they returned, displaying broad grins. Corporal Abikar saluted.

"Effendi, there were five men. One of them was in a hurry to return into the forest. Whoever it was collided into bushes and there were signs of where he had fallen down. There are signs showing at least four if not five other men couldn't have known the route. Like the first man there are clear signs of having run into bushes and fallen down."

Dundas nodded. "Excellent! So the tracks that you have found, how could you separate the single set of tracks from the other four or five men?"

Corporal Abikar, still grinning, said, "Very easily Effendi. The single man knew the route. Where he had not collided with bushes or fallen down, his tracks were wide spaced, so where possible he was running. The others were closer together."

Dundas gestured. "Are these tracks easy to follow?"

"Very easy Effendi!"

❖ ❖ ❖

From time to time Kipchumba paused and, using the barrel of his rifle, pointed out where someone had collided with a bush or slipped and fallen on the wet game track. After about half a mile, Kipchumba held up his hand, indicating that the patrol should halt. He then motioned Dundas to come forward.

"Effendi, look here. One man rested here."

Dundas noted the disturbed leaves and twigs. "Is it one of the four men?"

Kipchumba shook his head. "No Effendi. The prints just back there show where he had been running, so he must have known the route."

"Did the other four join him here?"

Kipchumba shook his head again. "Effendi, look here. Their footprints are on top of his. Now just look ahead. His prints are wide spaced, so even from here he started running again – yet their prints are normally spaced."

Dundas glanced at his wristwatch. "We need to move on."

The direction in which the patrol was heading would appear to lead to the Mau-Mau camp they had discovered previously. 'Is it possible that the same hideout is still being used?' Dundas wondered. If so, his ruse must have worked.

Sunlight was penetrating the overhead canopy, illuminating the rising moisture in its beams. Apart from the occasional birdcall, there was utter silence. The patrol was in extended formation, each man treading cautiously to avoid stepping on fallen twigs. From time to time Kipchumba would stop and indicate that they should crouch down and Dundas would feel his heart rate increase.

It was mid-day when Dundas decided to call a halt and the patrol formed their defensive ring. Kipchumba faced forward and Sergeant James to the rear, with the remainder of the patrol in the same prone position facing alternatively left and right.

In prone position, Dundas felt into his smock pocket for his Mars bar. Suddenly Kipchumba made a low whistle and cupped his right hand to his ear, then indicated with two fingers a walking motion. The bend in the game track concealed most of the patrol – there was no time to lose... Dundas stretched out his foot until it made contact with the man next down the line. The man turned his head and Dundas repeated Kipchumba's sign language, then motioned Corporal Abikar to come forward, indicating him to hide behind the nearest tree. Kipchumba glanced back at Dundas and gave the thumbs-up sign, then eased himself off the track. Dundas did the same and tightened his grip on the Sten gun. How many were heading in their direction and were they armed? The moments ticked by. Dundas cursed that he had been unable to alert the rest of the patrol. From his concealed position, he watched the track anxiously.

A solitary figure, walking very quickly, passed by, making no attempt to avoid broken twigs. The man was short-haired and looked like a farm worker. As he passed, Dundas saw Corporal Abikar quickly step from behind the tree and hit the man in the stomach with the butt of his Remington shotgun. The man gave a gasp and collapsed in a heap. Dundas waited a few moments until he was sure that the man was alone, then joined Corporal Abikar. Dundas rolled the man onto his stomach and quickly searched him. He was unarmed. Dundas turned to Corporal Abikar.

"Pass the word what has happened, then return here."

He knelt beside the prisoner. "Which Mau-Mau gang are you with?"

The man turned his face to one side and muttered, "Colonel Tom's."

Dundas continued to apply the handcuffs. "How many in the gang?"

"Four."

"Only four? So where were you going?"

Between gasps the man replied, "I decided to leave so I escaped."

"Escaped! Why did you escape?"

The man had difficulty talking. "Colonel Tom is always hitting us and threatening to shoot us."

The man continued to gasp and grimace in pain.

"Where do you come from?"

At first his prisoner didn't answer, then mumbled, "Bwana Fawcett's farm."

"Do you know who killed the old man?"

The man remained silent. Dundas looked up as Corporal Abikar returned. He turned to the man again.

"Is Colonel Tom in his camp?"

The man grunted. "He was in his hut."

"And the others?"

"Out gathering firewood."

"How many guns do they have?"

"Just Colonel Tom's."

Dundas glanced at his watch. They could be at the camp in under two hours. He spoke in a low voice.

"Corporal Abikar."

"Effendi."

"Take this man and hand him over to Sergeant James. Tell him this man is to be cautioned. Also I will come back and brief the patrol."

Dundas considered sending their prisoner back to Fawcett's farm under the escort of two of the patrol but decided against it. If the patrol or the gang sustained casualties, every uninjured man would be needed.

The plan to capture the gang was fairly basic. Move forward with caution and, barring mishaps, keep the camp under observation. Then, subject to the situation, at first light, take the camp by surprise and arrest the four men, or, if the opportunity presented itself, attack before the light faded.

Stealth would be of the utmost importance. In order to ensure that their prisoner could not raise the alarm, during the final approach, a small 'field dressing' would be used as a gag. It was time to inform the patrol.

Dundas stressed the need for stealth. Only when the camp was under observation could a decision be taken as to their course of action. If they attacked during daylight, the signal would be a long blast on his whistle.

It was now almost four-thirty. The patrol had been in concealed positions for nearly twenty-five minutes observing Colonel Tom's camp. It was evident that no guards had been posted, hence their prisoner had been able to escape. Security had been abandoned. Nothing of note had been seen. Beside the stream, at a distance of some 35 yards, three unarmed figures could be seen crouched around a fire that was giving off an abundance of smoke. There was no sign of Colonel Tom. Should they wait until daybreak or make a move now? Dundas weighed up the options. Where was Colonel Tom? He was conscious of a feeling of impatience to 'get the job done'. Perhaps Colonel Tom was in or near his hut. Dundas tapped Kipchumba on the shoulder and indicated by sign language that he would crawl over to Corporal Abikar. Kipchumba nodded his head in understanding. Having crawled to Corporal Abikar, he held up three fingers and pointed several times across the stream. Corporal Abikar nodded. Still holding up three fingers and making a circular motion with the same hand, pointing across the stream, Dundas conveyed that three members of the patrol should cross the stream to prevent any escapes. Corporal Abikar nodded again and then, with extreme caution, began to make contact with three members of the patrol. Dundas continued to observe the three huddled figures; they had hardly moved and were clearly oblivious to their situation.

Corporal Abikar crawled back and stopped beside Dundas. He pointed downstream and then pointed three fingers across the stream. Dundas nodded. Any escapes downstream were sealed off. Corporal Abikar tapped Dundas on the shoulder, then pointed to himself and Kipchumba. He pointed upstream in the direction of Colonel Tom's hut. Dundas nodded his approval and indicated that he would join them.

It took ages to crawl the distance. The hut was now some 25 yards below them at the base of a gentle slope. To their advantage there were no windows at the rear. But was their quarry inside? They kept the hut under observation for another five minutes. All was quiet. Dundas decided to make a move, realising that if Colonel Tom was absent, provided they were not spotted, there was still the opportunity for a dawn attack. No member of the patrol would make a move until they heard his whistle. He indicated that they should spread out and advance very slowly. As he stood up, Dundas felt his heartbeat increase. It was almost like walking on eggshells.

They were within twelve yards of their objective when suddenly there was the sound of someone leaving the hut. Instinct was to 'freeze' but every second counted. A scruffy figure, some five feet six inches tall, with a beard, long, plaited hair and wearing an ex-army greatcoat, appeared. Over his right shoulder was a double-barrelled shotgun. He was not aware of their presence and froze in his tracks as Corporal Abikar rushed forward and struck him in the stomach with the butt of his Remington. Colonel Tom collapsed to the ground and started moaning. Within seconds, he was turned face-down and handcuffed. Dundas picked up the shotgun and broke open the breech. It wasn't loaded. Suddenly, from downstream, shouts could be heard. It was time to check why the patrol had not awaited his whistle.

Corporal Abikar pulled their prisoner to his feet. The so-called colonel's face showed trepidation, no doubt realising what his ultimate fate would be. Dundas looked with disdain at the unkempt figure they had sought for so long. He was a singularly unimpressive specimen but in view of what was alleged about him, it was important to follow correct procedure, so, although it seemed unreal to be reciting such formal words in this idyllic woodland setting, Dundas read him the official police caution. Having completed his task, he added, "Do you understand?"

There was no response.

When they returned to where the three men had been crouched around the smoking fire, they saw things had changed. The three men were now face-down on the ground and handcuffed and the patrol was clearly jubilant. Dundas went over to Sergeant James.

"Well done James, but why did you act without hearing my whistle?"

"We had no choice Sir. All three men stood up and walked towards where we were hiding. We waited until they were within ten yards but they were still walking towards us."

Dundas nodded. "I understand James. Did they resist arrest?"

"We had no problems Sir. They didn't have time to even turn around!"

Sergeant James gestured towards the handcuffed prisoner.

"So this is the famous Colonel Tom?"

"Yes James, I have cautioned him, but he kept silent. This is his shotgun. Like your three prisoners, he was on the ground before he could make a move." Dundas glanced at his watch. "James, time is not on our side. We need to be at the forest edge by dusk. If we hurry, we can make it. Handcuff the prisoners in pairs in the usual manner, right wrist to right wrist. Have you cautioned the three men?"

"Yes Sir. All three have stated that it was Colonel Tom who shot the others."

Dundas nodded. "Hmm... no doubt they believe that he did, but what did they actually see? Have you searched the shelters?"

"Yes Sir, nothing was found."

"Right, any foodstuff heap onto the fire, then let's be off."

❖ ❖ ❖

The return journey was uneventful and they managed a reasonable pace in their usual formation, with the pairs of prisoners interspersed at the centre of the patrol. The forest edge was reached just after dusk. Dundas realised that the next step was not without its dangers. Major Fawcett would be armed.

The patrol stopped on the dirt road some 25 yards from the farmhouse. Dundas spoke to Sergeant James.

"We don't want any escapes at this stage. Lay the prisoners face down until I return."

Dundas noted that the farmhouse curtains were drawn and there was a solitary light in the lounge. He approached cautiously and mounted the steps. So far so good. It was time to knock. Dundas pressed his body against the stone wall framing the French door, then reached and tapped loudly on the glass.

"Major Fawcett!"

There was utter silence. He repeated the words again. He heard a floorboard creak, then Major Fawcett's voice responded.

"Who is it?"

Still shielded by the wall Dundas replied, "It's Chief Inspector Dundas Sir. We have met before."

There was the sound of a lock being turned and bolts being withdrawn. Major Fawcett appeared in the doorway clutching a revolver. His greeting was not very effusive.

"What do want?"

"I would like to use your phone."

The Major hesitated.

"Are you alone?"

"No Sir. My patrol is very close by and we have four prisoners."

Major Fawcett opened the door and stepped to one side.

"Come in, you know where the phone is."

Having called Headquarters and Njabini, Dundas returned to find Major Fawcett sitting beside the fire in the lounge with a glass in his hand. He looked up as Dundas entered the room.

"First my cook, then four of my men go missing. The Inspector from Njabini tells me that three of them are dead and your chaps wounded the other one. Then four more men go missing! You've stirred up a hornets' nest."

Major Fawcett stared at the logs crackling in the grate. Dundas decided to change the subject.

"Sir, some time ago you reported that an old man who had lived here for years was missing and his body was later recovered on this farm. One of our prisoners is the man we believe was responsible for his death."

The Major looked up. "When I left the army and purchased this farm, things were idyllic; a good life and a happy and contented labour force. At least some of them are left."

Dundas did not mention that following further investigations, it was highly likely many more would be arrested and charged with various offences. It was time to go.

# Epilogue

Many weeks of intensive investigations commenced to unravel the sequence of events and the persons directly responsible for the various murders. There was no doubt that 'Colonel Tom' would be hanged for his crimes, and as predicted more arrests took place at Major Fawcett's farm.

For Dundas, return to normal duties and domesticity had been very, very welcome. However, some evenings when dinner was finished and Stephen had served the coffee, his thoughts would return to the Aberdare Forest. Its smells, sounds, even the rain drops pattering onto his poncho. He had been lucky. During those many patrols no one had been wounded or injured. In his mind's eye he could picture it all so very clearly. One aspect of this former activity would always be with him - the thrill of the chase! His thoughts would stray to the Aberdare forest and the stream above Njabini. Perhaps one day when he retired he would establish a fishing camp where so many memories were embedded in his memory.

*~ End ~*